Village of Street Bells

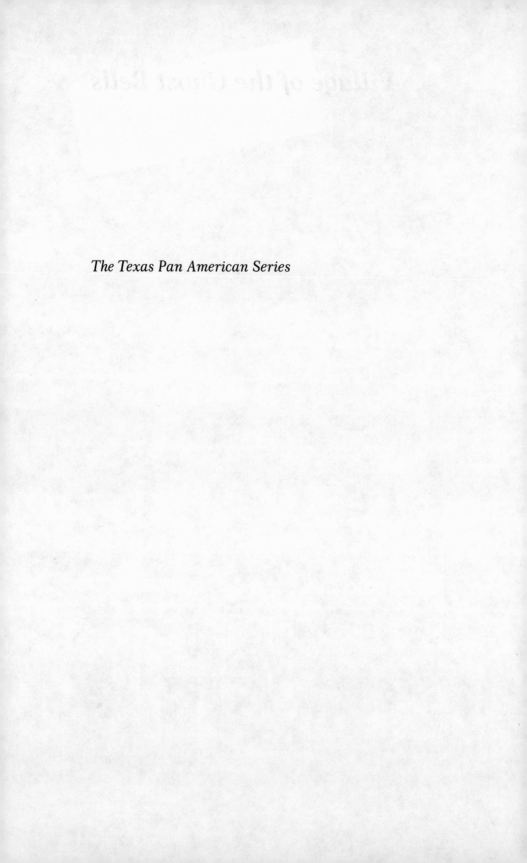

The Texas Pan American Series

VILLAGE OF
THE GHOST BELLS

A NOVEL
BY EDLA
VAN STEEN

TRANSLATED BY
DAVID GEORGE

University of Texas Press, Austin

Copyright © 1983 by Edla Van Steen
First published as *Corações Mordidos* by Global Editora, 1983

Translation copyright © 1991 by the University of Texas Press
All rights reserved
Printed in the United States of America

First Edition, 1991

Requests for permission to reproduce material from this work
should be sent to Permissions, University of Texas Press, Box
7819, Austin, Texas 78713-7819.

∞ The paper used in this publication meets the minimum
requirements of American National Standard for Information
Sciences—Permanence of Paper for Printed Library Materials,
ANSI Z39.48-1984.

The Texas Pan American Series is published with the assistance
of a revolving publication fund established by the Pan American
Sulphur Company.

Library of Congress Cataloging-in-Publication Data

Steen, Edla van.
    [Corações mordidos. English]
    Village of the ghost bells : a novel / by Edla van Steen ;
translated by David George. — 1st ed.
        p.   cm. — (Texas Pan American series)
    Translation of: Corações mordidos.
    ISBN 0-292-73062-4 (alk. paper)—ISBN 0-292-73063-2 (pbk. :
alk. paper)
    I. Title.   II. Series.
PQ9698.29.T34C6713   1991
869.3—dc20   90-22991
                                                        CIP

For Ricardo, Anna and Lea,
Angela and Marcos,
my children.

Sábato Magaldi,
my husband.

Foreword

Edla Van Steen was born in the southern Brazilian state of Santa Catarina on July 12, 1936. On her mother's side her ancestry, like that of many people in the southern regions, is German: family name, Wendhausen. Her father was born in Belgium.

She studied in a boarding school run by French nuns until the age of fifteen, when she began working as a radio announcer, reading and interpreting letters. A few years later she took up the career of journalist in Curitiba, capital of the state of Paraná.

In 1958, she was invited by director Hugo Khoury to star in his film *Garganta do Diabo* (*The Devil's Throat*). Critics praised her work and she won several awards as best actress in Brazil and another at an Italian film festival (the selection in the latter case was made by Roberto Rossellini). During the filming Ms. Van Steen had already begun writing her first book of short stories. Based on the letters she once read on radio, its title was *Histórias Incomuns* (*Uncommon Stories*). The book was never published—she inadvertently left the manuscript in a taxi cab. But she now had a son to take care of, and she was employed writing film scripts, dubbing foreign movies, and apprenticing as a film editor with *Cinema Novo* director Glauber Rocha, all the while carrying on her journalistic activities.

Her next book of short stories, *Cio* (*In Heat*), was published in 1965 by Von Schmidt Editora. The critics responded favorably to her literary debut. Wilson Martins, critic and later New York University professor, expressed this opinion in the newspaper *O Estado de São Paulo:* "As a writer, the author clearly possesses unusual literary qualities, such as a sharp sensibility and a personal style."

But who can live on literature alone in Brazil? Now the mother of three children, Ms. Van Steen founded and directed the Múltipla Art Gallery, while she worked on a novel entitled *Memórias do Medo* (*Memories of Fear*), which Editora Melhoramentos published in 1974 (a subsequent edition was published by Editora Record). The novel was written during Brazil's worst period of repression under a brutal military dictatorship, a time when friends were disappearing and dying. Reviews, once again, were highly favorable. The novel was cloaked in veiled language to get around censorship, and reviewers praised her implicit condemnation of the military's reign of terror:

The fear the author tells us about is not the result of phobias imagined by sick minds but rather the reflection of a situation that is much broader, absurdly real, characteristic of our present-day society. . . . The style is agile, the chapters are short segments that link the pulsating rhythm of the narrative. (Rubens Mauro Machado, writing in the Rio newspaper **O Globo***)*

The novel, ably constructed with a strong narrative flow, raises the reader's level of consciousness and alerts him to the increasing inhumanity that characterizes the violence of our urban society. **Memories of Fear** *is a strange and disquieting novel. (Lauro Junkes, literature professor at the Federal University of Santa Catarina, writing for the newspaper* **O Estado***)*

In 1981, *Memórias de Medo* was adapted for TV Cultura (public television) by playwright Jorge Andrade. According to a review in the newspaper *Folha de São Paulo*, it was "one of the best mystery stories presented by Channel 2."

Antes do Amanhecer (*Before the Dawn*), the author's second collection of short stories, was published in 1977 by Editora Moderna. Reviewers praised the book lavishly:

With this book the author enters the powerful mainstream of contemporary Brazilian story writers. (Professor and critic Fábio Lucas, writing in **Colóquio/Letras,** *Gulbenkian Foundation)*

The author has delved deeper into her themes, which could only emerge from a profound spiritual maturity, and she manages, almost always unflinchingly, her own style. (Leo Gilson Ribeiro, writing in the São Paulo newspaper **Jornal da Tarde***)*

All the author's fiction represents a broad stylistic renewal. Her plot lines, rather than being repetitive, are original variations on well-known fables. (Malcolm Silverman, professor at San Diego University)

That same year, Ms. Van Steen received the *Status* magazine prize for erotic literature, as well as an award from the São Paulo Association of Art Critics. She was also Brazilian representative at the Latin American Book Fair, held in Frankfurt, where she realized how little Brazilian literature was known abroad, and she convinced then São Paulo Minister of Culture, journalist, scholar, and University of São Paulo professor Sábato Magaldi—they would later marry—to sponsor a symposium to be called the First Encounter with Brazilian Literature, which she organized. Editors and agents from all over the world were invited to discover the country and its literary production.

In 1978, Editora Vertente requested that she organize an anthology entitled *O Conto da Mulher Brasileira* (*The Story of the Brazilian Woman*). There were two editions, in 1978 and 1979. The collection included short stories by Brazil's leading women writers, who, "with talent, technique, and varying degrees of experience, bear witness to a period in which one can no longer talk about women's art or men's art, but in which the artist's presence is affirmed: the question of gender then becomes merely grammatical" (writer Lya Luft, *Folha da Tarde*, Porto Alegre).

In 1979, Ms. Van Steen organized the Semana do Escritor Brasileiro (Week of the Brazilian Writer), which was sponsored by the São Paulo Ministry of Culture and included the participation of over thirty writers. The same year she organized and edited an anthology entitled *O Papel do Amor* (*Love Stories*), which was published in a dual English-Portuguese edition by Editora Cultura.

In 1981, she published two volumes of interviews with Brazilian authors entitled *Viver e Escrever* (*Living and Writing*), modeled after the Viking Press series *Writers at Work:*

*Edla has succeeded in eliciting from her subjects confessions in both the personal and literary realms. And her interviews do not follow the usual pattern of journalists who are unacquainted with the world of those they interview. Edla read their works, researched newspapers, magazines, and criticism, and she spent considerable time with the writers themselves. This invigorates her work with the life and energy of real people talking, which can be appreciated by those who love and study our literature. (Elias José, writer and professor of Brazilian literature, **Jornal da Tarde**, São Paulo)*

Edla Van Steen has always been in tune with her time and with the artists around her. She carries in her blood the solidarity and leadership of a movement that tries to move culture and its creators forward, this in the face of the most adverse conditions. Several Brazilian writers have seen their works in print due to her efforts on their behalf. . . . She defines herself as a cultural agent, which pertains to her continuing work in support of individual writers, organization of anthologies, collections, as well as editions of authors who constitute Brazil's historical legacy. (Cremilda Medina, writing for the **Estado de São Paulo***)*

There is not one Edla Van Steen, there are several, as everyone in this country who has any connection with culture knows. The dizzying trajectory of this Santa Catarina native with the aristocratic name and contagious good cheer, has gone from journalism, to the stage, to film, to the fine arts, a path characterized essentially by success. . . . Edla Van Steen is a mature writer at the top of her form. (Writer Moacyr Scliar, in **Zero Hora,** *Porto Alegre)*

Corações Mordidos (*Village of the Ghost Bells*) was published by Global Editora in 1983, and Círculo do Livro—the Brazilian Book of the Month Club—came out with a subsequent edition in 1986:

. . . fiction within fiction, novel within the novel, a questioning of the novel as a portrait of reality. The fictional game, the mirror, and the search for reality (narrated/lived) link a plot which unfolds through successive segments, in which time has another dimension, becoming a game of assemblage. The characters' memories create this world. . . . The Village of the Bells, the novel's setting, alludes mythically, starting with its name, to an ambient mystery, a kind of magic and curse, which vaguely threatens everyone. (Ligia Averbuck, professor of Brazilian literature at the University of Rio Grande do Sul, writing in the **Estado de São Paulo***)*

Edla Van Steen, in her guise as movie actress, is present in a construction based on short scenes, on cinematic montage. The Edla of the theatre, in the short, crisp dialogue interspersed among remembrance and interior monologue. Edla the journalist, in the clarity of her language, the precision of her words, the concern about current events. (Mário Pontes, writer and critic, **Jornal do Brasil,** *Rio de Janeiro)*

It is a powerful, dense, and denunciatory novel. . . . The skillful construction of the Village of the Bells will remain as one of the great creations of Brazilian fiction. (Lauro Junkes, critic, writing in the newspaper **O Estado,** *Santa Catarina)*

Edla Van Steen's magic realism lays down an unusual verbal path through a continual witnessing of human complexity. (Telênia Hill, professor of literary theory at the Federal University of Rio de Janeiro, writing in the **Suplemento Literário de Minas Gerais***)*

A delicate perception of the world around her is the key for the reader's entrance into the Village of the Bells and emergence at the end of the novel, his or her experience now enriched after having delved into so many lives. (Marisa Lajolo, professor of Brazilian literature at the University of Campinas, writing in the **Jornal da Tarde,** *São Paulo)*

Edla Van Steen is a star of the first magnitude in Brazilian literature. (Moacyr Scliar, **Zero Hora,** *Porto Alegre)*

Beneath the flow of an almost enchanting language the plot unfolds in a kind of ritual . . . (Fausto Cunha, critic, writing in the magazine **Status,** *São Paulo)*

Tereza Queiroz Guimarães has written a screenplay based on *Corações Mordidos.*

Manto de Nuvem (Cloud Blanket), a novelette for young people, was published in 1985 by Editora Nacional: "While creating characters based on autobiographical roots, Edla constructs a poetic and dense story, in which fantasy and reality complement each other" (Laura Sandroni, *O Globo*, Rio de Janeiro); ". . . sensitivity and tenderness in the telling of a beautiful story" (Tatiana Belinki, writer and critic, *Jornal da Tarde*, São Paulo).

The year 1985 also marked the publication, by Global Editora, of *Até Sempre (Until Always)*, a collection of the author's short stories:

A collection distinguished by the high level of quality and originality of its plot structures, for the most part cast in the classical mold of dramatic and atmospheric episode. (Wilson Martins, writing in the **Jornal da Tarde,** *São Paulo)*

The stories in **Até Sempre** *are very good, even those that are boldly experimental, since Edla Van Steen, in her constant search for innovation, in the end impregnates her fiction with her unmistakable personal touch. Her variations of new pathways, narrative focus, and point of view distinguish her among those who practice her craft. She is a short story writer who is always and absolutely true to herself. (Almeida Fischer, writer and essayist,* **O Estado de São Paulo***)*

Até Sempre *is a decisive step in a journey that continues to crystallize. Turning her attention toward making sense of the world, Edla Van Steen creates a language that only maturity based on constant exercise of craft can provide . . . (Bella Jozef, professor of literary theory at the Federal University of Rio de Janeiro, writing in* **O Globo***)*

The constant renovation of form and structure wedded to content, as well as the search for greater expressive powers, constitutes her most undeniable merit. Her variations on narrative focus, her treatment of time, her persistent plunging into the self, her parallel or alternating constructions, the constant presence of psychoanalytic symbols, the recourse to cinematic language . . . make up some of the incomparable values of Edla Van Steen's superb narrative artistry, values that place **Até Sempre** *among the most distinguished accomplishments in the contemporary Brazilian short story. (Lauro Junkes,* **Suplemento Literário de Minas Gerais***)*

Other Edla Van Steen short stories have been included in dozens of anthologies, in Brazil and abroad. Translations of her stories have appeared in such foreign anthologies and journals as *Nowe Opowiadania Brazylijskie* (Krakow, Poland); *The Literary Review* (1984, USA); *The Latin American Literary Review* (Pittsburgh, 1986); and *Sudden Fiction International* (W. W. Norton, New York and London, 1989).

The author has organized a series of collections of works by Brazilian and foreign authors for Global Editora (she is one of that publisher's directors): "Best Short Stories," "Best Poems," and "Unforgettable Stories."

Because she is a confessed "graphomaniac," Edla Van Steen translated and published, in collaboration with Eduardo Brandão, a collection of Katherine Mansfield's stories entitled *Aula de Canto* (Global Editora, 1984), and she translated and adapted Robert Louis Stevenson's *Dr. Jekyll and Mr. Hyde* (*O Médico e o Monstro*) (Editora Scipione, 1987).

She has done translations for the theatre: *O Encontro de Descartes com Pascal* (*L'entretien de M. Descartes avec M. Pascal le jeune*), by Jean Claude Brisville, with Italo Rossi and Kito Junqueira in the lead roles, staged in Rio de Janeiro and São Paulo, 1987–88; *Solness, O Construtor* (*The Masterbuilder*), by Henrik Ibsen, staged by Grupo Tapa, 1988–89; and in collaboration with Sônya Grassman, *Max*, by German playwright Manfred Karge, staged in 1990.

Edla Van Steen's first original play, *O Último Encontro* (*The Last Encounter*), was staged in São Paulo in 1989, with Kito Junqueira in the lead role. The work received Brazil's most prestigious theatrical award, the Molière Prize for Best Play, as well as the Mambembe Award in the same category and yet another prize, "Revelation of the Year," awarded by the São Paulo Association of Art Critics. The play was also published in 1989 by Arte Aplicada, São Paulo.

Edla Van Steen has brought to the stage the same intimate atmosphere she has explored in her prose. Faithful to her own concerns as a writer, **O Último Encontro** *deals with family ties, in a world containing several levels of reality. . . . The dialogue flows naturally. The action unfolds in intricate rhythms, in a complex structure, which superimposes scenes from past and present. . . .* **O Último Encontro** *reveals that Edla Van Steen is very comfortable in a theatrical setting, which one hopes will be translated into yet new works. (Alberto Guzik, theatre critic for São Paulo's* **Jornal da Tarde**)

Sixty concise pages of a play-writing debut were all the novelist required to make a valuable contribution to Brazilian theatre. (Jefferson Del Rios, theatre critic for **O Estado de São Paulo**)

Edla Van Steen's second play, *Bolo de Nozes* (*Nut Cake*), was written in 1990, in Aix-en-Provence, in the south of France, where she currently resides with her husband, a visiting professor at the Université de Provence. Ms. Van Steen is currently working on a new novel, tentatively titled *O Canto dos Anjos* (*The Angels' Canto*).

D. G.

Translator's Acknowledgments

This translation would not have come into being without the inspiration and perseverance of Edla Van Steen and a grant-in-aid from Lake Forest College. I warmly thank University of Texas Executive Editor Theresa J. May for her continuing support. I am grateful for the generous help, encouragement, and patience provided by Beatriz Zonis, to whom this translation is dedicated.

Village of the Ghost Bells

"Oh, sir, you know well that life is filled with infinite absurdities, which, shamelessly, need not have the slightest appearance of truth. And do you know why? Because those absurdities are true."

Pirandello

The fact is, Tina had been acting rather strangely. The gesture Greta found most intriguing was this: with her arms resting on the bathroom sink, she spent hours watching herself in the mirror. She drew her face close to the glass as if she wanted to touch her reflection. Nearly the entire metallic surface was steamed up, reducing the reflecting area to a minimum.

The mirror had three sections, two of which hid shelves filled with bottles and cosmetics. Tina positioned herself in front of the right-hand door section, precisely the one most damaged by mildew. Who knows why? Greta wondered if she was somehow trying to reveal the future in her reflected image. Not an absurd notion.

Ah, but her instability, that had been suspect for some time now. She paced back and forth, sighed, opened a book, discarded it, picked up another, a different one, went to the kitchen, heated some coffee—she drank over two liters a day—brought the cup into the living room and sipped slowly, which contradicted the nervous atmosphere she had created. Would that produce an inner pause, a self-interlude? Afterward she repeated the same actions; her anxiety was pitiable.

She didn't always behave that way. There was a time when the two women had fun together and took pleasure in each other's company. In the spring, for example, they enjoyed strolling about the yard, climbing the trees to pick hanging moss, an excellent kindling for the fireplace. Later they would cross the huge lot carrying baskets that overflowed with the dry moss, laughing heartily. The evenings were often pleasant too. They played cards, listened to music, and read poetry out loud.

During certain periods Tina would wake up in a happy mood and Greta could hear her singing as she watered the plants. Her youthfulness was something to see then. She gave the happy impression of someone who had just made love: the gentle expression, the smooth skin, the soft smile no one could resist. But there were other times when Tina aged suddenly. Her skin became rough and her voice sounded hoarse: she gave out a kind of grunt full of harsh and bitter words. Greta would ignore her then and entertain herself by watching television. The negative phases seemed to happen when no letters came.

One of Tina's tasks was to wait for the mailman, because she was always receiving correspondence and magazines. Greta took care of shopping and banking since Tina refused to go to town. She insisted the fruits and vegetables from the garden were enough for her needs. By fulfilling the tasks they took on naturally, the two women lived harmoniously. They kept a tacit agreement: no one would touch on the past, and Greta accepted the restriction that she not ask questions about the letters.

They say that Tina used to visit friends, give a few parties, and that her family was large and well-off. No one knows how she ended up alone. Greta respected the agreement—she shared the total reluctance to talk about herself. The present was more interesting.

But Tina began suffering from insomnia. She could not get to sleep before dawn. So she invented an odd system to make the hours pass: creating collages. At first she cut things out of magazines. Later she produced her own images by modifying the original meaning of the pictures. A patch of flower-covered meadow or section of ocean could be transformed into a rug or a tablecloth. Even a simple vase. She was meticulous, a perfectionist. She would spend night after night preparing the collage, unable to make up her mind about the innumerable options presented by the cut-outs. In the beginning she copied paintings by Rousseau, Chagall, and Marie Laurencin. She eventually gave up on mere reproductions, and the collages began to reveal imaginary compositions.

Greta had the best of Tina's works framed and hung them throughout the house. The picture in the dining room is her latest composition, a delicate and richly colored surrealist landscape. An upright open book suggests a house. In the foreground, the silhouette of two birds carrying suitcases on their wings. The title: Paradise.

Maybe Greta secretly attributed all her friend's changes in behavior to that collage. Just like that, she packed away in a box the scissors, paper cutter, glue bottle, and palette knife—she never made anything again. The interruption in the correspondence may have also been a decisive factor. Tina would wait for the mailman at the gate and later come back discouraged.

At first Greta paid no attention to the new odd behavior patterns:

2

observing the sky for hours on end waiting for the six o'clock plane. Then combing her hair, putting on makeup, and rushing out to the yard as if someone very special were going to enter through the gate. A lover or a father. Who knows? Greta was about to suggest she be the one to wait for the mailman, when Tina developed another strange gesture: she would pick up the portrait of a man and spend the whole day holding it and staring into it with total absorption. It was the photograph of a serious-looking man with black hair. (One day the photo showed up glued to the mirror.)

She never referred to the man by name. She would say: today he's like this or like that. There were occasions when she saw him with glasses but others when the glasses disappeared and she couldn't understand why. Some sort of memory magic? Or then she saw him with his eyes closed, asleep, and she asked for silence. Most of the time, however, she talked with him. At such times she spoke gibberish. She would address a certain Luís Leoni and call herself by the name she was baptized with: Cristina.

Finally, there was the business about the mirror. It was heartrending. Whatever was she looking for in that reflected face, Greta asked herself as she took away the tray, the food untouched. Tina tiptoed around, exploring, paying attention to the slightest sound. Three days and three nights without food or sleep. She seemed to be waiting for a miracle—what kind?

And then the inexplicable happened: Tina's eyes bored into the picture with a murky glow—the glow of someone about to undergo a metamorphosis—and they began to lose their blue color. They turned black.

At that point Tina let out a loud, frightening, masculine guffaw.

In the photograph the man's eyes became lighter. His hair became blond and grew down over his shoulders.

Δ   Could longing mean so much? Greta has been asking herself this question insistently. Some situations are beyond understanding. Mood is more exciting than fact. There are times when people acquire such individuality the best thing is to keep watch and try to decipher their enigmatic gestures. Greta ponders on her way to the clinic: could there be a good reason for this estrangement, this hiding place where Tina has taken refuge?

Tina transmitted an infinite sadness as she sat in the chair, stiff and indifferent. Why? Greta made an effort to chat; she brought news from home, she talked about the new sunflowers that bloomed in the garden. She'd heard the same small talk before, hadn't she? Greta changed the subject by reporting on the arrangements she had made: indispensable plumbing repairs (old houses are charming but so hard to maintain), painting the fence and gate as they had planned on doing for so long. Tina didn't show the slightest interest. She continued to stare into space as if she were there in body alone and her thoughts wandered through impenetrable zones. It's painful to see Tina in such a state. Greta is overwhelmed by a feeling of nostalgia for Tina's former light-hearted self. Really too bad.

♤   The nights are cold and starry. Logs crackle in the fireplace. If Greta turns out the light, a phantom—the man in the portrait?—may appear and embrace her, thinking she is Tina. After all, they can easily be mistaken for each other. And Greta loathes and fears illusions of any sort.

Better to think about something else, like her plan to clean the basement—oh, how tempting not to avoid the obvious solution of houses with mysterious basements! Let's see, should the old bureau in the hallway be cleaned? Who knows. It's a colonial bureau, one of those used in churches to keep priestly garments. It has a specific name—great chest? The bureau is being eaten away by termites. Greta injected it with poison once, then she waxed and polished it—it was like new. Tina wouldn't allow the drawers to be removed, claiming they contained forgotten secrets. She should've seen how much wood dust Greta swept up this morning . . . If you don't take a firm stand, the termites' path of devastation will lead right to the floor, and it's made of wood too, isn't it?

One of these days I'm going to satisfy my curiosity, Greta promised herself. She's resisting the desire to rummage through those old keepsakes. Fear of what she'll discover, remember, invent?

4

Maybe she should begin with the setting instead of with Tina. The name of the place: Village of the Bells. It sounds a bit precious but it has its purpose. Private enterprise does what it can to sell its products, and in this case the name of the venture should call attention to the location, with all its vegetation and church under construction. The area was beautiful, covered with native trees, as well as weeping-willows which had been planted by an uncle of Tina's whose idea it was to subdivide. All this surrounding an artificial lake.

It seemed reasonable to assume the old farm would make an excellent real estate development. Especially because it was based on the idea of a return to life in small housing clusters—far from the torment of the downtown area—a place where man could find his true self and be in touch with nature. The failure of the project is incomprehensible. If similar initiatives have been so successful in other countries, why not here?

Well, it doesn't matter anymore. The only thing worth mentioning is that the Village of the Bells ended at one row of houses, Palm Street, and at a cemetery that was added after the development ended in failure. A fortunate idea because the cemetery has prospered, thus guaranteeing Tina's income and ensuring a steady flow of buses and taxis on the avenue that cuts through the Village. Were it not for the Cemetery of the Flowers, the fifty families that moved here would be unable to stay for lack of transportation.

Viewed from above, the Village is an immense green area cut in half by the paved avenue. On the right you can see the skeleton of a church, the ruins of a four-story building, and Palm Street. The original streets slowly disappeared due to lack of maintenance; they're all overgrown with vegetation. A few twisted signboards hanging from eucalyptus posts are still legible. Streets named Mango, Pine, and Coconut Tree. On the left-hand side of the avenue, a lake. And the cemetery, which is quite lovely. There are no headstones. Each gravesite is defined by plants; the only thing visible is a cement plaque with the name of the deceased. The one upright structure contains the funeral chapel and administrative headquarters.

Some years ago there were rumors that the Village was haunted, that the dead refused to remain buried beneath the flower beds, a lot of nonsense. None of this bothered the residents, but the development stagnated. Doubtless, there are some strange goings-on. Apparently everybody has become accustomed to them. Or could it be that . . .

It may be worth mentioning that the Village was the subject of reports in the São Paulo newspapers. All because of a four-story building initially intended for the offices of the Fortuna Real Estate and Construction Company. Sales were ridiculously low, so the building had to be turned into eight apartment units, which sold immediately. City Hall, however, ordered the structure demolished because it did not conform to the building code.

It so happens that on the top floor lives Míriam, an odd duck who refuses to budge from the building. Fortuna has done its damnedest to get her out of there, because until it's torn down daily fines have to be paid into the municipal coffers. How can anyone be so stubborn? Tina came up with the theory that Míriam might be waiting for someone and that's why she insists on staying. Could be. The problem is Fortuna lost its patience, and except for her apartment it's a grim picture. All the windows and doors have been removed and the other floors turned into garbage dumps.

Tina suffered a great deal when the reporters were in the Village; she agonized over Míriam's situation and her stubborn refusal to accept—unlike the others—the Company's offers of relocation. Míriam, shut up in her apartment for a week, was photographed behind the window, the hateful expression on her face shocking. The reporters could get nowhere so they gave up trying to interview her. Tina—a shareholder in the Company—tried every argument she could think of, but the board of directors are an unscrupulous bunch and her words fell on deaf ears. Drastic measures were soon to be taken: a huge machine, a sort of tractor with a crane, was placed in front of the building.

Could the nonsense they were saying about the Village really be true? An unbelievable series of inexplicable events—bells that suddenly began to toll, when the church has no bells—the business with Míriam . . . A vexation for everyone. As if the Village possessed a kind of magic, a curse.

♁   By eleven o'clock at night all the houses were submerged in that silence and darkness which torments those still awake, particularly Greta and the man across the street, who also stays up late.

His name is Camilo. He's tall, with a wide nose and dark skin. His beard and mustache are white, with a few strands of black. He must be approaching seventy. He lives with a crippled child confined to a wheelchair, retarded. Greta makes a point of visiting him now and then because it makes Ivo, the child, very happy. He makes indescribable sounds. Could they be moans? No. They aren't grunts either. Strange sounds. During the visits, Camilo serves his own home-made liqueur to go with the small cake Greta has made a habit of bringing. Although they don't have a maid, the house is surprisingly neat. The floor is a mirror.

The house was intended for other residents—Tina went on explaining—a lively, noisy young couple who gave parties that lasted until dawn, a nuisance for everyone. No one could bear the constant revelry. One day they vanished from the face of the earth, and it was after that the man and the child arrived. In the morning, when the weather is nice, they go for a walk along the street: the old man pushes the wheelchair like a dignified Parisian out for a stroll. He wears a silk ascot and there's a certain solemnity in his slow footsteps. If someone addresses him, a few pleasantries and he's on his way. Now and then a relative shows up: his daughter? Perhaps. Greta always catches a glimpse of her from behind because she steps out of the car and goes right in, without looking back. Yesterday, Camilo said something that depressed Greta: "I have a horrible fear of dying. That's why I don't sleep much. Who's going to take care of my boy?"

Why do people choose certain friends or prefer one neighbor over another, Greta thought. There are so few people in the Village, yet Greta is very particular, as if the others were not worthy of attention.

The people at 508, for example. An ordinary family, apparently well established, five children. The man's name is Antônio; he owns a mattress factory. He leaves early, never has lunch at home, and on Sundays likes to take a nap in the yard, with a pillow and everything. Lord knows what kind of satisfaction he gets from lying on the grass like that. His wife, Jane, spends her time cleaning house, sweeping the sidewalk. She leads a quiet, uneventful life. She drops the children off at school, returns home, and picks them up at five because only the oldest can get around by himself. Except for one of the girls who is cross-eyed, they are attractive and healthy: one of the boys has a scar through an eyebrow, probably caused by a tumble or a cut. No big deal.

The children brighten up the street as they ride bicycles or play hop-scotch with their friends at 531.

Antônio is the current Village representative. He collects taxes, oversees street repairs, and maintains order in the community. His biggest problem at present: convincing the residents to sign a petition asking City Hall to change the numbers on the houses before the election of a new representative. The idea was his originally; he's the kind of person who takes pride in being helpful. It doesn't make sense for a street to begin with the number 500 and end with 600. If the plans didn't work out and they halted development on the other side of the street, where the numbering was supposed to start . . . The fellow's got plenty of reasons to want the change.

Greta goes to the window. The Village is sleeping. Except for Camilo, who's watching TV: the room emits a cold light, a slice of moon that fell inside.

And . . . Surprise! Sônia, the neighbor on the right, has her library lights turned on.

◊ The driver arrives every morning right on time. He gets out of the black automobile—who knows what kind of car it is; likely it's a classic because there's none other like it on the streets of the city— and, after opening the door, he assumes a waiting position. He doesn't enter the house, he doesn't ring the doorbell. He just settles in to wait, dressed in his black suit and impeccable white shirt.

Sônia will appear soon after. If she's in a good mood, she greets the chauffeur with a smile. If not, she gets in quickly with her head down and settles into the usual spot. People tend to sit on the right-hand side to have an open field of vision. She, however, chooses the seat behind the driver.

He could be any age, maybe fifty or sixty. He starts the motor quietly and shifts smoothly into gear. The driver must feel a special affection for the car.

They don't speak during the drive unless Sônia addresses him. Which happens on occasion. But usually she immerses herself in a book until the final stop, the medical office building.

Even now nobody's sure to whom the car belongs. It could be either his or theirs, meaning Sônia's and her mother's. Most likely he owns it. Maybe he bought it from the two women. The car isn't parked overnight at their house; he drives it there every day. On the other hand, he doesn't act like the owner, considering the way he serves them. He enters through the back door, and when they don't need his services he sits behind the wheel for hours on end. Or he stands glued to a cloth and polishes the hood patiently, like someone caressing a marine seal.

Sônia's job is to open the office, but if Dr. Bóris doesn't have an operation scheduled he comes in before her. They say he invited his niece to work with him soon after she entered the university. And he deeply regrets she gave up her studies. So suited for pediatrics! Neither could he understand why she accepted such low-level employment; she's been his assistant now for many years. She could hold more important positions. It would make even more sense if she used the money she inherited from her father and just took off, a carefree globe-trotter. Some folks simply don't know how to take advantage of what they have—he repeats constantly, simultaneously shaking his head no, which never fails to make his niece laugh. She always liked the office and nothing gives her more pleasure than books—her uncle should understand. Why didn't she read on the job? Look, if there's one thing she's learned over the years it's to digest her reading totally and not to squander it. It ruins the emotion when you're interrupted and have to return to a passage. If a patient called to make an appointment, it would mean switching from one mood to another in a matter of seconds, and that wouldn't do, doesn't uncle agree? She had a short memory; books were enjoyed in the act of reading, without further ado. Some she even reread five or six times without taking away the pleasure. She might be familiar with the themes, but she didn't remember the details . . .

"Interesting observation," the doctor mumbled; he felt deep down his niece was becoming a bit tiresome. "What about movies, don't you like them?"

No, she couldn't appreciate such a rapid succession of images. Films made you think afterwards, but she preferred to do her thinking as events unfolded. Was she explaining herself clearly? Besides, the books on your shelves could be enjoyed more than once.

"Well, my dear, I must be going. We'll continue this delightful conversation next time. My regards to Elisa. Come over and have dinner with us one of these Sundays."

She closes the windows, cleans the ashtrays, unplugs the sterilizer, and hangs up her white uniform. Afterward, she selects the filing cards for the next day's appointments.

With her light complexion, hair pulled back in a kind of bun, her tall, thin figure, Sônia reminded people of Ingrid Bergman. However, since she never went to the movies, she wasn't aware of the similarity.

And the truth is, appearance is unimportant to her: clean face, discreet clothing.

"Who's the lady with the glasses?" the fellow asked the doorman.

"She works on the seventh floor. Forget it," he spat, "she's a cold fish."

"I stood next to her on the elevator. She's worth a try." The man winked, craning his neck to see if he could locate her in the line of people waiting for the bus. What he saw was Sônia getting into a limousine, the driver making the usual gestures.

During the drive she merely rests her head against the glass or the headrest. The chauffeur once tried to find out what she was thinking; she seemed so sad. Sônia's first reaction was not to answer. Nevertheless, she must have realized that there, in front of her, was someone who had known her since childhood. He deserved respect. She wasn't sad and she wasn't thinking; she was sleeping. She gave her answer and turned her head back to its former position.

The driver swerved to avoid another car going the wrong way on a one-way street, forcing him to drive up a steep hill. On the horizon appeared a sharply drawn red line: a banal incident that would make him cry out. His impulse was to awaken his passenger so she wouldn't miss this spectacle of nature. He loved landscapes, and there was something ineffably beautiful in the red streak compressed between two dark surfaces. The spot quickly lost its intensity, as if it had lasted only long enough for him to notice it. Night was about to settle in fully; let the girl sleep her peaceful sleep.

But Sônia is not asleep. An idea circles about in her mind: buying dreams. Absurd? Not even original. One afternoon she read part of a story while waiting in a dentist's office. "The man who bought dreams." She was only half-way through when the dentist called her in. Afterward, the magazine had disappeared from the waiting room. And she didn't even know the author's name. From then on, she promised herself, she would never read anything she couldn't finish, because the desire to buy dreams kept coming back. Time after time she planned to imitate the story, but she couldn't make up her mind. Would people really be willing to sell dreams? What would she do with them? If she placed the same want ad in all the city newspapers, what would happen?

One of Sônia's personality traits was to attach herself obsessively to everything. For example, there was a period when she would fall in love with the characters she read about. In love with one protagonist, she couldn't accept a new one: she bent her entire will to keeping the old one alive within herself. The volumes piled up on the desk in her room, waiting for her passion to cool. Gatsby stood in line for quite some time. It was worth it; her devotion to him was unusually intense. Although rare, now and then she became enchanted with the authors themselves. When that happened she hurried to the public library during lunch hour, eating her apple on the run, in search of more and more information. Oh, if only there were as much information on the authors as on the characters they described.

It was Elisa who couldn't accept Sônia's indulgence. She was unable to understand her daughter, no matter how hard she tried. For nearly fifteen years she had observed painfully Sônia's withdrawal from society. She hadn't always been this way. To raise a daughter for that, instead of marriage and children . . . isn't that so, Greta? She'd rather have her be silly, flirtatious, anything besides a book maniac. Goodness gracious!

Elisa always went around talking to herself, poor thing, so lonely since the death of her husband. She amused herself watching television, playing solitaire, or serving tea and cookies to the neighbor ladies on Wednesdays.

Sônia never joined the tea parties; she appeared only when it was time to say good-bye. Today, she went directly to her room without greeting the visitors. She had to work on writing the want ad and she had no time to waste on those damn women—sorry, mother; she slammed the door.

That night, Greta noticed Sônia was shut up in her room, writing. Sônia wondered, should she choose a simple, direct text? "Wish to purchase dreams. Appointments on Saturdays and Sundays, from 8 a.m. to 6 p.m."

Afterward she locked up the house, lay down fully clothed, and went right to sleep.

♤ Thursday. Visit to the clinic. Tina's birthday—she heard the insistent honking of the horn.

"I'm coming." She waved to her neighbor.

If not for the ride with Sônia, she can't imagine how she would carry the chocolate cake. Could she hold on to the plate and drive the car at the same time?—She slammed the gate.

"Good morning, Sônia. You must have stayed up late."

Sônia shows the want ad to Greta, who praises what she considers to be a sensational idea, but wonders if there will be many sellers. One of the obstacles is distance.

"People have a way of finding what they want," Sônia responded. "Besides, I indicated the bus line and the stop. Don't you think the cemetery makes a great landmark?"

Greta agrees and wishes her success. Normally her neighbor Sônia doesn't go in for idle chatter but this morning she's all wound up. As she speaks she jumps from one subject to another. The likely demolition of the building, the selection of a new Village representative—who would it be?—the chilly morning. That woman was either crazy or very courageous. Her experiment as a reader who tests fiction by reproducing it would cause anyone to be envious, awestruck. How many people would have thought of it?

"Do you plan on making use of the dreams?" Greta asks. Sônia shrugs her shoulders, seemingly indifferent.

"I don't know."

Greta insists.

"You should. You'll get some incredible material, if anyone shows up. The opportunities to meet interesting people are few and far between . . . I don't know how many times I've heard people tell stories I was sorry weren't written down."

Unconcerned, Sônia smooths out her black skirt. Her white knitted sweater accentuates her chestnut-brown hair.

"You know what I think, Greta? If I really had any talent I would've written something serious. At one time I had intellectual pretensions." She made an ugly face. "At fifteen I fell in love with a poet. We'd spend hours on end discussing a book. He wanted me to be the Brazilian Jane Austen, can you imagine that? At that time we were living in the country and we made plans to write together, as a team. One day he got sick. I read aloud to take his mind off his illness. He died in six months. Of leukemia."

Greta almost thanked her for sharing the secret. Who would've imagined? We all have our reasons to be what we are.

"You still have time, Sônia, and this is a real opportunity."

"Forget it. Thank God not everyone's an artist. Otherwise who would practice the other professions?"

The driver stopped the car. Greta kisses her neighbor good-bye. A few sunbeams filter through the fog. The June day promises to be resplendent. Like yesterday.

Míriam also left the Village early. Right now she's returning home. The cold is bone-chilling and the icy wind is even worse in the vastness of the intersections—she waits for the traffic light to change. When the cars speed by like that, sometimes it's bad enough to knock you down, for God's sake.

Seen from behind, with her floppy-brimmed hat, long, tattered cape, slight limp, worn, misshapen boots, she's a disturbing figure, Greta observes, as she watches Míriam pressing the chicken against her breast while trying with the other hand to protect her cape, which the wind keeps lifting up.

Míriam hesitates now, but she chooses the dark alley that serves as a short cut to the bus stop. She wears her usual bewildered expression, like someone not sure if she'll be able to produce a smile. Or is it someone afraid to show she's a person? One never knows about private fears. Considering the way Greta is following her—they can have a chat on the way back—she might reasonably be afraid. Nevertheless, what character, god, what character she must have to live in that ugly, dirty, unfinished building, which they're threatening to demolish whether she's inside it or not.

Who is Míriam, where did she come from, how is it she wears that antique clothing in this day and age—those questions have given rise to long conversations between Greta and Tina. During their many attempts to unravel them, they came up with the idea of a ticket seller in a movie theatre.

"I don't know why, but there's something about those women selling tickets I find very touching," Tina said.

"She almost never goes out, so she couldn't have that job."

Greta got up her courage and went to visit Míriam: she was embroidering baby clothing.

"Oh, Tina, how delicately she filled the linen with bouquets of daisies, how carefully she stitched in the petals and leaves. She drew the cloth very close to her eyes, like this, or bent over it like a wilted plant. I was fascinated by the way she chatted both with me and her three dolls. Splendid dolls. One she calls Horácio; he's a chubby infant, made in Germany in the nineteenth century, I think. He's dressed in the most charming velvet clothing, with mother-of-pearl buttons. Daisy's a typical French peasant girl wearing a hood with a fringe. The baby's body and limbs are cloth, but her arms and legs are wax, with the color old-fashioned dolls have, you know, before they used that pinkish coloring. But the most incredible one is Elizabeth; she's an English lady, probably from the 1800s. With her mauve costume she looks like she's on her way to a royal ball somewhere. Her dress is made of pearl-colored satin, trimmed in white lace. Wonderful lace. Her head leans slightly to the right, her fan and gloves give the impression of . . . I don't know, a dream-like impression. Oh, Tina, if only you could see how pretty those dolls are. She told me that they keep her company, that Horácio likes chicken, Daisy prefers soup, and Elizabeth eats salads.

In the middle of the alley Míriam looks up and frowns: the piece of luminous blue sky between the buildings is almost a provocation—she turns around once, twice—someone was following her. Her heart begins to pound. A thief? She walks faster. Suddenly, she stops. Maybe the reflection in the shop window would show who . . . She quickens her step again and heads toward the park, taking the boulevard that cuts across it. In other circumstances maybe she'd sit on one of those benches and admire the ducks swimming in the lake. But not today. Because this isn't the first time she has suspected someone was following her. For days now she's had the shakes—she runs and gets on the bus.

The two neighbors spoke little during the twenty-minute return trip. Míriam still clutched the chicken to her breast.

"It's yummy, hot like this. Horácio's going to lick his chops."

Greta agreed. It really must be deliciously hot. Something in her memory reminded her of a sensation similar to what Míriam was experiencing at that moment. When? How? She would talk about it the next time she went to the clinic. In the meantime, she ought to think about whether or not she's going to open that chest. So simple, all she has to do is decide. She doesn't even need a key. She observes Míriam: her nose is thin and her neck long, but her hands are coarse with those short fingers and chewed nails. She notices her face has a pale, yellowish cast; there's no blush to her skin. Her lips are two narrow slashes; seen from this angle, her eye is a restless sphere in its socket. What's she frightened of? Outside, the day is rapidly coming to an end.

"Five o'clock and it's already dark."

The other woman hasn't noticed. Greta remembers vaguely that Tina once told her about a diary she had written, a kind of secret report on the boarding school—where could it . . . She also mentioned at one time that she had aspirations to be a nun. Was there ever a girl in a parochial boarding school who didn't at some time want to be a nun, Greta argued. They all aspired to be brides of Christ, under the influence of mystical aggravation. Tina smiled mysteriously. She had this obsession with closing herself up in a smile as if to declare, I–have–nothing–more–to–say. You–don't–understand–me. Why–do–I–have–to–be–what–you–imagine–me–to–be?

Talk was unnecessary. She knew that smile very well.

Δ   Greta turned on the television after dinner. There was a gloomy and oppressive feeling in the living room. The cold wind came in through the cracks in the floor. She turned off the set and took out the plaid blanket to wrap around her legs. There in the corridor was the bureau. Why not tonight? I don't feel up to it; maybe tomorrow. But what harm can it do? I won't linger over anything. I'll pick up the pages tied with blue ribbon—imagine remembering such a specific detail. Oh, of course she had actually seen a photo of Tina at age ten with the ribbon in her hair. Where the hell was that photo? In the album. Where's the album? Somewhere around here. OK then. Go open the drawers and look for the old leather-bound book. And don't stick your nose into anything else.

Mozart's *Requiem* filled the house and echoed through the Village. Greta got out a bottle of wine and sat on the sofa, wrapped in the blanket.

Intimate Portrait in Search of Identity: 1963—Greta was astonished. That was written when Tina was twenty-five years old. It was, therefore, not a diary.

I'm scared to death of going to school. It's seven o'clock on a cold, cold, morning, March first, 1945. I'll never forget that day. I put on the uniform—pleated skirt, sailor-style blouse, the collar stiff with starch, beret, everything navy blue, except for the white gloves and stockings.

I see a seven-year-old girl in the mirror, with straight blond hair and eyes wide with terror.

I examine the bedroom for the last time: the bed is made, the quilt is pink. It's a pretty room. I'll miss it, and the dolls, too. They've been put away in the closet, except for the one I received that Christmas, my favorite, sleeping in the cradle. She looks like me, that's why she has my name. I kiss her like someone saying good-bye to a daughter. And I feel a lump in my throat.

The rest, does it matter? The kitchen. I open the door—my mother has just wrapped an apple. New black suit. Porcelain complexion. She's lovely, I think, as I climb into the taxi.

I don't look back—I know every nook and cranny of the house—nor do I listen to my mother's advice; I know it by heart. What matters to me is keeping a clear mental picture of her. We're holding hands, mine a little bird enfolded in hers. My mother's hands smell like Vaseline. Vaseline of course has no smell, but I breathe in the strange odor of that transparent cream. A transparent fragrance, that's it.

A rhythmical, soothing voice. A crystalline laugh. My mother's laugh protects me, even from far away. It's funny; whenever I think of her she's laughing. With her hair pulled back in a bun, her face is exposed completely. A round bun, with a hole in the middle.

"That building up there, on the left, that's the school. See?"—she pointed. Slowly, I leaned out of the car window, and I managed to see the building as the car skirted around a wall where the thick ivy climbed the stone to catch a glimpse of the other side.

Confused, I stepped out of the taxi. A whole lot of people were going into the convent. The driver carried my suitcase up the stairs. I looked inside: I couldn't distinguish features in the semi-darkness, only shadowy forms. My first thought is to yell and run out. The only reason I didn't is because the fat nun came up to us tamely, like a sneaky cat. I don't understand what she and my mother are saying: I'm deaf and paralyzed with fear. What's more, there's a low whispering sound, just like you hear at a wake. At least quite similar to the murmur of voices I noticed at grandma's funeral last year. If she were alive there's no way I'd have to go to boarding school. She'd take care of me while mama went to work, I'm sure of it. My mother smiles politely at the nun, but I can tell her lips are trembling.

Suddenly a bell tolls right above our heads, sharp and penetrating. Everyone in the room stiffens in expectation. As if there, at that very moment, something very special were about to occur.

Mama squeezes my hand tightly and my eyes fill with tears: the little bird was going to suffocate to death. I try to confront her—you-shouldn't-leave-me-here-please-take-me-away. Someone moved and a ray of light illuminated her face. A humid sadness radiated from her blue

*eyes, those unbelievably blue eyes. I swallow the recrimination, throw
my arms around her neck, and hang on for dear life.*

Greta stopped reading; she too felt the emotion. I need a sip of
wine—she got out the corkscrew. She hates drinking alone, but tonight Tina is keeping her company through the story. The text is
handwritten in pencil, with tiny, nervous lettering. The odd thing is
the sudden, restrained, unadorned style. Which has nothing to do with
Tina—or does it?—for she talks about herself as if she were construct-
ing the identity of a character. Is that good or bad? She doesn't know.
There's something growing out of those pages that creates a sense of
distance . . . Which brings us to another question: what was her emotional state at the time of writing? Intimate portrait: truth or fiction?
The house is the same. Maybe she could make use of that and describe
the architecture . . . That's what she, Greta, would do, not Tina. She's
now in the boarding school. If she is going to give some description, it
should be . . . The sip of red wine warmed her stomach and made the
blood rise to her soul.

*The school building: a huge square shape with a patio in the middle.
I don't know how to judge architecture. The bars on the window project
a sinister, oppressive atmosphere. The paint on the walls has faded and
the doors, made of native wood, have been varnished. The classrooms
are located on one wing; on another the dormitory rooms, bathrooms,
kitchen, and dining hall; the third is the province of the nuns and novi-
tiates, and it houses the laundry as well; the fourth wing contains the
office and visiting room, which has direct access to the chapel. The basement serves as an orphanage, while the second floor has been reserved
for the medical and dental offices, and for the residence of Father Ferdinand, who is responsible for the daily masses and catechism.*
　　*I admire the priest and his French accent. I often sit next to him,
beneath the fig tree in the patio or on the veranda that surrounds it.
I like to listen to him talk about France; that is, about Avignon. No,
he does not miss his native land, not at all. He does, however, miss the
French countryside.*
　　*The dormitory: fifty beds separated by head tables. The space is too
confined for the larger girls to kneel in the dark to remove their uniforms
and change into their nightgowns. As they say their Ave Marias they
pull off the sleeves, then take off the blouse, they slip into the nightgown,
and finally they let the skirt fall to the floor. With the lights on, we hang
our clothes in the closet and brush our teeth. Everything is timed.*
　　Oh, how curious I am to see Sister Olga—the same one who took

me in tears away from my mother—remove her clothes. She sleeps in a separate space behind a curtain that hangs from a steel frame. A rosy-cheeked, good-natured, friendly nun. When the lights were out, I heard the sister drop her skirts, of which there were three. Perhaps because of that, because of the number of skirts she wore and the baths she didn't take, she gave off such an unbearable acrid odor. During the summer months the nuns stank.

The habit: long and black, made of wool, with a white wimple covering the head, spilling down the neck and ending in a large bib on the chest. A black veil is attached to the wimple by a pin, a speck of light surrounded by darkness.

I never heard Sister Olga combing her hair. I think she shaved her head. But I always waited for the sound of her dentures dropping into the glass of water: in a few minutes her snoring would echo loudly through the dormitory, like a net covering the beds.

Poor Sister Olga. She wouldn't be at all pleased with what's been said about her, Greta thinks. An astonishing detail: the prevalence of smells in Tina's childhood. As an adult she has no sense of smell whatever.

Seven years old. I think about myself and it makes me want to cry.

Eight years old. It's my birthday. I run across the patio and up the stairs three steps at a time. Boy oh boy, the Mother Superior gave me permission to go out. A heck of a privilege.

Mama and I are going to the movies. When I grow up, I want to have a boyfriend as nice as Van Johnson. And be as sweet and loving as June Allyson.

Nine years old. A mystery. Why the chronology? Silliness. Anyway, this is the age where I'll go through the mystical phase. It really doesn't matter—it could be at eight or ten.

On one of my solitary visits to the chapel, to which I had been devoting myself lately, I felt a strange presence—was someone watching me? I shivered, my hair stood on end, I didn't dare look around. Recreation period. Could another girl be seeking peace in the silence of the chapel? I turned around: no one. Although I had never done so before, I began to pray fervently. Someone was hiding back there: I was sure of it.

Suddenly, a man approached me. He was distinguished looking, dressed in suit and tie, hat in hand. An understanding man. For some reason I thought he looked familiar. He remained standing in the aisle as if he knew me well and was only waiting for me to ask him to sit down. I stared at him numbly, unable to utter a word. Then he patted me gently on the head. A soft, delightful caress—I closed my eyes. When I opened them, he had disappeared.

I was deeply affected. I asked the nun in the visiting room if she had seen anyone entering the chapel. No, she hadn't. I must have been dreaming.

Intrigued, I returned to the bench. Could it have been a hallucination? I was about to ask Saint Judas Thadeus, when I noticed there was something in his face reminiscent of the man I had just seen.

During that whole year I attended chapel diligently in the hope that it would happen again, that the man would return. And I discovered my desire to be a nun, which I declared openly to Sister Ofélia, the music teacher. After that, we became friends and had long talks about my unquestionable vocation.

I was always inclined toward Sister Ofélia. Maybe because she played the piano, or maybe because—according to hearsay—she entered the convent after becoming disillusioned in love. One day I asked her if the rumor was true. She smiled sweetly at me; she didn't deny it.

Many years later, far from the boarding school, I came across a photo of my father. I had found the man in the chapel at last.

That imaginary visit was the only one I ever received from him.

Greta takes another sip of wine. Will she be able to deal with the need she felt for her father? Will there be any resentment? Or will she simply face the problem without dramatizing it? She notices the *Requiem* has ended. She gets up and flips the record—how long has it been spinning like that? She goes to the window. A mist covers the Village, a sign that tomorrow the sun will be out. She sits down again.

Ten years old. I spend July vacation in the convent. I feel indignation against the world's injustice and against God.

August brings the first opportunity to go out. I open the closet— the dolls are sitting on the shelf as usual. Cristina has grown, her neck is so twisted . . . I look disdainfully at the dolls and yank the ribbon from my hair.

I constantly give in to the temptation to lie—to myself?—and I must reexamine the memories that have come to the surface. Or is it just my imagination?

There's one thing I can't deny: I learned to lie in that school. I lied out of fear. A morbid fear. Everything was a sin. Even chewing your fingernails. And I bit my nails until they bled. Soaping your skin directly was an error we were supposed to confess but never did. The rule: enter the shower in your nightgown; leave the door open. We rubbed the soap on our nightgowns, made of a loosely woven diaper-like material, under the watchful eyes of the bathroom warden.

"I forgot my towel, Sister. Pray bring it to me."

Bath days were Wednesday and Saturday. The girls took turns asking the novitiate to get something. When she turned her back we soaped our skin. To this day I don't know if she was on to the trick. Her not noticing was probably another lie. Probably.

One night we were returning to the dormitory from daily mass. I was about eleven. Father Ferdinand had just given a frightening sermon about carnal sin. I left the chapel terrified, since I had acquired a few notions about sex from conversations with the older girls. How could I sleep in such a panic? You sinned against chastity in your dreams. In your dreams!

Around that time I suspected my mother was planning to remarry. Instead of taking me out on my Sundays off she sent chocolates and other sweets, which I received with deep hatred. Awake or asleep, I wove dark visions of my mother loving some man. Widowhood: life-long temptation. At least in my understanding.

During the priest's sermon, cold sweat ran down my trembling body. As if I had a fever.

Waiting in line, where talking was categorically prohibited, I tried to tell another girl about my torment. The nun whirled around indignantly.

"Who's talking?"

Intimidated by her authoritarian tone, I did not confess my troubles. I kept my guilt secret and what is even worse I started the whole business over again. A dreadful fear about what Father Ferdinand had said: hands disintegrating with leprosy, lips covered with sores, a vast panorama of hideous diseases. Sister Olga did not hesitate to apply the prescribed punishment. Before going to sleep I had to write one hundred times, 'I must not speak in line.'

There was a writing table between the dormitory rooms reserved for that punishment. It was nicknamed 'the gallows'. After prayers and changing clothes, I faced the corridor of death. Pale with terror. A long, deserted corridor.

Writing fifty sentences wasn't so much trouble, but the rest . . . it was painful for the fingers and for the soul. I was easily distracted and my words were constantly interrupted, sometimes by a soft knocking on the window—was someone trying to get in?—which made my heart beat wildly; a fig-tree branch—I sighed in relief; sometimes by sister Olga's snoring, which that night failed to give me protection: it frightened me. It sounded like a toad croaking; I opened the sash window. The frigid

June wind cooled my burning face. A lighted train raced in the distance.
Writing a column of 'I must not's' might be less distressing than the
whole sentence. I try it out. What if I ran away on that train? An or-
phan, no parents, no school, no friends, no nothing, disappearing from
the face of the earth? They'd all regret it, the nun, mama, all of them. I
imagined myself ragged, filthy, unrecognizable. My hysteria stained the
paper and smudged the ink. Just when I was starting the column with
'speak in line.'

I had to do the whole page over again. I don't know how long it
took to complete the penance. I know I suffered long and endless hours—
was it getting light on the horizon when I went to bed?

I got sick for a week. I had done my penance just before coming
down with a severe case of the mumps.

If older people and our educators understood that children have
memories, maybe human relations would be less difficult, Greta declared to herself as she poured more wine. The second glass. She must
change that agonizing record. She's not dead, not yet, so enough *Re-*
quiem. Or could it be . . . Chopin. *Etudes* for piano. Homage to a great
pianist—cheers: Cortot.

She can hear Tina saying: I hate romantic films because they
affect me so much. Especially if they're about families that fall apart.
Or about love. I always cry.

It makes sense. Some people are capable of placing sensibility
above reason. Tina's one of them. Imagine someone with that trait,
how complicated she must be. There's no place in this world for ro-
mantics. (Are they all put away in asylums?) Only in our imaginations.

I have doubts about whether or not everything I'm telling actually
occurred. I could simply be making it all up. But where in heaven could
I find so much material? A short time ago I considered dumping these
pages in the wastebasket and to hell with this search for identity. One
small detail is bothering me . . . Something that happened or that has not
yet taken place?

Nowadays I'm absolutely horrified by lies; I can't forgive them, no
matter what the excuse. Therefore, I declare my mother's widowhood is
not genuine. My father is alive. The two of them are only separated. But
I never knew him.

Thirteen years old. I'm in the infirmary again. The day is so long
when you're sick, I say to Neusa, an orphan, who has sneaked in. She's
seventeen. At eighteen, she'll leave the orphanage. She can't wait. Mama
promised to find her a job, if nothing else helping around the house. Neusa

dreams about the moment when she'll receive her first paycheck—the or-
phans do the cleaning at the school, which pays for lodging, food, and a
primary education. She slips her alibi, a dirty bedpan, under the bed. If
a nun shows up, she's on duty: the students are forbidden to socialize
with the orphans, lord knows why.

Neusa wears gray sackcloth. Brown skin, black hair cut short to
avoid lice. An ordinary face. What gives her character is her sweetness
and her extraordinarily soft voice.

"Feeling better?" She approaches the window.

"So-so. I had awful stomach cramps this morning. You think I have
appendicitis?"

"At your age? I bet it's your period."

"What?"

"Menstruation, like you people call it."

"I'm already a young woman," I lied, because I pretended I had
started menstruating several months ago—so I wouldn't seem different
from my classmates and I could enjoy the privilege of relating to the
older girls.

"Well, then I don't know."

Neusa picked up a brush and began to run it through my hair.
Nothing could have given me more pleasure than that—I closed my eyes.
Grateful.

"You have such fine hair. Mine's thick as a broom."

The walls in the room, pink. Outside, a red sky. I loved sunsets, but
there's nothing like the pleasure that brush gave me—I closed my eyes
again.

"Have you kissed a boy yet, Tina?" Neusa asks.

"Of course." I lied again: she might reveal to the girls that, in fact,
I had never kissed a boy.

"What's it like? Don't whiskers hurt?"

I remembered Jussara, a day-student, explaining the facial irri-
tation.

"His beard scratches but it's yummy."

"What do you do with your tongue?"

I blushed. How would I get out of that one? To gain time, I asked
Neusa to open the curtain wider because it was getting dark.

"Wait a minute." The orphan knelt by my side. "What do you do
with your tongue?"

"Depends. Everyone has their own way of kissing . . ." I considered
that a brilliant answer.

"Could you teach me?"

"Me?"

22

"Yes. I'll kiss you on the mouth and you show me."

Our discussion was interrupted when a strong cramp forced me to double over in pain. She made me lie back and delicately massaged my belly. The pain became intense and, odd thing, I began to swell, to float. Suspended on a thin wire. Something was about to burst inside me. Something I couldn't distinguish—I groaned loudly. A thick liquid began to flow as if I were suddenly a plant or a flower, snipped off.

Greta stopped for a few moments. One becomes a young woman in many ways. Each is unlike the next. Greta never even felt her first menstruation. One day, pop, she woke up in discomfort.

The Chopin piece has ended; she doesn't feel like getting up—she checks her notes. Not far to go. At least tonight.

Does the idea of weeding the past, as if childhood were a kind of garden, really have anything to do with my present identity? I doubt it. One has not been; one is. Do scars condition feelings? Justifying certain peculiarities in one's behavior may be a sign of . . . it's like looking "through" the mirror rather than "in" the mirror. What other person could I be but the one I glimpse there?

Sundays. Group outings in town; the black shepherdesses lead their submissive beasts down the pavement. I'll be leaving in six months. Goodbye, school. Goodbye, girl friends. Goodbye, childhood. The world is waiting for me.

But somehow I don't fit in. My mother has a man I can't stand. When he comes into the house I hole up in my room. She has moved to town, so the house is different. I miss the farm.

Am I pretty? The mirror says I am, some days; on others it says I'm not. My mouth is too big. They stare at me on the street. I'm terrified I stink like a bitch in heat. And I douse myself with perfume.

Sixteen years old. My first boyfriend is blond—a kind of brother? My Van Johnson. He holds my hand at the matinee and brushes his arm against my breast. I promise myself I'll marry him so God won't punish me. See you Sunday. They'll be showing **Million Dollar Mermaid**, with Esther Williams.

At one o'clock I'm waiting anxiously by the entrance of the Avenida Theatre. I'm wearing a new dress. At half-past one I see Murilo coming toward me—what a letdown—holding hands with another girl. I return home in tears. Men are wicked.

Other names: Kiko, Dirceu, Almir, Carlos, Emílio, and João, who suffered from epilepsy. Just like that he would faint, his trembling lips gave the warning, and he frothed at the mouth and his body writhed.

After the crisis had passed, he'd say he was going to die. I felt like a Sister of Charity. A radio announcer. I listened to his well-modulated voice saying, 'good night, dear listeners,' with the solemnity of one listening to God.

Wedding. With my veil and garland, lovely as an angel—in the words of my mother-in-law. Much ado. The church full of people I didn't know. Frozen with panic. It lasted three years. One day I woke up, packed my bags, and hid away in the village.

"No one can make me go back," I yelled at my mother and at him, my husband. "No one."

Not even my uncle, when he decided to subdivide the farm. I accepted the challenge of remaining here during construction. I felt deep regret as I watched the bulldozer's path of destruction. The rape.

During that time I went to town every day. It was then I fell in love. The only time. But I can't talk about it yet. My heart starts bleeding again.

"Passion seems intense when it is brief," my mother stated sententiously.

She was ill, her blood pressure dangerously high. It had been a long time since we'd spoken, each living her own life. I sat in a rocking chair, a bit distant from her bed, and I felt our roles were reversed. At that instant I assumed a certain power; I was the mother and she the daughter. That's why I decided to express my opinion. (I'm amazed I did it!)

"As far as I'm concerned, passion is a dramatic representation of love. I believe in happy endings."

"And does he deserve all the romanticism?" She looked at me sadly.

"I don't know. What does it matter?"

"All passion has a bad ending, dear. Afterwards there's nothing left."

(Poor mother, how wrong she was. There is indeed something left: an enormous sense of failure.)

She died of arteriosclerosis. She regressed so far. A newborn child. She lost the ability to speak. Only her eyes remained alive, because she cried so much. From joy, when I arrived; from sadness, when I left.

She was all wrinkled up when she died; I managed to control myself.

But I dissolved into tears on another occasion as I looked at a picture of her: she was thirty years old, her smile radiant.

On Saturday, Sônia woke up early and read aloud to her mother the want ad section, "Business Opportunities."

"Isn't it too bad, Mother, that the address and telephone number are in such small print?"

Elisa asked excitedly how much her whim had cost.

"Almost nothing. Why are you bringing up money?"

"Because I want to know, dear. Are want ads very expensive?" She tried to hide her irritation.

It was eight o'clock in the morning. In spite of the cold, the sweat ran down Sônia's body.

"What's the temperature today?"

"About sixty degrees, I think." Elisa went out on the veranda to check. "Can you believe it?" she shouted. "Thirteen degrees. It's really cold out." She saw Greta at the window and waved to her.

A gust of wind blew into the room, reinforcing her words. Sônia turned up the collar and huddled in her woolen robe.

"Mother, hurry up and close the door. The coffee's going to get cold."

"This is going to be a rough winter," Elisa said as she returned to the table. "It's only June and already the weather has turned cold. I'm going to have to send for some wood for the fireplace."

"Nonsense." It was Sônia's turn to get up. "The mist is a sign it's going to be a lovely day."

The optimistic tone astonished Elisa. Her daughter is truly amazing. They've lived together for so long and . . .

She'd make a good wife. So sweet, so proper, a heart of gold. She's not exactly pretty, but she's certainly not ugly either: healthy skin, teeth white and shining, sparkling eyes. With a little makeup she'd be attractive. The interviews, a wonderful pretext.

"Makeup? Whatever for? I don't even know if anyone will show up. What time is it?"

"A little after eight."

"Then we have time."

Elisa wiped off the table and quickly checked over the living room. Everything was in order, in spite of the fact that the maid had weekends off. And why not? The two of them can get along just fine by themselves. The important thing is that the driver show up to take them shopping.

"Are you going to receive the people here?"

"In the library . . . it depends . . . if anyone has to wait . . ."

"Of course, Sônia. Should we serve coffee and cookies?"

"Perhaps."

"I have to go to the supermarket. If you need anything, let me know."

Shortly, Elisa was ready to leave.

"Daughter dear, I don't mean to intrude, but what are you going to do with other people's dreams?"

"I don't know yet, Mother."

"Please, Sônia, trust me at least this once. You never open up with me, you never tell me your problems. We're like a couple of strangers."

"Not now, Mother." She gives her an impatient look.

"Whenever you feel like it."

She thinks for a few seconds, and then changes her tone of voice.

"I promise I'll tell you." She goes up to Elisa and strokes her hair. "You know, you looked better with long hair."

"Don't change the subject. It's nine o'clock and the telephone should start ringing soon."

"I hope so."

"And how much do you plan to pay for these dreams?"

"So we're back to money again."

"OK, I'm sorry."

"Oh, Mother, I forgot to buy pencils. Would you pick me up a dozen of those sharpened ones with erasers? You know which ones I mean? Hurry up. If anyone shows up without calling first, I don't even have a pen."

"There's one hanging on the note board in the kitchen, above the sink."

"Thanks, Mom." She kissed her on the forehead and went to get dressed: gray skirt, black sweater, white blouse.

Once she was ready she opened a packet of note cards and arranged them on the desk top, next to the telephone. The library, her favorite room in the house. The walls are hidden by shelves filled with hardcover books with worn and faded spines. The wicker chairs facing the window look like two friends having a chat—she sighs in satisfaction. A beam of light suddenly brightened the library. The telephone rang for the first time.

Wrong number. She hung up in relief. Her voice quavered. For heaven's sake. She almost regretted taking out the want ad.

The second call: a pastry maker offering cream puffs for sale. Amused, Sônia explained to the kind lady the word was dream, not cream. She was looking for the dreams you have in your sleep.

"Now why would anyone want to buy such a thing?" The caller slammed the phone down.

What a mix-up of words. If everyone thought like that woman just now . . . The worrisome thought was cut off by the phone, which rang again. This time it was a man's voice. He made an appointment for eleven o'clock. He sounded dignified, perhaps a bit hesitant. Did the seller understand what she was looking for?

She must decide quickly whether to assign different values according to the quality of the merchandise, like in the story. Or should she pay by the session? A short dream could be as good as a long one. Besides, it would be difficult to judge the quality in front of the sellers. She would pay by the session, she decided. The thing to do was to put the money in an envelope. She would sense at the proper time if someone was faking it. People who wear glasses have certain advantages—she puts hers on—they can hide one's reactions. If the dream doesn't interest me, I'll get rid of the person immediately. I'm very good at seeing through con artists.

"Did anyone call?" Her mother interrupted her thoughts.

"There's someone dropping by at eleven o'clock."

"A man?"

"Yes. Why?"

Elisa didn't answer. Maybe her daughter would actually meet someone; suddenly filled with hope, she began arranging cookies on the silver tray.

"Shopping on Saturdays is awful. That's when everybody goes out," she grumbled from the doorway before going back into the kitchen.

Sônia arranged the pencils in rows inside the drawer, leaving only one on the desk. She picked up a book with photographs of Venice. A present from her uncle. She spent a long time studying the first reproduction: lord knows what she was thinking about, with such an air of concentration. What did she see? Venice, fog-shrouded. Golden reflections in the choppy water. A man holding a broom sweeps a piazza. He's wearing gray coveralls—in the original they must have been blue but in the reproduction they have a lead gray color. A cigarette hangs from his mouth and his shoes are old and dusty. A desolate image of Venice.

The sound of the doorbell made Sônia turn pale.

Elisa brought the visitor ceremoniously into the library.

"I'm Mateus. A friend told me about the ad. I was intrigued . . . I think she'll be coming by, since she makes a practice of writing down her dreams."

"Really? Have a seat." Her voice faltered as she spoke. He looked like someone . . . I know, like Kafka. That's it, Franz Kafka. She clearly remembered a photograph.

"Do you mind if I smoke?"

"Not at all." She swiveled the chair toward the yard but then turned back to her original position, facing the desk.

Mateus glanced at the bookcase without focusing on any single work. She noticed his trouser cuffs were frayed and he was sitting at attention.

"There's a Truman Capote story about a dream merchant. Are you familiar with it?"

She excitedly wrote down the name. What luck, receiving a visitor who knew the story!

"Do you know what book it was published in?"

"*A Tree of Night.*"

"Is there a translation?"

"I don't know. If there is, it probably carries the original title: *A Árvore da Noite.* If I remember correctly the story's called 'Master Misery' in English."

Sônia gave him a straightforward account of the incident in the waiting room at the dentist's office. The experience had aroused her curiosity. Now that she knew the name of the author, she could look for a Portuguese edition and take up her reading where she left off—suddenly embarrassed, she bowed her head. The fact that she had discovered the source of her plagiarism chilled her enthusiasm. Was there something in his manner that suggested annoyance, or could he be mocking her?

"If you'd like, I can translate the story. I have a copy of the book at home."

"Yes, I would. You charge by the page for translations, don't you?"

He agreed. Feeling quite at ease, he lit his second cigarette. His manner was that of someone visiting an old friend—or an aunt. His movements were delicate, almost feminine, as he inhaled and blew out the smoke.

"There's a dream I can't seem to recall. My mind's a blank. You see, I dream a lot . . ."

"I never do. I mean, rarely."

"That's not possible. Everyone dreams all the time."

"Then I guess I forget," she quickly recognized.

And she thought to herself: dreaming is a creative act of the subconscious. I must be mediocre even in my dreams.

"There's one coming back to me." He paused at length, as if he were reconstructing the dream mentally before telling it.

At that moment, Elisa brought in coffee and cookies. She placed the tray on the desk, her eyes fastened on her daughter, her face alight with expectation. A face suspended, if that is the proper definition.

Sônia poured the coffee without a sound so as not to interrupt the flow.

He picked up the demitasse mechanically, as if he too were trying not to lose track of the story.

"I dreamed the moon had split into several moons. A sort of vision of the end of the world, you know? The sky had shrunk and I could touch the horizon line with my hand if I wanted. The general impression of the image was that of a cataclysm about to happen. I woke up in a nervous sweat. And I had this dream several times, I don't know why."

"Would you care for more coffee?"

"Yes, thank you. It's delicious. What are you going to do with the dreams?"

"Put together a file."

He did not act surprised. Quite the contrary. He seemed to accept her answer naturally.

"Alice is the one who has good dreams. You'll see."

"Who?"

"My friend. The one who told me about the want ad."

Sônia noticed a wrinkle slanting diagonally across his forehead, a wrinkle deeper than the others; she saw he had long legs and short, slender fingers. She must look ridiculous the way she stared at him—she lowered her eyes.

"Funny, I'm trying to remember what the buyer in Capote's story did with the dreams, but I can't. In any case," he lit another cigarette, the fifth, she counted the butts in the ashtray, "I'll find out when I get home."

"I never found out because I stopped in the middle. Just the other day I was making precisely that point to my uncle. You should never stop reading . . ."

"I agree."

A few more moments of silence and Mateus got up, promising to have the translation ready in a week or ten days. Before he said good-bye, she asked for his address so she could pick up the translation after work, around seven.

"Next Tuesday, ten days from now, all right? Here's the payment for your dream." She tried to hand him one of the envelopes.

"By no means. I told you nothing of value. I spent a very pleasant hour, thank you. See you soon."

Sônia walked him to the door. She tried to smile but was unable to.

That afternoon no one else showed up or telephoned. Greta came by to chat at the gate. Going over her meeting with Mateus, Sônia saw nothing unusual in the fact that they hadn't once referred to each other by name. Human contact means embarrassment; why should Greta find that peculiar? You can't be on a first-name basis the first time you're with someone. You need a certain degree of ceremony.

Elisa had a premonition at bedtime: her daughter opening books and drawers, feverishly searching for an old magazine clipping with a photograph of Franz Kafka.

A short time ago Elisa mentioned that she and Sônia don't have a maid on weekends. Only two or three families in the Village of the Bells have exclusive, full-time housekeepers; the others have made do with cleaning women who work day hours and who live in the *favela* behind the cemetery. Household help is really necessary only for those who work in the city; for folks who stay home it only gets in the way. Physical activity, in fact, helps to relieve anxiety. For example, when you're bustling about you don't have time to think about the church bells—that's what the Village representative's wife was saying yesterday. The hours fly past and she just forgets to listen. Now there are people who deny emphatically that they hear the mysterious tolling, either because they don't wish to discuss it or because they don't want to encourage malicious gossip.

And as if the problem with the bells wasn't enough, strange objects have begun to appear at the intersection of Palm Street and the Avenue: dead chickens, bottles of sugar cane brandy, effigies of scowling voodoo gods, burnt candles. Devilish business. They say that the girl who is a maid at number 580 performs the witchcraft, that she's a priestess from a famous voodoo temple. She acts more like a mad woman than a witch. Some cynic claimed those were the doings of Fortuna to scare the residents. Can you imagine anyone in Fortuna commissioning spells?

Once Greta discussed the matter with Tina, who said that one shouldn't be skeptical, that there exist supernatural powers unknown to us. The two women were enjoying the fresh air in the yard, seated under an arbor that had once sheltered an orchid collection. That arbor is one of the most delightful places in the world. You have to have sat there and watched the fading light of a summer afternoon to appreciate the feeling of peace and beauty it brings. Gnarled roots twist enchantingly around its time-corroded wooden latticework. A dilapidated slatted bench is covered with dark, humid moss; many different species of worm promenade across it. A most enjoyable pastime: observing the comings and goings of the tiny creatures, up and down, down and up. Some are sluggish, others hurried.

When Greta heard Tina admit she believed in the supernatural nonsense, she gave up on intelligent arguments. She had already wasted her breath on a former cook who suffered terrible stomach pains and was frightfully pale. The woman was convinced someone had cast a spell on her and her lover, a married man and a ne'er-do-well. Poor thing. People who hold such beliefs can never be convinced otherwise.

But blaming the poor maid at 580 was really too much. If they said she was amusing, Greta would agree. She's an odd duck. There's always a turban covering her head and she wears shoes with extremely high heels; that's how she earned the nickname Carmen Miranda. She gets roaring drunk on Saturdays. No one minds because she's always well behaved on weekdays.

A sharp, cackling sound approached—Greta went to take a look. Speak of the devil, Carmen Miranda was staggering back home. It's funny how a simple laugh can produce sensations so different from its actual meaning. At that moment, the laughter gave the impression she was making fun of all the villagers. Or did that shrill and eerie sound only herald further misfortunes?

Tina seemed so downcast the last time Greta visited her in the clinic. Not even her birthday celebration helped. Everyone ate a piece of the cake, the nurses, the group of friends, except for her. She remained listless, cold. At one particular instant she stared at the doctor as if she were watching herself in a mirror. Or looking at a portrait.

♎ Sunday morning the sky was clear, Sônia observed as she tried to make out the forms drawn by the cirrus clouds; sometimes one could discover animals, objects, even words. One day the clouds wrote the word "I." Today, unfortunately, the patches of cloud dispersed uniformly in a long veil. With her elbows on the window sill, she had the impression it was not exactly she who was there, but herself as a little girl—she smiles. As we grow older, some childhood experiences come back as clearly as if we had relived them, she recognized before going into the shower. Feeling lazy.

She dressed in the same clothes as yesterday, gray skirt, black sweater, white blouse—no, this one won't do—she changed into a beige blouse and settled in the library to wait for the telephone

Upon her return from mass, Elisa dismissed the chauffeur and took her usual Sunday stroll around the yard. She was ashamed to admit that she talked to plants. She had learned about it from a television program. And she firmly believed plants had feelings, to the point that she couldn't understand people who would allow themselves to cut branches or flowers to decorate vases. Practically a crime, killing them for no reason—don't you agree, Greta? She would never do such a thing. Plants belong in gardens, she insisted. In gardens.

And she went in to prepare lunch, which was eaten in almost total silence. Sônia was trying to figure out the readers' lack of interest in her want ad: no one telephoned this morning. Elisa thought about her garden.

The doorbell rang as they were finishing dessert. It was a woman of about forty with extraordinarily white skin.

"Excuse me for not making an appointment. I don't have a telephone and it's impossible to use those payphones. They're always out of order."

"Please, it doesn't matter. Come this way, let's go into the other room. Will you bring the coffee in there, Mother?"

The visitor noticed the rugs and stopped briefly before an armoire.

"Lovely piece."

Sônia thanked her and showed her into the library. The woman's appearance was unusual, not only because of her bizarre manner of dress—black, with the sun so hot!—but also because of the personality she projected. Her dress was a silk tunic fastened at the waist with a braided cord whose two ends dangled loosely. Along with her purse, she carried a straw bag.

"My name is Alice Gross. My parents are Austrian . . . What a marvelous garden!" she exclaimed. "I love gardens like that, without flowers. Are you a psychoanalyst?" She gave Sônia a cordial look.

"No." Sônia was enjoying this. "Do I look like one?"

"Never mind." She sat in one of the wicker chairs and Sônia in another. "What I want is to get rid of this notebook." She took it out of her purse. "I've been writing down my dreams for years although I don't know what for. When I read the newspaper on Friday I gave a sigh of relief."

Sônia took the brown spiral notebook. She paged through it; the notebook was nearly filled.

"Can you lend it to me for a few days? There's a lot of material here. It'd be a bit difficult to read it now."

"Listen, I want to be free of the notebook. My conditions . . ."

"And the price?"

"I want absolutely nothing in exchange. It's a present, if you can call that rubbish . . ."

Sônia gave her a look of surprise. This was the second person who had answered the ad and wasn't after money.

"Well, I have to go." She got up.

"Stay a while longer." Sônia almost shouted, fearing she was really leaving.

Alice accepted the invitation immediately and sat back down.

"Have many people shown up to sell their dreams?"

"You're the first, I mean, the second."

"Was Mateus here?"

Sônia nodded her head.

"Oh, I knew it. He was so curious. If the want ad had been about kinky sex, you would have been in for a surprise. People would've been knocking down your door."

"Really?"

"The world's full of perverts." Alice bent down and took a crochet needle and a skein of wool from her purse. She began to work as if that were exactly what she had planned on.

The pause gave Sônia a chance to page through the notebook again. The dreams had titles: *The Pearl, The Shop Window, The Babies*.

"Can you read my handwriting?"

"Perfectly."

The writing is steady and slants to the left.

"Are you left-handed?"

"Yes."

Elisa brought in the coffee. Instead of simply leaving the tray on the table, she decided to serve. Perhaps she could stay and chat for a bit. She knew several crochet stitches. But Alice, with her head down, carefully examined her handiwork and refused to acknowledge Elisa's presence. Sônia was taken aback by Alice's attitude of rejection and the smile of connivance she flashed as soon as the door was closed.

"Any problem?" she asked, facing her visitor.

"No. I was distracted and almost messed up a stitch."

The notebook should be read from the beginning, even if the order didn't alter the content—Sônia placed her cup on the tray.

The Pearl. I was standing with T. and several other people I didn't know. I ask: who has what I want? They all raise their hands. T. hesitates, but he raises his, too. I examine their hands one by one: they are holding seashells, which open as I approach, revealing pearls. T. holds out his closed hand. He looks at me lovingly, to see if I'll order him to open his hand. I wait, unconcerned, and he finally has no alternative. I can hardly believe it—the shell is empty. I ask: What? You don't have a single pearl for me? I turn my back on him. The others could have thousands of them, large, small, colored, I wasn't interested. I wanted him and him alone to have a pearl for me, even a tiny one. Suddenly, I hear T.'s voice calling me. He holds out a lovely pearl necklace for me. I ask if the pearls are his. He says they are. I see it's a lie, because all the shells that were previously filled are now empty. Infuriated, I hurl the necklace, which bursts on the ground. T. is both angry and shocked: what is it you want? The people begin laughing and shouting: he doesn't know, he doesn't know. Dancing and singing, they form a circle around T. He puts his hand on his head and cries. I feel sorry; I want to go up to him but I'm unable to.

"It's strange," Sônia observed, "and well narrated."

"I always wanted to have a child with him. I think the dream reveals that fact, don't you?"

Elisa came in to remove the tray. Alice again ignored her.

"Sounds likely," she said, noticing that the woman crocheted with her right hand.

"I learned to use this hand after several thrashings."

"By whom?"

"Adults, of course. I had a hard time learning. I stuttered, had colic, you name it. Now I can use both hands for a variety of tasks. For example, I write with my left hand, I embroider and crochet with my right, which is also good for stirring. But if you hand me something, I'll reach for it with my left, and so on."

"What're you making out of that strip you're crocheting?"

"It's the last section of a blanket. I use leftover pieces of wool."

"Who is T.?"

"My husband. I dream about him all the time. I don't know why."

The Shop Window. I'm walking along a downtown street when I notice a crowd of people in front of a store. I approach and the people withdraw. A man is lying in the shop window. He stretches and walks in my direction. I realize it's T . . . I tap on the glass, I need to speak with him. T. shows he neither hears nor sees a thing because he turns his back on me and moves toward the bed. I knock more loudly. He then turns toward me, but he no longer has T.'s face. I shake my head, that's not the face I want, and he turns his back on me again. I tap on the window

again and he shows me yet different features. I don't understand and I
continue knocking on the glass, and each time a new face appears in re-
sponse. I cry in sorrow for T. He turns around for the last time and what
do I see? A face without features, without eyes, without a nose or a
mouth. Smooth as bread dough, white and raw. I scream and wake up.

Sônia observed the accomplished dreamer with sudden tenderness. How pleasant to be there with such quiet company, with someone who knew how to entertain herself with her hands.

"Have you finished reading the second dream? I never understood that one. I can explain some of them, at least to myself; others I
can't. They remain obscure. Excuse me, do you have a radio here? I
love music."

"There's one in my room. I can get it if you like."

"No, please. I can sing."

"Can you?"

A clear, trained, enchanting voice filled the library. Sônia listened
attentively to the strange melody sung without words.

"Music is the most fantastic of the arts," Alice exclaimed. "A person doesn't need education or refined sensibility to appreciate a song.
It's enough to have hearing." Alice gave her opinion and smiled.

"What was that?"

"One of those short Medieval pieces. I learned it in school. It tells
the story of a fisherman who lures the fish with his singing. I forgot
the lyrics."

"Can you hum it again? Maybe I can learn the melody . . ."

As she sang, Alice was the exact image of the friend she never had.

"Look, I'm almost done crocheting this piece. As soon as I finish
I'll be on my way."

"Would you like another cup of coffee?"

Sônia didn't wait for an answer. Elisa was asleep on the sofa with
the television on. Her daughter turned down the volume and went to
the kitchen to get the thermos and the cookies.

Alice remained in the same position, her fingers deftly moving
the crochet needles.

"Tiago loves to have a blanket to wrap around his legs, and the
one he has now is falling apart. That's why I decided to make this one
from leftover pieces of wool. It'll be versatile because I can use it too,
right?" she asked tentatively.

Sônia praised the result.

"Please. Read out loud *The Operation*. I think that dream is one of the most complicated . . ." Alice looked it up in the notebook, which she handed back opened.

The room is huge and its walls are shaped like steps, on which people are sitting in absolute silence and with looks of expectation.

Suddenly, a large man comes in; he's dressed in white, with a doctor's mask. Then two nurses enter with a very fat lady, naked from the waist up, who carries her breasts in a wicker basket. She's tired and out of breath.

The large man bows to the audience, which applauds. He raises his hand and the two nurses place the basket on the floor. Each one seizes a breast and takes five steps forward, until it's completely stretched out. The man takes a length of wire from his pocket, shows it to the audience, and twists it around both breasts.

He then snaps his fingers and a tall, thin man appears; he's dressed all in black and holds a pair of long scissors in his hand. He cavorts, leaps, pirouettes, as if he were a dancer. The man in white again snaps his fingers and the thin man hands him the scissors. He executes a few pirouettes in the air and one, two, he cuts off the fat woman's breasts.

The two sweating nurses drag out the pieces of breast that have been cut off and are now spraying blood on the audience. The man bows in all directions, but instead of applause he receives loud boos. The remains of the breasts on the woman's body look like wrinkled daisies.

After that he takes a green coconut out of his pocket and cuts it in half. He blows in it three times and throws it at the woman with all his might. When the pieces of coconut hit her chest, a report is heard, a gunshot. The man in black runs to the woman and quickly paints the coconuts red. The public cheers.

Each breast had gained a lovely red nipple. Now everything was truly in order.

Sônia closed the notebook.

"Amazing."

Alice laughed, her left eye closed more than the right, the muscles attached to the ear by invisible threads and supporting a face about to crack.

"I think so, too." She reassembled her face. "Look, I've finished the blanket. A good thing; Tiago hates it when I get home after dark. The sun will be setting soon."

Sônia walked her visitor to the gate.

"Thank you so much for the notebook. I wish there were something I could do in return."

"Never mind that." She takes the notebook out of Sônia's hands and writes an address on the cover. "Drop by. Tiago will enjoy meeting you."

Walking slowly, Alice stopped now and then to examine a garden. She snapped off a spring bough at Camilo's house—she turned around to wave good-bye; Sônia watched closely as her unexpected friend moved off into the distance toward her own world.

The parenthesis of the visit to the Village, closed forever?

🔔 Six o'clock. The bells are tolling. Greta turned her back to Sônia's house—yes, she felt her neighbor's loneliness—and felt a tightening in her chest as her eyes scanned the street.

The architecture on Palm Street is redolent of the past. Tina's house is almost completely hidden by acacia shrubs. The ivy has climbed up to the veranda's tiled roof and back down, forming a curtain that brightens the living room in the summer but darkens it in the winter. Being the oldest building in the Village—the manor house?—it still shows traces of its colonial past: the windows and doors have those wooden lintels in the shape of ox yokes. At the main entrance a stairway with eight steps leads to the habitable floor, since the bottom floor serves only as a basement—in times past it would have been used for servants' quarters, storage, and laundry room. In the kitchen, a table battered by use and an old retired woodstove keep alive an orderly family atmosphere. In the beginning Tina considered taking over the kitchen for her collages. In the end she settled for the living room; it was cozier and when the weather was cold it was heated by the fireplace. And that way she didn't have to keep changing places and have pieces of paper scattered about.

Sônia's house is also ivy-covered; Camilo's is painted blue and the windows have natural wood trim and louvered shutters. Personally, Greta prefers more modern architecture, the concrete structures they build nowadays. Still, she can't deny the street's charm, with its 1950s look. Really, the only awful building is the corner bar. A perfect example of a tiled façade, each porcelain fragment a different color. If some of the residents were a little more conscientious they'd have the cracks in the plaster fixed, which would help tone down the general look of ruin . . . wasn't the decaying apartment building enough? Ananias's house had been deteriorating, but after he died it was spruced up beautifully. The new resident painted the walls himself. When the folks at 515 painted their house, they tried to match the same shade of ochre. If everyone followed their example . . . At the same time Greta is thinking this she's doubting she'd like the effect: brand-new neighborhoods have no soul. The Village projects a dense atmosphere; it has personality. Míriam and her tattered cape, Camilo pushing the wheel-chair as if he were on the Champs Elysées, Sônia's driver, haughty as a prince, Elisa conversing with her plants, the opera singer at 520 . . . In spite of the problems, Greta wouldn't trade the Village for any other neighborhood, oh no, she'd never do that. The Village of the Bells was her paradise, with or without loneliness.

Is living a conscious dream?

🔔 Tuesday Sônia woke up with a headache. She couldn't even get out of bed. Maybe she was really ill—she took the thermometer from the bedside table. After a minute she checked her temperature: normal. The gadget wasn't working. She stuck it in her armpit again. There had to be a fever. She had the symptoms: chills, migraine, weakness. She must take some medicine. And she didn't want to hear her mother's usual rigmarole about hypochondria. She was tired of arguing. For heaven's sake, if you don't feel well it's because you're ill.

The thermometer refused to confirm her fever. Well then, why was she sweating so much? Anyone could see she was dehydrating. She placed a hand on her stomach: the gesture brought back her nightmare. Incredible—she too had dreamt!

She stretched out her arm to reach for one of the books on dreams she had borrowed from the library yesterday. Her eyes scanned several paragraphs and came to rest on one that discussed self-censorship as a way to explain the symbolic forms of dreams. Freud can go to hell— she selected another volume and opened it at random. When she read the word "moon" she pictured Mateus. "In Egypt, it was considered a favorable sign to see the moon shining and it revealed a sense of forgiveness. This astral body generally exhibits a feminine, and particularly maternal, aspect. As Caligula writhed in his bed he would call the moon to share his bed and his passion. The moon, in that case, might have an incestuous meaning. But in spite of its maternal dimension, it does not refer to the mother. It remains a heavenly sphere which the ancients transformed into a deity. Caligula wanted to become one with the mother-goddess, which implied a desire for sacred marriage, transcendent incest, religious union. Incest with his real mother would never have satisfied him. The moon, in dreams, always involves a mystery, the unidentified face of a woman or a mother. At the same time, the mystery contains the idea of rapid change due to the quick succession of the moon's phases. Finally, it is associated with intuitions of death, because it is a lifeless, burnt-out orb."

Could the dream be a sign of Mateus's personality? She again visualized him with unbelievable clarity. What about trying to figure out the meaning of her own nightmare? She wouldn't know where to begin. She's vaguely aware she was trying to escape from a deep stone tunnel. She struggled to hold on to the sharp edges, but when she succeeded the pit became deeper. Well, was it a tunnel or a pit? She can't remember. Both, she thinks. And she has no idea what it could mean.

Sônia, get up: a heavy blanket of fog covered the Village. No, she wasn't going to the clinic. After all, she was sick. She deserved the rest. Her mother advised her to have something to eat before she made up her mind. She was well aware of her daughter's emotional disturbances: indolence, an unmistakable sign. Who was going to help uncle with his busy appointment schedule? Sônia knows how much she'd be missed if she didn't show up. Wasn't she supposed to go over to Mateus's, she muses, anxious to break out of the dreary mood.

Her morning at the clinic wouldn't have been so bad if her waiting-room game had worked out the way she planned: asking the children about their dreams. Surprisingly, they withdrew like clams into their shells the minute she mentioned the word dream. "I don't know, I don't remember," was the prevailing attitude.

She gave up on her research when a blond girl, about ten years old, answered: "I dreamt my dog Boni died. And I didn't want him to be buried in the backyard with my father."

"Was your dog pretty?"

"Not wasn't, Miss Sônia, he is pretty. It was just a dumb dream. It's a lie to have my father be buried. He just brought me here to get my shot. Dreams are secret. You're not supposed to tell anybody."

Secret? Sônia was mystified.

She wandered the streets for a while at noontime. She had two free hours. She usually sat at the nearest lunch counter and ate while she read the newspapers. Then she would kill time browsing in the bookstores. She preferred secondhand booksellers on days she wasn't hungry. Which was not the case today. And if she were to check the shop windows for the latest fashions? It's been ages since she bought any clothes.

The mannequin looked marvelous with its leather boots, riding breeches, and bandana tied around the neck. She went into the store and tried on the entire outfit. She liked it so much she had her old clothes wrapped up. Certain things are capable of bringing a corpse back to life, she recognizes, and new clothing is one of them.

She felt unexpectedly happy when she walked out of the store. Well now!

A small pleasant restaurant. It was still empty. A frail sunbeam struck the table she picked out. Instead of the usual sandwich, she decided on fish fillet, vegetables, and she screwed up her courage to stammer, "Half a bottle of white wine, dry." She didn't bother to open the newspaper; she just let herself relax and watched the passers-by in the street. Ashen, peaked, and worried faces, bodies bent against the icy wind. The fog lingered in the air, lighter, more rarefied. An unreal landscape—she searched for her glasses in her purse—perhaps a result of nearsightedness, usually responsible for visual hallucinations.

The waiter brought the bottle and she tasted it. Wine is the nectar of the gods. A trite saying now and then never hurt anyone; it's a manner of speaking. Or . . .

As she sipped the wine she accepted her loneliness with no feeling of shame. The totality of her being had come to the surface. She purposely turned to the mirror on the wall next to the table; it showed her a simple face. A face painted in an academic style. She beheld a lonely woman looking at herself kindly. Who am I? And she continued to study herself in the mirror, slowly perceiving herself, as if she had just met herself.

🔔 Oh my God, incoherence, Greta thinks. Someone conveys an image and just like that it changes into something else. Could Sônia, with her passion for literature, become feminine and frivolous by a stroke of magic? Multiplicity of character. No one is as linear as people think. The error, or mediocrity, consists in exactly that, in our one-dimensional view of individuals. Sônia, beneath that shell or layer of the obsessive reader, must still be a woman. Anyone passing by Palm Street that Saturday who noticed the two of them chatting in the library would immediately think, what a pleasant, refined pair! The scene observed from the outside, a photograph. A meaningless snapshot. Sônia, like all of us, is more than a coherent whole. And if she were suddenly to go over to Mateus's and seduce him? Unlikely, but what if she did?

Greta let out a sigh. You can't fool around with other people's lives. Sometimes coherence is a defense mechanism, a form of protection. Could Sônia be defenseless? Why not look into Elisa more carefully, who has played only a walk-on role so far? Because Elisa lost her identity when she was widowed. When her husband was alive they bickered from morning till night. He complained about everything, from the Milk of Roses fragrance she wore to the way she seasoned his food. She hated the fact that he wiped his nose in the bath, the ugly way he used toothpicks, and other things she was ashamed to talk about. They both depended on minor dislikes for their mutual survival. After her husband died, she lost her motivation and let herself become widowed forever.

No, Sônia is more intriguing: for her incoherence and for the lopsided way she fits into the world.

♊ The postman arrived while Greta was sweeping up the dry leaves in her yard. A letter for Tina. From Spain. If only it were from the man in the portrait. The envelope was addressed in precise masculine script—of course it could only be a man's handwriting; she shoved it into her pocket. There was also mail for Elisa.

"It got here late, didn't it, Greta?"

Míriam runs down the stairs. The mailman checks. Nothing. She clutches a German baby doll to her breast. She crosses the street.

"Do you see that?" She points to the tractor. "If they think they can frighten me they've got another think coming. Antônio told me as long as he's the Village representative he won't let Fortuna do anything drastic."

Míriam wears a long, full, faded gypsy skirt and a flannel blouse mended in several places. Greta admires the way her hair is parted in the middle and pulled back tightly.

"We've got to make sure Antônio gets elected for two more years," Greta says. "His term is almost up."

"Yes." Míriam starts rocking the doll as if it were a child. "But it so happens he doesn't want to continue. The Company's been a constant headache. They haven't repaired the pavement on the street, or cleaned up the lake, or any of the things we feel are important. Besides that, he wasn't able to get the night watchman we proposed at the last meeting. As far as he's concerned he's through and the homeowners association will only function in someone else's hands."

"Modesty. He's been an excellent administrator. Next week is the last meeting. Let's insist he accept the position for another term."

"Can't you help, Greta?"

"Me? I'm the person with the least influence. Fortuna thinks I should set an example by moving out of here."

Greta makes believe she is continuing to sweep the yard. But noticing that the other woman lingers because she wants to chat, she leans reluctantly on the broom.

"Excuse my asking, Míriam, but why did you refuse the Company's offer to move?"

She shakes her head, a gesture of annoyance.

"Basically because they offered me a pigsty in the center of town. A filthy two-room apartment on a noisy street full of nasty little dives. I used up my savings when I came here. I bought the apartment and the philosophy of a life with clean air they sold in their ads. I wouldn't mind if they gave me another place here. But Fortuna shouldn't get away with trampling on our rights, don't you agree?"

Greta recognizes Míriam is right. Entirely.

"How can you stand living in all that filth?"

"Oh, Greta, don't even ask. The rats and the cockroaches make so much noise at night I can't sleep. I get this feeling they're gnawing at the beams and the supports and any minute the building's going to collapse. It's awful."

"And if we all helped you clean up the other floors?"

"It's no good. How're we going to clean up the trash from the demolition? The flagstones are covered with smashed bricks and broken sections of wall. That's men's work. Men with strong backs."

"The homeowners association can find someone, Míriam. We'll all chip in . . ."

Camilo appears at the gate and waves at the two women. Once a week he gets a letter. Greta suspects it's a check, because the next day he goes shopping.

"Have you met our new neighbor?" Míriam asked. "They say he's an artist. What else could he be, the way he painted the house?"

"Who said he's an artist?"

"Antônio did, yesterday."

"Does he live alone?"

"I don't know. See you, Greta. I have to go."

She watches Míriam stop in front of the tractor for a few seconds: what could she be thinking about?

The children from 508 run after a ball that rolls under the tractor. The smallest boy lies on the ground to reach for it. Suddenly, Greta remembers . . . She had so much wanted to have a child. By this time she might have had one. It is unsettling to have the memory pop into her head that way—she tries to suppress the thought and goes back to piling up leaves in the yard.

The church bells toll slowly, lazily, maybe in sorrow. Greta quickens her step and hurries into the house.

She closes the windows to keep out the mosquitoes and thinks about whether or not to light the fireplace. The weather has improved quite a bit. Perhaps she won't need a fire this evening, but it's so pleasant and such good company! She kneels down to arrange the logs.

The hot bath made her ravenous. What should she eat? Vegetable soup—she opens the refrigerator—damn, she forgot it was the day to go to the supermarket. Then . . . baked potatoes and cheese omelette. Got the menu figured out, hop to it—she turns on the radio. How strange. She hates the radio any other time but this, when she's cooking. Ancient memories; she smiles. Old Aurora, while she prepared lunch, used to turn on the National Radio Station at full volume and listen to those awful live-audience programs. Greta tunes in an Eldorado Radio program: late afternoon piano. Too pretentious. Excelsior Radio: disco. The news will be on in a while. Right now she could really go for a program with samba music, especially those songs about love and jealousy. She turns the dial. Italian music. That'll do, corny enough. Now, to the potatoes.

Whew, tough work; she sits down. The sound of paper crumpling reminds her of the letter in her pocket. She takes it out carefully so as not to tear the envelope, trying to conceal her indiscretion.

♤ *Dear Tina,*

It's raining. I mention it because I feel a little like that inside: dark and wet. I've wanted to write you for months (I tried out several letters in my mind). Problems? Many. I still haven't gotten over some petty feelings: anger, for example. Anger because it was so futile to have believed in you, though I do accept a large part of the blame for the failure of our relationship. Patience. I was born out of focus. I offered union and construction, while at the same time I had neurotically started the destruction.

You offered me the impossible: me here in Madrid, you there in the Village, out there in the middle of nowhere which you think is some sort of paradise. Long distance love doesn't work. You have to be together when you go to sleep and when you wake up to face the daily grind. I know it won't do any good to talk about this. I can still hear you saying love doesn't exist, only passion is real. Maybe you're right. I know I made you suffer, I'm emotionally unstable, but you didn't give a second thought to tearing me out of your life as if I were just another piece of paper in one of your collages. What kind of love was that, if you couldn't deal with the slightest hassle? I don't have an answer. I looked deeply into your eyes the last day we were together. I saw love and suffering there. I'll never understand the ambiguity of all the Tinas that share your body. How are all of you in there? Everything's fine here. I spend hours walking around the city, which I won't describe because I don't like it (the only thing that saves it from immediate evacuation is the Prado Museum. Absolutely fantastic).

The hotels are cheap. I can spend three months in Spain with the money I have left or I can lose myself in the wide, wide world. (And my name's not Raimundo!)*

As soon as I arrived, I wrote two acts of my next play. I got stuck on the third act. My characters feel like stale bread: hard, lifeless. And more complex than they should be . . . So far I haven't been able to reach them. Or is it the other way around? Pirandello exhausted that theme. After him, you'd have to be a genius. Besides, I think I took the wrong path. What I'd really like to do is write a novel in the form of an immense dialogue (as you know, I hate descriptions of character and/or setting), so I wouldn't have to think about stage effects, theatricality, and all that other technical bull. I still don't know. Writing plays doesn't satisfy me anymore. I've dried up. I said everything I had to say in my first four plays. Yeah, I think my well's gone dry. And talking about this just made me remember a character I've got in mind (you see how contradictory I am?). The character is a lonely woman, a hermit, who lives by the side of the road. She has no neighbors or relatives. She lives off the vegetables from her own garden and fish from the river. The period of the clothes and manners is undefined, like those women in Cuevas's engravings. One day a stranger knocks on her door (his motorcycle broke down) and he moves in right away. An urban type, running away from civilization. And the conflicts start. One important detail that knocks me out: I want the woman to be a deaf-mute. Just think. It's incredible. A film script? Who knows. I'm in love with the character. And suffering. I want her physically identical to you singular/plural. A bit rougher around the edges. I mean, less "civilized," in a purer state, like the Tina I'm in love with. (Never mind.)

I've been reading my fellow Luís, Cernuda, and listening to Piazzolla.

---

*Translator's note: the writer repeats a pun here—mundo (world) / Raimundo—from Carlos Drummond de Andrade's poem entitled "Poema de sete faces."

I find "Adiós Nonino" very moving. I wish I could write something as solid and with as much sensibility.

Don't miss Brazil a bit. Miss you, though.

Kisses, Luís

Greta slowly folded the letter, put it back in the envelope, licked the flap to seal it. She remembered the potatoes and smelled something starting to burn.

It had just gotten dark. What could have happened to Sônia?

🔔 Sônia rings the bell to Mateus's apartment. It's seven o'clock. The twentieth floor in one of those old buildings with long corridors lined with doorways; his door faces the elevator. While she waits she moves over to the stained glass window. A last glimmer of light shines on the black roofs of the concrete city. The television antennas, wingless dragonflies. She'd never get used to living perched up there, she thinks.

The sound of a key in a lock. Sônia perspires nervously—sudden doubts about her visit. Unfortunately or fortunately the door opens; it was the next apartment over. An old woman in slippers shuffles listlessly down the hall to put a bag in the garbage can by the stairway.

"You can just forget about it, miss. He left less than fifteen minutes ago." She points her finger. "And when he takes to the streets there's no telling how long he'll be gone."

Damn, fifteen minutes—Sônia feels let down. Mateus has been inconsiderate, to say the least.

"Can I leave a message with you?"

"Sorry, young lady. I'm too old to remember messages. Sometimes I even forget who I am." She smiles. "Anyway, I don't like him. Every time I try to watch my favorite soap opera, he plays those lousy classical records just to upset me." The woman scratches her thinning hair. "And he knows very well that I'm half deaf. He does it on purpose."

The elevator stops. They both watch the door expectantly. A teenage girl, dressed in her gym class uniform, with an armload of textbooks and notebooks. The old woman approaches Sônia, unexpectedly confidential.

"You by any chance a relative of his?"

"We're friends."

"You don't say. I thought that guy didn't have any friends!" She scratched her head again. "The only person ever comes by is a young man with long hair . . . And also his brother. He lives in the interior

47

and shows up now and then. Even so, he's better off than I am, because nobody visits me. Not even my grandchildren. Ungrateful wretches, the whole lot of them. Got a cigarette?"

"Sorry, I don't smoke." Sônia pushes the elevator button. "Thank you for the information."

Squinting, the old woman examines her from head to toe.

"Fancy clothes you're wearing. In my day people used to wear those riding boots. My father had a plantation back when coffee was king. If he were here to see the dump I've ended up in . . ."

Sônia smiles, politely mumbles a "see you soon," and gets on the elevator. The old woman says good-bye and wishes her all the best.

"Do come back again, young lady. I enjoyed the chat."

Unbelievable. Poor thing. Old age is so sad. In a few years . . . She suppresses the thought. Although she tries not to, she has to admit she feels disappointed. She had imagined everything but the possibility of Mateus standing her up like that; she crosses the street with her head down. The driver has dozed off.

"Back already, Miss Sônia?"

"Things didn't work out. Let's go home."

She was horribly depressed. But after all, what had she expected? That Mateus would be kind and generous and drop everything just to meet some mad woman who was after a short story translation? Sônia sighed. That wasn't the issue. She had been thinking for days about the fragility of her life, about her absurd pose as the heroine out of some melodrama who romantically devotes herself to the memory of her first love. A ridiculously widowed Doña Rosita. And her passion for characters, at least for authors? That wasn't betrayal, only transference. If Maurício had loved Zelda, Emily Brontë, Emma Bovary, she wouldn't have been jealous. How could she be?

The driver braked suddenly behind a line of cars. The traffic was awful! Patience—Sônia leaned her head back—too soon to decide how she felt.

Flower-covered veranda: the roses were blooming.

The fifteen-year-old girl is reading aloud. A teenage boy beside her leans back in a wicker chair. The boy pulls the girl toward him for a kiss. On the lips. Elisa appears at that instant. Awkward situation. Shouting. The girl cries.

Sônia lifts her head and tries to erase the unpleasant image. That's all it took, just that scene, an excuse to hole up in her room and read. A kind of revenge, a form of daily aggression against her mother who drifted through the house sighing because her daughter hadn't married? Did Elisa recall that long-ago incident too? Could the role of romantic heroine be a silly excuse for retribution against a mother who repressed, humiliated, and wounded her deeply over a simple adolescent kiss? Enough of that—Sônia unbuttons her blouse and loosens her scarf: the sweat runs down her neck. She hates cheap psychologizing and she's just indulged in it; she takes off her glasses and then puts them back on. Who's that woman there in the mirror? The soft, gentle, pitiful creature who saw herself in the mirror at lunchtime as if for the first time? No. A ridiculous woman stood up by a guy she secretly wanted to seduce. A woman who would soon be alone, who enjoyed working as a nurse in her uncle's clinic even though she was taking the place of someone who really needed the job. An insignificant woman, not even able to put the fortune her father left her to good use. A woman hiding from the world, full of contradictions, who never did anything in her life, someone totally bland and colorless. A complete failure; she blew her nose.

"Catch a cold, miss? Here we are. Want me to pull the car in?"

"No. Good night, Mário. See you tomorrow."

Sônia got out and slammed the door as if she were leaving a nightmare. She didn't have the least desire to go in and see her mother.

"You took so long, dear. What happened?"

"Nothing. Is dinner ready?"

♤ Greta was reading quietly when Sônia arrived. Heaven-sent. She hadn't expected her this evening. So nice to have someone to talk to; she got up to stir the fire.

"Large open spaces, no matter how full of stuff they are, make people feel more lonely. Don't you agree, Sônia?"

"I like this room." She looks around.

"Sometimes I think it needs redecorating, or at least a wall separating the dining area there, you see? I could put the piano here and the space would be less . . . I don't know. At night I can actually hear the echo of my own breathing." She opens the cupboard. "How about a glass of wine?"

Sônia thinks about the pleasure the wine at lunch had given her, and accepts.

Greta takes out the two red crystal glasses.

"How lovely," Sônia exclaims.

"They're Baccarat crystal, the last ones left." She uncorks the bottle. "The red wine's nothing special, but the glasses improve it. Health."

"Great," is the other woman's compliment.

"I love wine. White or red, it doesn't matter. The hell of it is, if I don't watch how much I drink I'll turn into an alcoholic."

"Do you drink all that much, Greta?"

"Almost every day. I'll be doing my writing and reading and suddenly I realize the bottle's empty. Wine warms the soul."

"And ruins the liver." Sônia laughs as she holds the glass in front of the fire and examines it. The crystal takes on a fantastic coloring.

"A toast to your trip to Europe."

"Oh, Greta, I wish I could get excited about the idea."

"After everything you've told me about what you've been thinking, I don't see any alternative. Even if it's only to make Elisa happy."

"We have relatives in Switzerland, a great uncle and some cousins who send us Christmas cards every year. Mama would love to meet them."

"Well, what are you waiting for?"

"Courage. An attitude that means I've changed inside, don't you see? I might even get married."

Greta is about to express an opinion about marriage but keeps it to herself. Not all marriages fail. And this is not the right time. The two women remain silent for a few moments. Abruptly, Sônia asks:

"What about you, Greta? Why do you live alone? What happened to your family?"

She refills the glasses. She doesn't want to be impolite or dishonest. But the point-blank question has left her completely flabbergasted. She would rather listen (or suck dry?) than talk (or give?).

"Sônia, you're the theme of this evening. Some other day, who knows . . . Besides, I'd rather not say, for reasons you can understand."

"I'm sorry if I was indiscreet." Sônia is visibly embarrassed.

"It's OK."

"Are you writing in the first person?"

"In a way. Sometimes yes, sometimes no. For now I'm recording the Village. Isn't it great material?"

"That depends. Nothing goes on here."

"Don't you think you make a good character?"

"Me? I'd walk out of the book in a second."

Greta laughs out loud.

"And Míriam?"

"She's an interesting figure but she's impenetrable. I have the impression there's something incestuous about her; I don't know why."

"Incest? I hadn't thought of that. I've kind of left her hanging . . ." She interrupts the phrase as she spills wine on herself. "Excuse me, Sônia. I'm so stupid, I stained my sweater. I'm going to rinse it out."

Sônia gets up too. She walks around the room, opens the piano keyboard. Two keys make a timid sound. And if she were to play a bit of "Für Elise"? She swivels the stool around.

The sound fills the house and echoes through the Village. Greta turns off the water and stands listening. She imagines Tina playing the piano in the school's small music room, her heart full of hate. There was nothing she hated more than piano lessons. Once again, Greta sees the schoolyard, the fig tree. Truth or fiction, it all lives inside her now.

Sônia stopped playing.

"It's no use. My fingers are rusty. I think of the note and I hit the wrong key. It's crap."

"Too bad. I was really enjoying it. Nobody's played that piano for years. I thought it needed tuning."

"No, it doesn't, but you should call someone to . . . Oh, I almost forgot. Can I have the notebook with the dreams back?"

"Sure. Wait a minute, it's in my bedroom."

"Have you read it yet?"

"Of course."

Sônia feels her face reddening and her feet getting hot. Until she gets used to those boots . . . She unbolts the door to adjust gradually to the outdoor temperature.

"Here it is. Thanks. Some of the dreams are strange. The one about the shop window . . ."

"My favorite one is the dream about the breasts," Sônia declared.

"Are you going to keep on publishing the ad?"

"I don't know. I think it's accomplished all it's going to."

In front of the house the two turn simultaneously to face each other.

"That guy's weird. I can't imagine what those floodlights in his yard are for," Sônia commented.

"I'd like to meet this painter. You think he could be a relative of old Ananias? Poor thing, I keep thinking about him getting run over . . . He seems to live alone, because since he moved in nobody else has been at the window or in the yard."

"What'll you use as an excuse?" Sônia rubbed her hands together.

"I'll suggest he hire Zaíra. She's an excellent cleaning lady and she hasn't filled her calendar yet. She asked me herself. Besides, I'm curious to know if he did that aluminum sculpture by the doorway. It reminds me of a globe by Morelet, a French artist who had a show in a gallery I used to own. I hope the birds discover it and use it as a perch. It's incredible how many there've been in the Village lately. Can you hear the *bem-te-vi* birds singing in the late afternoon or early in the morning? When you cross the Avenue on hot days you can see a flock of them diving into the lake. Even if it is dirty it's still a lake, right?"

Sônia agrees.

"Bye, Greta. Thanks for the wine. It's really gotten cold out. It's time you went back inside."

Greta went into the house shivering, but it was warm inside. It was ten according to the clock. She could work for a while yet.

☊ As a child, Míriam runs through the fields. Slight body, small eyes, she appears and disappears among the corn stalks searching for six of the fattest cobs for supper. The Polish farmer, his face sunburned, is also returning, his basket filled with fish. Father and daughter do not speak on the path home up the hill. They walk quietly side by side, sensing the silent landscape of the southern state of Santa Catarina. He's a tall man, tough and solid: his boots go crunch crunch on the gravel.

The mother sits on the porch embroidering a linen sheet, while her son chops wood for the fireplace. She's a refined woman with delicate gestures, her hair tied in a long braid that hangs across her breast. In a little while, the old servant woman will announce that the soup is on the table. And they'll eat by the light of the fire, as the father talks about the rice field or the birth of another settler's child. After supper the parents will play double solitaire and the children will play old maid or dominoes until the grandfather clock strikes ten.

Because the large wooden logs crackle loudly at night, Míriam is always afraid; she leaves her room to go to her brother's bed. She slides under the sheets and, trembling, cuddles up to Gricha.

The brother leaves home at eighteen to serve in the army. When he returns he finds that Míriam is now a young woman—how quickly she's shot up! "Take care of her, my son," says the father on his deathbed. "The men around here have their eyes on her." Twelve months later the mother passes away, bitten by a poisonous snake. Alone, brother and sister discover each other and become lovers. They would never have left the farm if the government hadn't expropriated their land to put a road through it.

Gricha and Míriam came to São Paulo to stay with a widowed aunt with whom their mother corresponded.

And the dolls, where could they have come from? From Míriam's maternal aunt. She is the one who told the story of the family tragedy.

Olga, her mother, fell in love with Ivan, her father, who managed their grandfather's large estate in the south, near the state of Paraná. Olga's pregnancy created an uproar. Míriam's grandfather was willing to put up with anything except his daughter's marriage. She could choose a trip to Europe or hide out in another estate near the town of Laguna, under one condition: she had to give the child up for adoption. Olga wouldn't budge, she cried, she raised a fuss. In the end she ran away from home and for several years no one heard from her or her husband. Then World War II broke out. The old man, a German, transferred his property—no one knew whether all of it or just some of it—to the family attorney, who betrayed him. We lost nearly everything. In those days women weren't allowed to deal with business matters, as if we weren't capable of thought. Can you believe it? By then I was married and living here, so I never found out exactly what happened. One day I got a letter from your mother saying she was living quite happily and now had, in addition to you and Gricha, another girl. That's why I kept these dolls which belonged to your great-grandmother. They're foreign dolls, and I never had any children . . .

Míriam and her brother moved in temporarily with their aunt while they looked for a place to build their own nest. The aunt lived off her husband's pension; he had been a high-ranking officer in the Air Force. So Gricha could leave Míriam in their aunt's care if he wanted to go find out what had happened to the family property. Like her mother, Míriam started doing embroidery to save money and keep busy. She almost shouted with joy when she saw the newspaper ad about the new building opening up in the Village of the Bells. She and Gricha would have a home at last.

♌ An act of generosity or hostility, apprehension or searching, isolation or communication? Dr. Oswaldo refuses to discuss the magic of creation: Tina, Greta, Alice, Luís, Sônia, Elisa, Míriam. Into how many personalities can a single individual be divided?

♌ Greta knocks on the painter's door with her left hand because in her right she's holding a bunch of foliage. An indecently large bouquet, and he probably won't have a vase and she'll be embarrassed . . .

He's surprised to see Greta standing there uncomfortably behind the branches she's picked from her yard. She explains she's his neighbor and has dropped by to welcome him, but he, attracted by the greenery, pays no attention. She notices his hands, pants, and shoes are spattered with paint. All painters are the same, she thinks, and she recalls one in particular who stank of turpentine from his head down to his toes. The artist points to a wicker chair by the window and disappears from the room.

She studies the familiar setting: books are piled on the floor waiting for shelves; canvases are turned backward against the wall (could they be paintings?); a board placed on bricks is used as a table for brushes, tubes of paint, and cans.

A drawing board and a rack to hold paintings in one corner. Across the room, a broken-down cabinet filled with jars. Objects sculpted in a wide range of materials—iron, wood, bronze, acrylic, stone—are strewn around the parquet floor, creating an air of improvisation, an air of someone in transit, who hasn't really moved in. Greta is struck by one of the works: on the easel, a mirror with a landscape painted on it in gouache. She moves closer and her image is reflected as if it were part of the composition.

The artist crosses the room a few times. Busy doing what? Greta wonders. I only seem to meet the weird types.

"This can is the best I could do. Sorry I took so long but I wanted to touch it up so it wouldn't be so ugly," he said as he placed the black painted can on the painting rack. The foliage seemed to be floating.

Greta praises the arrangement. "It looks very nice."

They sit down facing each other. He lights a cigarette. Dark with kinky hair, balding on top. Lanky, tense. About forty? He seems nervous, mistrustful. His name is Alexandre. He asks politely about the Village residents. He expresses interest in Míriam, whom he finds attractive with her eccentric clothing. A character right out of Poe.

"More like someone out of Lúcio Cardoso. Have you read him?" Greta asks somewhat aggressively.

"No. I knew Lúcio personally. He was a diabolical figure. I hate reading Brazilian novels."

"When was the last time, I mean, what was the most recent one you read?"

"I don't remember."

"Maybe that's why. We have fine writers. Like a lot of people, you're prejudiced. I can lend you a few if you want . . ."

He laughs derisively.

"When another Chekhov appears on the horizon, lend me a copy." He gets up and takes a bottle of sherry and two goblets out of a trunk.

"We're in Brazil, not Russia. Our literature is creating an identity for us . . ."

"Now that we're speaking seriously, how about a little drink to lighten things up?" he interrupts bluntly.

Greta accepts the glass without saying a word. His disdainful, contemptuous attitude halts conversation. One to nothing in his favor, she realizes. She'll take a few sips and be on her way.

The Village bells toll six times.

"Did you hear them too?" she asks.

"What? Your thoughts?"

"The church bells."

"What bells? What church?"

"The ones that just rang."

"I didn't hear a thing." The artist shrugs his shoulders.

"That happens in the beginning. Later on you'll hear them. Some people hear the tolling at night and others during the day. What time is it?"

He cranes his neck and looks toward the open door—the kitchen?

"Five o'clock."

"I usually hear the bells at six. I hope this schedule change doesn't mean something terrible's going to happen in the Village."

She sighs theatrically.

"You buy all this b.s. about witchcraft in the Village?" Again he gives her a sarcastic look.

Greta struggles to control herself. Her host is not at all pleasant.

"I have to confess that my common sense rules out the possibility but my feelings tell me something else." She stares into the goblet.

"You must be dying to tell me the story. Go ahead."

"There's not just one story; there are several. There've been some shocking tragedies here. The fire, for example. Three years ago an entire family was burned alive."

"That can happen anywhere. Where was the house?"

"On Magnolia Street. The only house not on this street. Two blocks up that way. It burned in half an hour—the construction was prefabricated. Only the ashes were left, and soon they were overgrown with vegetation."

For reasons Greta herself can't understand she feels an urgent need to talk about the Village's misfortunes. Between sips of sherry, she spins her tales.

"And finally, there was that terrible business last year, on the thirty-first of December. We were already celebrating twelve months without any incident, when old Ananias, who lived in this house, was run over on the Avenue by the funeral hearse. We stayed awake all night."

"Only a coincidence," he says brusquely. "If it hadn't been for the death of my old uncle I'd still be in Araraquara, out in the sticks. So you see; the house was heaven-sent. Was it ever!"

He stands up again, grabs a piece of cloth and begins dusting a sculpture. Greta waits silently for a few moments: no one in the Village knew of any relatives. It was generally believed that old Ananias had no family because he was eighty and yet cooked and washed and ironed his own clothes. He lived in near poverty. As far as anyone knew, he never received visitors. How did the nephew find out right away about the death of his uncle?

"My sister lives in São Paulo, and Fortuna let her know. Someone had to take care of the burial, right?"

This was a detail that hadn't occurred to Greta. Of course someone had to make the burial arrangements, even if they didn't show up themselves.

He interrupted her thoughts.

"What do you think about that?" He pointed to a sculpture and turned on the lights.

He had obviously asked for the hell of it, indifferent to whatever opinion she might or might not have. She decided to show off her artistic knowledge by analyzing it and other pieces. Most of them couldn't stand up to analysis. They were modernist clichés.

"Excuse the criticism. You don't have to agree."

"I agree with a few things. Your point of view is solid but your concepts are too rigid. Professional distortion, am I right?" His look conveyed his sarcasm.

"How do you . . ."

"I've been in that gallery of yours. At an opening, years ago."

"And you recognized me?"

Two to nothing in his favor, Greta admitted. What a character. Why didn't he say so before?

The art business would be the next subject. He had a deep hatred for auctions, the criteria for selection, and the poor performance of the galleries.

"When I decide to show my work, it's going to be in the street. I'm not going to get caught up in that gallery scene. They're basically useless—they just rent a space and take a percentage of the sales. I swear I'd starve to death before I'd get mixed up with any slimy art dealers."

"Aren't you overdoing the sainthood bit? Look, there are several galleries that sponsor exhibits, make contact with the collectors, and generally do a good job. It's not what you think."

He looked at her closely. For the first time.

"Don't move. I want to draw you in that position." Hurriedly he grabbed a blank canvas and began making a quick charcoal sketch of Greta. The charcoal made a grating sound as it moved across the canvas—like a rat scratching on the floor? She felt intimidated by the artist's expression. It was as if he could see right through her; she looked down in embarrassment.

"Look at me. Just another minute. Now you can look where you want, but don't move."

It was then that Greta saw it: that woman, the one he was drawing, was not her. Not at all. It was Tina emerging from the artist's strokes: the same languid, dreamy posture, the other woman's aura. Right away, before she could stop herself, she imagined Tina and Luís with their arms around each other as they took a romantic walk around the lake. Feeling left out, Greta watched them with envy and a heavy heart. Suddenly, Tina had become a threat, as if she, Greta, were about to lose something of great value; she changed position.

"I'd give anything to know what you were thinking. It must've been something important because you almost disappeared."

Greta tried to change the subject by joking that she wanted the drawing.

"It doesn't matter. You look incredibly beautiful when you're pensive. And sit still."

They both laughed.

"I'll give you the canvas when it's ready."

Unable to sleep that night, Greta took a long walk in the yard. How far did the symbiosis in the drawing go? Can an author be jealous of her characters? What was the meaning of her selection of protagonists in the micro-universe where she had placed them? Did they make any sense? She was distracted when she heard the aria from *Rigoletto*. Gino, the opera singer, was belting it out at the top of his lungs.

♤ Gino di Carli's parents came to Brazil from Italy around 1920. They learned the language, listened to advice, and before their money ran out they opened a restaurant in São Paulo's Bela Vista district. A cantina featuring fresh pasta made by Assunta, from the province of Potenza, who had grown up watching her grandmother and mother prepare all sorts of cheeses, breads, and salamis. She knew the recipes by heart and was a talented cook.

When Gino was born, Giuseppe made a vow: his son would be

an opera singer like Beniamino Gigli, his idol. He would live to see his son on stage, if only once. At age fifteen, Gino went to his obligatory private singing lessons after school, which he kept secret from his friends and classmates because they didn't approve of such things. He went reluctantly, complaining all the time.

"*Io ho fatto un giuramento, figlio mio,*" his father insisted almost imploringly. I have made a vow, my son.

At last the old Italian maestro gave Gino a chance to sing a small part in *The Barber of Seville*. The young man was about to turn twenty and this was all he needed to be free of his father's vow. On opening night, Giuseppe and Assunta climbed the steps of the Municipal Theatre, proud as a king and queen. After the performance, the Cantina di Carli gave a cast party. Gino didn't attend, stricken by one of the migraines he had suffered since childhood.

But when his father died, he took over the management of the restaurant and began to sing for the customers—he himself never understood why. The cantina became famous, for its food and its singer. They say even President Getúlio Vargas ate there. In 1945, Gino married Graziela, a distant cousin who had come to spend a holiday at her relatives'. They had three children, all with their own families now. Assunta died in 1970 and the restaurant, in a state of decline, was sold. Gino used the money to buy an apartment for each of his children, as well as the house in the Village of the Bells. Sometimes at night he liked to sing passages from operas, and his baritone voice filled the silence of Palm Street. He would also sing duets with recordings, as he was doing now. When the aria was over, Greta would go to bed. Lately he sang less and less and only then when his wife was spending a few days with one of their children.

♤   An atmosphere of peace in the Village. The days drag on endlessly. The temperature has gone up, the thermometer registers sixty-four degrees. Zaíra has given the house an unusually thorough cleaning—was she planning a trip? She moved the furniture and the books and at noon she pointed to the bureau.

"I'm going to clean out these drawers. They're a complete mess."

Greta was taken aback, but before she could object Zaíra was kneeling down to show her.

"Take a look at these papers. This is cockroach food." She dumped the drawer's contents on the floor.

Greta was horrified to see the mortal remains of everything she had kept hidden so carefully in the chest. A mound of shredded paper rose from the floor.

"It's no use to keep all this paper. It's really no use, Miss Greta. Except to the rats—they love it."

The covers were about the only thing left of the account books from the gallery.

"You can throw them out," she said.

Greta thought briefly about the gallery. The remodeled house, her desk, the typewriter. How had she managed to get mixed up in that damn business? She'll never understand it, no matter how hard she tries. Was there actually a time when she could put up with the art world? In her conversation with the artist two weeks ago she had discussed the subject so naturally one would have thought she still believed in the future of art, in the art business. No truth to that at all.

The drawer was pushed back in its place. And that pile of junk on the floor? Zaíra waited for her to make up her mind. A wooden box—she opened it—eraser and paper clips, broken picture frame, brass ring, metal buttons covered with verdigris, old telephone tokens, rubber stamp, rusty tweezers, a frightful brooch without a clasp, a jammed padlock—what did it lock?—useless old keys, worn out batteries, a torn piece of purple silk with a floral pattern.

"Chuck it all in the trash," she said with disgust. Could her soul be a reflection of that junk? Why had she hung on to it?

The housekeeper obeyed the order and quickly swept the litter into a dustpan. And she proceeded immediately to pull out another drawer. Sheet after sheet of multicolored paper slid onto the parquet floor. There were envelopes and stationery—some even had printed letterheads. How and when had she been able to afford that?

"Throw it out!"

"Oh, Miss Greta, I'll give it to my kids to play with."

"It's all stained, Zaíra. It's worthless. I don't know why I kept it . . . You can have some of the better stuff if you want . . ."

They repeated the operation of putting back and slamming the drawer shut.

"That's enough. You'll wear yourself out with all this trash."

"I'm not gonna stop. What do you think I'm here for, ma'am?"

"I'd rather you washed the windows. The shutters are filthy . . ."

"On Thursday. I'm already halfway through this." She pulled out the third drawer.

"Not that one!" Greta nearly shouted.

Too late. The maid leafed through miscellaneous photographs, including a pile tied with a faded ribbon.

"What a shame, Miss Greta. They're so old you can hardly make 'em out. This one here I think is you, ma'am, with your school uniform. Darn, these photos are stuck together. What about these letters? You still want 'em?"

Greta felt like throwing the woman out. How dare she? Her face, pale with tension, must have given away her momentary crisis, because Zaíra delicately put the packet of letters aside as if she were handling a child. Greta's entire body shook.

"Please stop."

"So what should I do with all this junk? Everything's mildewed. At least I could take the stuff out of the drawers and clean it up before I put it back. Look, the back of this plywood is peeling off."

"No. No thanks. I do not want you to touch those things." Her voice was hard, authoritarian.

The cleaning woman forced the drawer in until she could hear it closing. Greta went to the window thinking that it was wrong to meddle in other people's lives. Those drawers contained the story of her life.

"Come over here, Zaíra. Someone has set fire to the grass."

"My lord." She opened the window.

Clumps of sedge crackled. You could hear the grass burning from quite a ways away. The line of flames drew the shape of a balloon in the field.

"Some nut did that. What you call those folks who like to set fires?"

"Pyromaniacs. But look over that way, Zaíra. The people from the cemetery are putting it out . . ."

The maid picked up the broom, ready to sweep away the destruction left in the wake of their cleaning.

Greta looked back at the flames, which had begun to die down. A dense fog still enshrouded the eucalyptus trees. Small hills were visible in the foreground but the mountains disappeared in the mist. In the nearby yard the ferns resembled great fireflies. It hadn't rained for three months. And the plants needed water.

△   The invitation to the homeowners association meeting—moved up fifteen days—came typewritten: that was a new twist. Perhaps Antônio wanted to make everyone feel obligated to attend; he was either going to propose his reelection or announce his resignation as Village representative. Greta folded the piece of paper. It would be a shame if he resigned.

Elisa's voice interrupted her thoughts.

"Hot isn't it, Greta? Who would've imagined it this hot in mid-July?"

Antônio's son waited for the old woman to sign the receipt for the letter.

"Wait a minute, Greta." She turned to the boy. "How's your father, young man? And your mother?" She took a piece of candy from her pocket and gave it to the boy. "I'll read the letter later on. I forgot my glasses."

Greta laughed as she stood next to the azalea bush.

"It's an invitation to a meeting tomorrow night."

"The invitations are by letter now?" She came closer. "Oh, how terrible. The grass dried up completely during the last cold spell. It looks awful."

"This hot weather will bring everything back. All we need is a little rain," Greta remarked. "The azaleas are thriving."

There were no walls dividing the lots, and the residents had found several ways to mark their boundaries, at least visually. Elisa put in a hedgerow of azaleas, Camilo planted mahogany trees, which had grown quite tall, and Tina created a wall of potted ferns on both sides of her property. The decoration of the yards gave Palm Street a special charm.

"If those clouds don't blow away it could rain."

"Well, that would be the end of our Indian Summer."

"That's right. Nothing's perfect in this world. Know who came to see us yesterday? Ananias's nephew. He's a nice young guy, very proper. He talked about his uncle, about Araraquara, and said he was very happy in the Village. He told me he was visiting all the residents because he wanted to get to know his neighbors. Isn't that thoughtful of him?"

Greta agreed.

"He said you've been friends for a long time. Is that true? He must be a good catch." Elisa winked.

Greta neither confirmed nor denied the friendship. She decided to cut down right away on her visits, indignant at the fellow's insolence and lack of integrity. Friends!

That night, seated at the table, she recalled clearly her chat with the neighbor woman.

♩ Míriam's story turned out to be more melodramatic than Sônia's. Why? Tomorrow she'd try out another version. How could Míriam's brother find her? When and under what circumstances? And what if she really did work in a movie ticket booth?

♌ Maybe because the night was pleasant—in spite of the black clouds—or because the invitation had been typewritten, almost all the residents showed up at the association meeting. As people arrived and exchanged friendly greetings, the hostess served passion-fruit punch and delicious butter cookies. The house was overflowing with people. The latecomers would have to stay in the garage.

It's obvious Jane has taken great pains to make both the house and herself look good: black dress, pearl necklace, and makeup. Flowers in a vase on the coffee table. Furniture divides the large living room into two separate spaces. The velvet sofas are heavy, and so are the curtains, reminding her of the home of some provincial aunt who got her furniture ideas from those home decorating magazines. Velvet, provincial aunts can't do without it.

More people arrived. Antônio checks his watch and opens the meeting by apologizing for the crowded conditions. He promised to make his administrative report brief; he didn't want to tire those who were standing up. In fact, he would dispense with the roll call, since it was obvious that more people were present than the two-thirds required by the bylaws. He would just pass around the guestbook at the end of the meeting. He would also skip the usual formalities and take the opportunity to present Mr. Alexandre Ribeiro, the nephew of old Ananias (may God rest his soul), as of this month a member of our little Village.

The artist is standing next to the hostess and discreetly greets the association members (is he intimidated by all the curious or unpleasant stares?). His caramel colored suit and brown tie show that he considers the occasion to be very important.

Antônio then goes on to read the report on his activities as representative. It's not necessary, since everyone knows perfectly well what he has accomplished. As he reads the record of his service in a measured, full, and strong voice, Greta wonders whether or not she ought to bring up Míriam's request for a clean-up and security system for the apartment building, just in case Antônio refuses to accept re-election. Míriam knows how the majority of the residents feels, which is why she hasn't shown up. "That spineless bunch wants the building torn down just because it spoils the view. No one takes my problem seriously. If Dr. Alceu would grace the meeting with his presence, then I'd go for sure. After all, he does represent Fortuna. Do you think I'd give up the chance to confront the s.o.b. who's taking advantage of me? He invented this homeowners association for a purpose. So instead of having to listen to individual complaints and demands, he uses the Village representative as a go-between or a lightning rod, you know, to avoid unpleasant situations. That's all there is to it."

 Greta could see Míriam's point, but that evening it was going to be very hard to intercede on her friend's behalf. Sure, the homeowners organization was suspect. In the first place, the deeds had been tied up in red tape for years. When the project was initiated the property owners were supposed to be purchasing not only their homes but theoretically also shares in the public areas; the sites, to be precise, where they were putting in the lake, the church, the sports center, the streets, etc. Because of some error or carelessness in the initial planning, it turned out that the real estate company would have no power to act in case the venture fell through. The whole thing got fouled up and Fortuna was saved from bankruptcy because the cemetery land wasn't part of the public area. Otherwise . . .

Antônio was now coming to the end of his report. He explained that he had received authorization to hire a night watchman, as long as the residents shared the expense. The fellow from 512, an insurance broker named Tancredi, stood up immediately and asked for the floor to lodge a complaint. Considering the increase in taxes and maintenance fees, who had any money left to pay for a night watchman? Antônio let him talk and gave others time to make their usual asides. Finally he said that the matter should be taken up with the new Village representative after he was chosen.

Camilo said impatiently to Greta:

"If this nonsense doesn't end soon I'm not even going to sign the guestbook. The boy isn't used to all this commotion." He buttoned his black blazer.

Greta was about to tell him to calm down when the host raised his voice and shouted for silence.

"My friends, may I please have your attention. You're all aware of and accept my decision not to continue as Village representative. Nevertheless, several association members have asked me to serve another two-year term. I appreciate your confidence but I truly believe change is always positive, even necessary. My dear friends, I'm tired. These four years of struggle to solve our many problems with the real estate company and City Hall have kept me from the things that matter most to me. I believe I deserve, like everyone else, time to relax, be with my family, and take care of my business. I've consulted with several of our neighbors about the possibility of their accepting this difficult position, and I understand why they aren't willing to. Which is why I now submit to you the name of the only resident who has offered to fulfill these duties: our new neighbor, Mr. Alexandre Ribeiro." (The audience was astonished at the nomination. Why would he want the position, Greta wondered.) "Although he's unfamiliar with our problems, I'm confident of Mr. Ribeiro's abilities. It is therefore my pleasure to nominate him, because I'm convinced he'll strive to serve our community. And to conclude, I would like to express my gratitude to all those who have supported me."

Thunderous applause broke out in the living room and the garage and went on for several minutes. Antônio had without a doubt done an excellent job. He was fair, humane—in Míriam's case—and efficient in resolving the constant crises with Fortuna.

"Although I understand Mr. Tancredi's objections, shall we all sign the guestbook . . ."

Greta amused herself for a few moments with Ivo, who held her hand.

"Our secretary, Gino di Carli, will pass the book around. My best wishes for the new representative."

Applause again, although much weaker. Camilo wheeled Ivo's chair up to the artist.

"I don't envy you, my good man. I was the first to fill the position, and the headaches are endless. If you need any help don't hesitate to ask. Good evening."

Ivo, drooling, refused to let go of Greta's hand, and she was forced to stay with him. Sônia and Elisa joined the three of them. On the way home, Camilo mentioned that there was something about the look of that Alexandre character that he didn't care for.

"Did you notice how superior and mistrustful he acts?"

The observation was probably valid. There was some kind of impenetrable intention in the artist's look. As if he were waiting in ambush—Greta gave a brief sigh. In ambush for whom?

◬ Everyday routines—like the meeting—are tiresome, especially when they're narrated in such a lifeless way. Could the meeting have any purpose?

◬ It was raining hard when Greta left the clinic. Dr. Oswaldo sent the patients on their way with an impersonal, professional "See you next Thursday." Boy, what a cold fish. They've just opened up their heart and soul to him, so why couldn't he at least show a little human warmth on his face or in his voice? Greta huddled against the wall to keep out of the rain that dripped from the roof. Tina might fall in love with him, but not Greta. Never. She considered skipping next week's appointment and felt a pain in her chest. So many people were able to live with their conflicts—why not Tina? Poor Cabral, drowning in anxiety, spent two-thirds of his salary on that innocuous therapy. He even went without eating, imagine that.

Dr. Oswaldo glanced at Greta indifferently as she stood beneath the overhang. Go take your obnoxiousness and . . . A long blast on the horn: beepbeepbeepbeepbeep. The doctor ran. Greta watched the peroxide blond kiss him on the mouth. Either he was completely selfish or he was very ill-mannered.

Cabral appears with an umbrella.

"Will you take me to my car?"

The young man, thirty, offers his arm. He's a gorgeous male creature. Too bad he's so unhappy and contradictory.

"Where is it?"

"Across the street."

"Are you going to take Pamplona Avenue?"

She nods yes.

"Great. What about a ride to Estados Unidos Street?"

The large raindrops sliding off the umbrella ran down Greta's arm—she shook them off—while the two waited for the light to change so they could cross the street. Finally they climbed into the car. The traffic was totally tied up.

"How's your masterpiece coming along?"

"Terrible. A lot of the time I can't find the right words to express what I want to say. I keep having to use the dictionary to find the meaning of words that pop into my head, or I have to look for other words that are more precise. It takes a tremendous amount of time. Sometimes I give up and sweep the floor, dust the furniture, sharpen my pencil, anything to take my mind off my writing."

"Precision isn't what matters, Greta. It's spontaneity that counts."

"If you want to be spontaneous your technique had better be pretty damn good. If you're not careful, everything sounds cheap and trite. I'd like something else from Dr. Oswaldo. An interpretation . . ."

"You're funny. You want him to define the creative process as if he were all-knowing, like some kind of prophet, a sorcerer, a philosopher."

"That's not quite it. Anyway, what gets me is that consciously I'm one person but I'm someone else when I write. Yesterday I wrote a short piece kind of aimlessly—I was trying to sketch out a character from the Village. I swear I don't know who wrote those words down. It wasn't me."

"I don't understand much about that, but there has to be something supernatural or extrasensory perception, otherwise everybody would be an artist, don't you think? Watch out!" he shouted anxiously.

Greta slammed on the brakes, narrowly avoiding a collision with a pickup truck.

"Whew, that was a close one. A sissy like me, a few more like that and I'll die of fright, sweetie."

She smiled, but inside she could feel her heart pounding.

Cabral got out a little further on.

"Now don't you get too worked up, girl. See you on Thursday. Bye."

Greta turned on the radio. "Il mondo in Tasca." Can't stand those Italian songs. Mentally she began to compose a letter to Luís. A tender letter. Of love. Of friendship. And she knew she'd never send it.

It rained the whole week: a calamity for the Village. The cemetery, which is being developed on high ground, was the only area unaffected. Everything else was covered with at least a foot of water. (The radio reported parts of the city where the floodwaters rose to three feet.) Apparently the sewer system for the Village and the surrounding areas couldn't handle the runoff, either because the pipes were clogged or because they weren't designed for such heavy rainfall. The situation on Palmeiras Street was intolerable. No one could get out, and most families' homes were inundated.

Greta ran back and forth struggling with buckets and pans to place under the many leaks that appeared in the roof. Worse yet, the wind blew a tree down on the veranda, channeling the rainwater outside the gutter which filled with leaves. You could see the water rising in the yard. It was bound to flood the basement. The only solution was to put on a raincoat and clean out that gutter to prevent catastrophic damage. The yard simply disappeared. At night she fell exhausted into bed. Write? Are you kidding? All she wanted to do was sleep.

The weather improved on Friday. The sky was still cloudy but the rain had stopped. Finally it was possible to assess the full extent of the damage in the Village: tree branches fallen across electric and telephone lines, hedgerows carried off by the floodwaters, the sidewalks a damn swamp.

The families worked all day cleaning up the houses and the streets; their determination was admirable. Only those who had to go to their offices didn't participate in the community effort. Camilo gave everyone a skillful helping hand; his own house was very well built and was raised about two feet off the ground. Míriam, who obviously had no problems with her own apartment, cleared away the debris from the building's entrance with a shovel and a trash can. To some extent, the floodwaters had cleaned out the apartments on the first floor by carrying away some of the lighter rubble. By late afternoon the Village was regaining its normal appearance, the damage was less obvious, and the residents could get their cars out of their garages and restock their pantries.

Strangely, a spontaneous *ad hoc* meeting took place at Greta's house. Tancredi, the insurance broker, was the first to ring the doorbell.

"Forgive the intrusion, but I think we should . . . "

"Come in, please."

In half an hour, twenty people were sitting in the living room. Greta thought it had spread by word of mouth . . .

"Since there's so much concern," the broker raised his voice, "I think the best thing is that we all discuss the situation, don't you agree? That way we can all voice our complaints and concerns."

Antônio was dispirited; he seemed more upset than anyone else as he paced back and forth.

"It's time we considered what we've been through this week because of the rain," the insurance man went on. "As for myself, I've decided to put my house up for sale. The good woman doesn't want to live here anymore. We lost our carpeting, and our furniture is ruined."

Sônia, who usually never opens her mouth, interjected:

"I can't even guess how many books I've lost."

"Since we've all lost something, maybe a great deal," Camilo said, "we should draw up a petition asking Fortuna to take steps to prevent this from ever happening again. This is our chance to clarify the situation about our lots and the repairs we were promised. It's true the rainfall was unusually heavy and several areas of the city were affected, but that's City Hall's responsibility. In our case, it's Fortuna's. We're within our rights to demand they fulfill the contractual agreements on street maintenance. Our streets are overgrown with vegetation and overrun with murderers, prostitutes, and thieves. The public areas also need fixing up. As far as I'm concerned, if the Company doesn't come up with drastic and urgent measures, we should denounce it in the newspapers and bring a lawsuit against it. The new Village representative, and I have no idea where he's been hiding all week, should be our spokesman and present our demands."

"I knocked on his door," said Ribeiro's neighbor, a retired dentist named Soares, "but he's not back yet. He hasn't shown his face since the election."

"Maybe he hasn't finished moving yet," Greta ventured, "and he had to go back to Araraquara."

"Is that where he's from? That's funny, so am I," stated the dentist's wife, a woman of about seventy and a grandmother several times over.

"Selling our houses won't solve anything, especially since our deeds aren't in order yet," Camilo went on.

"All the buyers have to accept the same contractual obligations with the Company when it comes to transfer of title."

"Tancredi, my dear fellow, you know that's not so," Camilo insisted calmly. "The real estate people are trying to block us, to stop us from selling our homes. It's not in their interest to keep this project alive, because it's gotten in the way of their plans to use the land for other purposes."

"Well, then they should buy my property back. I'd rather lose the profit on my investment than see my wife suffer. I made a mistake, fine, I'll pay for it," the insurance agent concluded.

Everyone in the living room began talking at once. The notorious titles to deed were a sore point in the Village. Either they stuck together and hired a lawyer or nothing could be done. The uncertainty had dragged on for years without benefit to either party. On the one hand, the residents believed they had a claim to a theoretical portion of the total area and therefore would profit from rising property values. If there were no development, on the other hand, increase in property value would be slow, maybe illusory. The best thing would be to set up another meeting of the homeowners association, the retired dentist suggested.

At that point, Antônio decided to tell them about the research he had done on the Village. His purpose had been to assess the damage they had suffered, but more importantly he had wanted to find out what caused the flooding. This is what he discovered: someone had purposely blocked the drainage gutters with the obvious intention of unleashing the floodwaters. Even a less severe rainfall would have produced the same result.

The revelation was a shock. Who would do such an evil thing? And why?

"There can be only one reason: the use of violence to force the owners to abandon the area and sell their houses and their shares to the Company."

Those at the meeting were indignant, outraged. Only a criminal, a gangster, a mafioso would behave that way.

The neighbors said goodnight, each one committed to the idea of convincing the absent members to share the cost of hiring a lawyer and possibly bringing a lawsuit against Fortuna.

Greta's whole body felt sore; she wasn't used to all that physical exertion.

She had a glass of wine and before going to bed she saw Sônia and Elisa chatting quietly in their living room. At that hour?

🔔 "That's it, Mama. It's all set. We're going to Switzerland in October. They say fall there is lovely," Sônia sighed.

"And what about Bóris, my dear?"

"I talked to him. I haven't shown up these past few days; it's been raining and I haven't been missed a bit. The truth is he doesn't pay much attention to the clinic. He plans to see his patients in the hospital. How old is he, Mama?"

Elisa thought for a few seconds.

"He's five years older than I am: he must be fifty-nine. The same age your father would be now."

"He's too young to be so neurotic about the traffic."

"He's had a heart attack, Sônia."

"Anyway, we're going to Switzerland no matter what happens with the clinic."

Elisa trembled with joy and excitement. An old wish was about to be fulfilled. She could hardly believe it. She wouldn't even ask Sônia why she had decided to go. Her daughter had changed so much. Her head was filled with completely crazy ideas, like publishing those ads—she crossed herself—imagine that!

"We have a zillion details to take care of: documents, charging our tickets, itinerary . . . I dropped by the travel agency today."

"How much are the tickets?"

"I don't know. I'll find out tomorrow. Do you want to go by plane or by ship?"

"I've never been on a plane, my dear. Ships are safer, aren't they?"

"It's twelve days to Spain by ship. It's one night by plane—we go to sleep and when we wake up we're in Switzerland."

"What a difference! But why charge the tickets?"

"In a country with runaway inflation it's a good investment."

"I won't make any suggestions. I don't understand anything about that. You take care of everything and I'll write to my cousins and tell them we're coming. Now what's this itinerary business?"

"The countries or cities you want to include in the ticket."

"Visiting Geneva and Zurich is quite enough for me."

Sônia remained silent. Wasn't she excited! That whole week, shut up in the Village, had taken its toll. She had really become aware of the isolation and futility of her life. The agency had scheduled an excursion to Paris, London, Amsterdam, and Rome, including local tours. When she returned she would figure out what she was going to do. Maybe open a bookstore.

Elisa stood up and kissed her daughter's forehead affectionately.

"God bless you, Sônia, for the happiness you're bringing me. Do you think we could give Greta power of attorney so she could represent us in this legal stuff?"

Sônia agreed.

"Sleep tight, Mama. We'll take care of that tomorrow."

That night Sônia had an unusual dream in which she flew. She could just open her arms and take off. First she tried flying over Palmeiras Street and back. Next she went over to the lake. Instead of the moon, she saw the sun mirrored in the dark waters, which disconcerted her. At night the sky and the lake were the same; she continued on toward the church. Where are the bells? They appeared to the left of the bell tower—tiny, silver—and they tinkled softly. To the right, the inside of the tower was completely empty. She circled around a few times and the same image persisted, even though she remembered that the sound, when heard from down below, was that of an enormous brass bell.

🔔 A clear Saturday. The weather has stabilized. The garden has to be replanted. Must buy some seeds.

Twenty days passed during which Greta took no notes. Extreme list-lessness and a measure of tedium. A period of good will toward the Village. She spent several days going to Fortuna's offices, requesting meetings, discussing the problem of the gutters and the tractor in front of the apartment building, alleging intimidation, abuse of their rights, you name it. She tried to take a fighting stance but deep down she knew it wouldn't do any good. Still, she fought. She was behaving differently at the clinic. Cabral joked: beware of Greeks bearing gifts.

She would return to the Village breathless and emotionally drained. She went so far as to take up knitting. When the needles fell from her weary hands, she would fall asleep.

Tina's getting better. She may even come back home. For sure.

Oh, this weather. Can you believe it's turned cold again? Tiny daisies have started blooming in the fields, suddenly challenging the winter: stars on the ground. Clouds moving slowly in the transparent blue sky glide swiftly across the dark lake. Why?

"With all these burials, the grave diggers never put down their shovels," the director of the cemetery remarked yesterday.

Camilo was uneasy.

"Elderly people can't tolerate these sudden drops in temperature, Greta. Any day now I'm going to kick the bucket. And then what'll become of my little boy? I can't sleep when I think about that."

Míriam goes downstairs when the mailman comes, a daily exercise in futility.

I'm going to write a letter to Luís, Greta promises herself. Now.

Luís, thank you very much for the letter. I'm glad to know you're enjoying the trip and your head is filled with so many plans. It looks like things will turn out fine. Especially the story about the man who meets

*the deaf-mute. It sounds stimulating. It could work if he spoke for the
two of them. As if he were the unconscious mind of the civilized man on
the motorcycle. The man suddenly confronts everything he had absorbed
in the big city, and examines his own duality. The pure emotional being—
she—as opposed to the rational, sophisticated being from the urban center. I know what you're thinking: after all, ambiguity has always been
my favorite theme. Maybe it is. In any case, the fact that his reflection is
female should enrich the dialogue quite a bit. Keep up the good work.*

*My ties with São Paulo have weakened considerably. Besides prac-
tical problems with the Company, which will probably be resolved (un-
happily), I go to the clinic. The truth is, Tina couldn't bear certain as-
pects of the real world and she needs treatment. Which was to be
expected. Considering the obsession that's possessed her, there was no
other way out. "Love, your burden is great."*

*Finally, I'm taking notes on the Village, on my world: incoherent at
times, contradictory at others; monotonous maybe for restless souls hun-
gering for excitement; alienated, for those who can understand only one
kind of social commitment. But I have no pretensions. I scribble down
my observations, as if I were telling stories to myself. Outlines to see if I
can draw or see some pattern in the fragments. And here comes a confession (a rather uneasy one): I find the outlines more interesting than a
completely worked out development. And mood is especially provocative
for me. That's a lot of what the Village is, a series of moods. For the time
being. Well, Luís, as you can see I don't have anything interesting to tell
you. Were you able to find Cavafy's poems? A great poet. Be sure to read
him. Make the best of your trip.*

Hugs,

Greta

⚕ Hallucination, madness, or some other illness—she sat down,
her mind finally made up. It's impossible to control one's feelings. Suddenly, the certainty that she should continue. The Village was there, a
constant source of information.

⚕ Month of August, month of augury. Gino di Carli killed himself.
A shock to everyone. No one expected such a desperate act.

As soon as he got home Sunday night, Gino put on a record—he
never did that on Sundays—and stood at the window and sang the aria
from *Il Trovatore*. Greta thought: on Sunday? She opened the door

and went out on the veranda. All of a sudden she heard a shot. A few seconds later Graziela was in the street, screaming in despair. Eleven o'clock.

They called emergency right away but the ambulance took too long. The police took charge of the body and didn't release it until the next morning. Most of the residents on Palm Street stayed up all night with the inconsolable widow, while her children made funeral arrangements. Gino was buried at five in the afternoon in the Cemetery of the Flowers. The group of neighbors walked back slowly as if they were following a procession and stopped at the entrance to the Village. Looks of expectation: the church bells tolled sadly. Although he was home, Alexandre Ribeiro didn't attend the wake or the burial.

A strange suicide, so unexpected. It seems so unlikely that a person who sings, who cares about music, would kill himself. Graziela once mentioned to Greta that her husband had some financial problems. He loved to play the horses and his vice was going to the Jockey Club on Sundays, his pockets always stuffed with betting slips. Maybe that's why he didn't sing or listen to records on Sundays. Graziela never went with him to the racetrack. As far as she was concerned, it was a ridiculous waste of time to sit and cheer for the horses as they huffed and puffed around the track. A few years ago Gino had actually been a Jockey Club board member. Profligacy. His name was involved in a case of embezzlement that was never cleared up. Which was deeply disturbing to this model husband, parent, and grandfather. He had nothing to do with the matter.

There were other troubles during the month of August besides the singer's suicide: the new representative refused to hire a night watchman, maintaining that there wasn't enough money, and he wouldn't submit the petition requesting the measures agreed on by the residents. One day, Soares saw him leaving Fortuna's offices in a suspicious manner. Moreover, he seemed overly friendly with the president, who was one of those working hardest to throw the residents out of the Village.

It's important to emphasize how strange Ribeiro's behavior was: after the election he went from door to door speaking against Antônio. As if he wanted to ruin his predecessor's good reputation and accomplishments. If anyone offered a dissenting opinion, he changed the subject, patted the neighbor on the shoulder, and claimed it was only a joke and so on and so forth. And he promised a plan that would revolutionize conditions in the Village by establishing a fund for home improvements. What did they have to lose by waiting, he would ask. The preliminaries would be discussed at the next meeting.

But setting up the meeting was easier said than done. He didn't want it to be held at his house because it was in no condition for visitors, he being a bachelor and all. The way to do it was to arrange a place in the city suitable for such a purpose. This took everyone by surprise. The meetings had always been social gatherings, a chance to converse. Everyone struggled to get by, going from home to work and back, but at least once a month the neighbors could meet socially to chat. Of course there were private gatherings, people visited each other. Elisa had her teas, some people did their shopping together: they bought boxes of fruits and vegetables and divided them up. A practical way of doing things for those who lived far out, as well as an attempt to redefine human relationships, to make them less selfish. If the meetings were held in the city, the women who didn't work outside the home wouldn't be able to come. Camilo couldn't leave Ivo alone either. In short, very upsetting. It wouldn't work. In fact it seemed like a scheme to make sure few people would attend. The dentist resolved the situation by offering his home.

Once they got beyond the impasse, the meeting took place on the twentieth of August. Míriam showed up in the company of a skinny fellow.

"This is my brother. He just got here from the South."

Greta looked at him in amazement. The brother really existed. Now Míriam could never work in a ticket booth, or have any other destiny. She looked very pretty that evening, a figure out of Klimt, with that flowered shawl and her braids wrapped in tight circles around her ears. For the first time Greta saw her neighbor wearing makeup. Her serene face shone with a peaceful light.

Gricha, with his arm around his sister's shoulders, seemed softer than her. Maybe because his eyes were blue. A bit unsteady in his gangling walk? He constantly tightened his facial muscles, showing an inner tension. Or could it be shyness?

The Village representative entered the living room carrying a stack of drawings. He was the only one dressed in executive costume; everyone else had taken off their suits and changed into their most comfortable jeans. Which in fact was a kind of uniform, too. He greeted no one, as if he were in his own home and had been there the whole time. He glanced quickly at Míriam and her brother.

"Quiet. I'm going to start with a demonstration of the project I've put together to reduce expenses and turn the Village of the Bells—an awful name, by the way—into a place that will attract more people. That, however, is a matter to be dealt with later."

Some of the residents exchanged wary glances. Could it be this character wanted to change the name of the Village? He unfolded the first drawing. A view of the unfinished church. Beside it, a large circus tent. The general reaction was expressed with a prolonged oooooh. Greta wasn't sure if it was a reaction to the colorful drawing, or shock at the circus.

"Well, this is it. I propose renting out the land to a circus. I've looked into this matter carefully and there's a lot of interest in spite of the out-of-the-way location. The People's Circus has made an offer. There are several advantages: free police protection for us, publicity for the Village, and income for the homeowners association and for Fortuna."

At first glance, as they stared at the drawing, the residents liked the proposal.

The dentist decided to speak.

"Interesting but . . ."

Ribeiro cut him off, "Wait till you've seen the whole proposal."

And he showed them a second drawing.

"The circus will generate a series of stands selling food and drink and the space will be utilized more fully."

The drawing: another view from a more distant point and with a wider perspective; plastic modules had been inserted around the tent, similar to the newsstands in the city. In this drawing the church had disappeared.

"What about the church?" asked the insurance broker's wife.

"Please, don't interrupt me. If you'll make a mental note of your questions, we can discuss them afterwards," the artist spoke sharply.

And the third drawing was laid out. Besides the circus and the food stands, they could see a Ferris wheel, which indicated that an amusement park had been included in the project.

He had filled this drawing with human figures to give it a lively sense of movement. Men and women with colorful clothing, children holding plastic balloons, a celebration of color.

The audience exclaimed once again in astonishment. The impression he had made didn't escape his notice.

"I don't bother with unimportant things but only with great projects. I leave insignificant practical details to whoever wants them. I'm a man of creativity, as you can judge for yourselves."

"Very good," Tancredi applauded.

Greta looked around for Antônio; dignified, he pretended not to notice anything.

In a few minutes everyone was talking at once with the people next to them. Jane, Antônio's wife, expressed admiration. Míriam and Gricha argued quietly. Sônia and Elisa listened in silence as the red-faced dentist held forth in a blustering rage.

"Who authorized him to talk to the People's Circus?"

The representative again raised his voice.

"I see everyone's excited about the project. My dear neighbors, you have demonstrated your intelligence and good sense."

A fellow who never said anything and always approved everything, Dilermando Canudos, a ham radio operator, decided to leave. He took the arm of his wife, a heavy-set woman with a happy face and beautiful teeth. He was clearly incensed.

"What's this, my dear friend? Are you going to leave without giving me your invaluable opinion?" Ribeiro shouted.

The radio operator glowered at him before answering.

"My dear sir, until now the Village has been a peaceful place, and I imagine all the residents came here for the same reason. Your project, to say the least, goes against the purpose of our lives here. It's a violation. It wouldn't benefit us in any way. Quite the opposite. The profits would go to Fortuna, which is the largest shareholder, but we'd suffer the consequences because we'd have to live next to a circus and an amusement park. Do you by chance work for Fortuna? How much did they pay you to put together this project? Has it ever occurred to you how unpleasant it would be for us to have to put up with the stink of animals right next door? Can you imagine the total chaos we'd have around here?"

Ribeiro smiled sarcastically. The ham radio operator's words had suddenly revealed the proposal's terrible meaning. Camilo approached.

"If I have anything to say about it, this nonsense will not be approved. Have a nice day."

Bedlam ensued. No one understood anyone else. Míriam and Gricha went over to Antônio. They needed his advice. They couldn't bear the pressure from Fortuna anymore. Yesterday they had given her ninety days' notice to leave the building; otherwise, they'd tear it down whether she was in it or not. What should she do?

"You need to hire a lawyer."

"I had one, but the crook works for the Company. In the beginning he said I had a case and I could get Fortuna to meet all my demands, but then he turned around and said the problem was too complicated and I should reach a compromise settlement . . ."

"Get another lawyer, Míriam. Your brother can help you."

Gricha lowered his eyes in embarrassment. Míriam whispered

something in his ear. They both moved away, toward the representative. It was impossible to talk to him at that moment: he was vehemently defending his plan.

"And this business about the blocked sewer, what about that?" Soares questioned him.

"My dear sir, I have just presented a great idea and you want to talk about this petty nonsense? We'll deal with that matter in due time . . . Don't you think my proposal is important?"

The dentist turned his back on him without further ado. Fortuna must be behind this. Who knows, maybe they even paid the artist to make those drawings. Which should be looked into.

"And what about you, madam? What do you think?" The representative kissed Elisa's hand obsequiously.

"I was just arranging a discussion over tea tomorrow with my neighbor from 580. The women are going to get together, aren't we, Clotilde?"

Alexandre refused to give up.

"I can explain my plan to you in detail, if you wish. Women are the pillars of the earth," he declared slyly.

"I'm sorry, Mr. Ribeiro, but our teas are for ladies only."

Sônia chided her mother.

"Don't forget about the trip. You don't have time to get involved in anything."

"It's in our interest, dear. Our property is at stake."

Clotilde, a forceful and energetic woman and owner of a lingerie factory, threatened the representative.

"Even if our husbands do nothing, you can be certain we women will meet this issue head on. You failed to respect even the church! What will become of it, eh?"

The representative thought a moment before answering.

"We have two solutions: the first is to demolish the building. It's ugly and falling apart from lack of maintenance."

"We will never agree to that solution."

"If you will only let me finish, madam. And the second solution would be to invest part of the profits in completing the construction and buying a real bell so people will stop imagining . . ."

The woman, red-faced, interrupted:

"No one is imagining anything, my dear sir. The bells do ring."

The representative didn't argue. The subject would only stir things up. Then he tried to hurry off, as if he needed to speak urgently with someone.

Greta didn't wait until the meeting was over. There are times when it's best to keep one's distance, to get away. The fellow's project would simply destroy the Village. The whole business fit the Company to a T. Dilermando's questions were valid: who had paid for the artist's work? It was no use guessing. She would ask the directors to their face. There was no doubt someone was trying to take unfair advantage of the situation. Her steps echoed on the asphalt. She thought she heard footsteps; she looked back. Whose? She stopped. No one. She resumed walking. She heard the footsteps again. Suddenly she felt afraid. Horribly afraid. Of what? Of the unforeseen?

🔔 "I'm sorry to barge in on you like this, Greta. You can't imagine how upset I am. Gricha's gone back to Santa Catarina. He found out about an abandoned farm in Laguna belonging to my grandfather. He's occupied the house, claimed squatters' rights, and started fixing it up. He wants me to go there. And what about the problem with Fortuna?"

Greta looked at her neighbor compassionately. The happiness of a few days ago had disappeared; her eyes were puffy and her skin looked wrinkled.

"Come on in, Míriam. Want some coffee?"

The woman stammered but finally accepted the invitation.

"Two heads are better than one. Sit down. I'll put the water on."

"I'll join you so we can talk while we wait."

They went into the kitchen. At that hour the sun shone directly on the sink. Greta filled the teapot with water. Míriam sat on a stool at the wooden table.

"Do you wax the table often, Greta?"

"Once a month."

"It's lovely." She ran her hand delicately over the table. "Old things are always prettier."

Silence. Míriam, like a child, propped up her head with her hand, a troubled look in her eyes. Greta stood leaning against the cupboard while she waited. Her friend really was an inscrutable presence, with that old-fashioned hat. A felt bonnet tied at the chin.

Míriam broke the silence: "I stopped doing embroidery. Gricha said I'd go blind. Now I won't have to put up with that shrew at the store. Gricha brought me some money. I'm so tired of living alone. My aunt's gone to Santa Catarina, too. I don't have anyone left here. I asked her to stay . . . Poor thing. She wants to be buried in the city where she was born. Before she left she told me if she were to die in São Paulo there wouldn't be a single person to put flowers on her grave. At least in Santa Catarina her relatives would remember her, if only on the Day of the Dead."

"So what have you decided?"

"Well, I don't know." She straightened up. "If I just pack up and leave the apartment, Fortuna will go ahead and have the building torn down. Then how will I ever get my money?"

"Why don't you accept their offer for an apartment in the city? It can be rented out . . ."

"Well, the fact is I gave Dr. Alceu a hard time and he's going to want to get back at me."

"No he's not. I'll talk to him tomorrow. I have to go to the clinic and I'll drop by his office on the way."

"Can I go with you? I'm terrified of those people."

"Of course," Greta said as she poured the boiling water over the powder in the small aluminum pan.

"You make coffee like that? How strange." Míriam stood up.

"Hillbilly coffee. It's stronger and tastes better. When the water boils and the powder starts to rise to the top—you see?—I pour it through the cloth filter. It won't work with a paper filter because the powder passes right through it."

"Where are the cups?"

"In the cupboard. Will you get them?"

They sipped their coffee slowly. The yellowish sunlight tinted their forms and their surroundings.

"For the past few days the smell of wet vegetation and coffee has been making me think of my childhood, my father, something."

Greta wanted to answer but couldn't think of anything to say.

"So I'm sure," the neighbor woman continued, "there's someone else hidden inside me. As if I were only here in body."

"Everyone's like that, Míriam. Nobody's only one person."

"My other self is violent, obsessive, full of uncontrolled, wild passion. Good thing it doesn't come out very often because it'd be unbearable. I need Gricha close to me. He makes me feel secure." (She thought—I love him so much, the last night he slept in the apartment I imagined I could hear his dreams.)

But it was as if she had said it.

♤   Later on, as Greta recalled the conversation with Míriam, she realized she would have preferred talking with Tina. The mood was Tina's; the obsession, ditto.

And could that be of any importance?

♤ Elisa talks to her plants while she sweeps up the dry leaves.

Mateus parks his motorcycle, hangs his helmet on the handlebars, and goes up to the house.

"Good morning, ma'am; is Sônia home?"

Elisa takes off her rubber gloves and offers her hand to the visitor.

"No, she's gone to town, young man. We're going to Europe, did you know that?"

He didn't answer.

"Would you like to come in? I don't know what time she'll be back and . . ."

"No thank you. I stopped by to deliver this envelope. I thought she was coming over to pick it up."

Elisa looked Mateus over: an interesting man.

"Very nice of you. We do live in such an out-of-the-way place. Would you like to rest a bit? How about a glass of water? I was getting these flower beds ready," she pointed, "because we're going to be away for a long time. My poor plants. Did you know they can feel lonely, too?"

He stood there thinking, not knowing what to say. Lonely. A reasonable idea. He had once had a fantastically decorated vase filled with begonias. He spent the weekend on the beach, and when he returned the flowers were withered, almost dead. And they hadn't lacked either water or air. In a few days they straightened up and regained their vigor and gaiety. Although he wouldn't admit it openly, that had convinced Mateus that loneliness wasn't good for plants.

Finally he said something. "Do you buy the seedlings, ma'am, or do you grow them yourself?"

"Sometimes I buy them and sometimes I grow them. Last year the lizards ate all the leaves off the arum lilies and the creepers. Those over there, you see? Was that a lot of trouble!"

"In my house in Rio—I used to be from there, but I don't know where I'm from anymore—we used to have a garden. My father was the one who took care of it."

"Really?" Elisa brightened up. So pleasant to chat with someone. "And was he good at gardening?"

"He had a green thumb. I don't know if it's true, but my older sisters claimed he used to talk to the flowers."

Elisa's face lit up.

"So they'd grow happily."

Mateus was taken aback by her reply.

"Well, ma'am, I'm off. I have a lot to do and I want to be on my way while the weather holds. Goodbye. Have a nice trip."

Elisa waited until he was out of sight down the Avenue. Sônia would be sorry she missed him. She is certain.

♤   Yesterday the German shepherd at 530 died. No one knows why. A fat dog with shiny fur, gentle eyes, and a sensitive tail. If anyone from the neighborhood met him—he roamed the streets at night—he'd approach affectionately, wagging his tail to show he wanted to be helpful. An excellent watchdog. His name was Duke. A young dog. He couldn't have been more than five years old. A mysterious death.

♤   Míriam versus Fortuna. An unpleasant situation. Greta acted as go-between. The deadline requested by the Company to decide whether or not to accept her offer: thirty days. Míriam has asked for her money back, with interest and monetary correction, or an apartment of equal value in the city.

Greta believes the Company will offer this: only the return of her initial investment, without penalty. Which is outrageous.

Alexandre Ribeiro knocked on the door, holding a canvas.

"Excuse me for dropping by so early in the morning. I finished your portrait and I wanted to bring it over."

"Very nice of you."

"You see, my dear lady, we artists are impatient." He unwrapped the canvas. "As soon as we finish something we want someone to see it and approve of it."

Greta looked at the painting uneasily. It was Tina, in every way. A Tina she knew and detested. The tender, romantic Tina. In the background, the lake and the willows, in gray tones. In fact, the entire composition was grayish, as if the landscape and the person were covered with a veil.

"Interesting," she exclaimed, and immediately regretted it. Interesting isn't an adjective, it's an impersonal observation.

"Is that all you have to say? I'd say it's a beautiful painting."

"That's what I was thinking."

"You want to buy it?"

She was taken aback by the question. Buy it? She took Tina's collage down from the wall and hung the canvas in the same spot. They both moved back a few steps to check the result.

"If you don't want it, no problem. Don't feel obligated."

The light falling on the painting accentuated the streaks of dirty paint and the sloppily applied finish. From that angle the picture was ugly and poorly painted; the drawing helped, but not that much. She would never have bought it if she'd seen it in an exhibition.

The painter, with an air of superiority, removed the canvas from the wall and rehung the collage. Greta tried to find something polite to say and then gave up. He saw the pieces of paper piled on the table.

"What's this?"

"Nothing important. Just something to kill time."

She considered offering him some juice to get him off the subject. But he was already staring at the stack of newspapers wrapped in plastic, which the paperboy left in the yard every morning and which had never been opened. Greta merely dumped them on the bench until the pile got too high and then put them in the trash.

"If you don't read the newspapers why do you keep up the subscription?"

Greta smiled.

"Someday I might feel like reading them. I used to read several, including the Rio papers. Since I moved I've become less and less interested and I gradually got out of the habit. The world doesn't change. The radio and TV news are enough for me."

He went to the window, looked out at the landscape, and settled into the couch. Greta sat facing him in a sagging armchair with worn leather: her favorite. He crossed his legs. His woolen pants pulled up, exposing a torn sock. A fashion plate on the outside and a ragamuffin on the inside, she thought.

"What did you think of my project?" His expression was hostile. "I've received a number of favorable opinions. Tancredi has offered to help me put together a written report. A wonderful individual. He suggested we put in a parking area, which he would manage on behalf of the Village. The stumbling block is Antônio and his influence on the other residents. I know he's trying to turn people against me."

"Oh, I don't know about that. What would he gain from doing that? He's the one who nominated you for the position. He's a man of principle and a loyal friend. He truly has a heart of gold."

"Principles, heart of gold! He's doing everything he can to undermine my efforts."

"Why would he do that? He was so dedicated: along with running a mattress factory he sacrificed his weekends to deal with Village problems. He must be relieved not to have to worry about anything except his personal affairs."

"I can see the way he looks at me. I can sense underneath he blames me for that night watchman business and for not being here during the flood. If you doubt it, what about the fact that he's going around saying I'm the one who plugged the sewers?"

The painter stood up, clearly agitated. Greta spoke slowly and tried to clear up the misunderstanding.

"Antônio isn't capable of discrediting someone, even in thought. We care about him because he's always been helpful, attentive, understanding, and efficient. He's a man of character. No one has any reason to cast doubt on his integrity. Not even Tancredi, though they had a serious dispute a few years ago. Tancredi was about to earn a huge commission buying aluminum trash containers for the Village," she also stood up, "but the Village representative blocked him when he found out about the shady deal."

"What are you talking about?" He seemed surprised.

"I'll tell you in a minute. I'm going to get us some juice, or would you rather have wine? It's all there is to drink in the house."

He checked his watch.

"Wine."

Greta opened the cupboard and took out the red crystal glasses. She talked as she struggled with the corkscrew.

"Some company or other, I forget its name, sold aluminum frames, containers, something like that, to hold trash cans along the street. The firm belonged to a cousin of Tancredi. Before spending Village funds, Antônio did some comparison shopping and discovered the prices for Tancredi's merchandise were twenty percent higher than the going rate. So he got in touch with the company and figured out that the extra amount was the insurance agent's percentage. He ended up not making the purchase so he wouldn't have to inform on his neighbor."

"Come off it." He picked up the glass and took a sip without offering a toast.

Suddenly, he looked furiously at Greta.

"I don't believe a word of what you've said. I think you're trying to discredit Tancredi, my principal associate. The one person willing to help me. You're up to the same scheming tricks as Antônio."

Greta stared at him in amazement.

"Me? No way. I mentioned the incident to illustrate Antônio's character and ability, to show you why he's loved and respected."

"That's not what I've heard. I know some residents who don't share this great admiration, just the opposite. He's not the saint he makes himself out to be. By the way, I'm checking last year's monthly balance sheets because I found the treasury empty. He made sure he paid all the bills so I wouldn't have a chance to do a single thing until more money comes in."

Alexandre Ribeiro shoved the picture irritably under his arm.

"See you around."

She walked across the yard with him. Without waiting for her to unlock the low gate, he jumped over the fence like a ballet dancer.

"Your legs are light as a feather." Greta smiled.

He didn't hide the fury in his look.

"Tell that cleaning lady of yours I don't need her anymore. I want to keep my distance from people who gossip every chance they get. And you," he shook his finger, "watch what you say about me to the Fortuna people. Dr. Alceu is my ally."

Greta didn't give the warning a second thought. It could only have come from a sick person. First, his unreasonable suspicion of Antônio and the others. Second, his overblown image of himself and whatever power he might have. Third, his illusions of grandeur, such as the proposal for a circus and amusement park. Fourth, his inability to accept criticism. And finally, his persecution complex. Even his way of walking revealed his paranoia. Pathological schizophrenia?

He walked right past Camilo without so much as a hello. If Mr. Alexandre Ribeiro is not careful, he may wind up in a mental hospital. *L'être suit son vice.*

♧ Time off from the clinic. Tina slowly disappears from memory. An egocentric creature who lived off her fantasies. There's so much suffering in the world and everyone's entitled to a scream. Tina let out hers. An obsessive scream of despair in the form of a guffaw before the mirror. Why a guffaw? Could she have foreseen the absurdity of the situation? Everyone has her own brand of madness.

September. Foggy morning. Gino di Carli's house is shuttered. A few acacia branches poke in through the window. The widow neither made arrangements to move nor revealed her intentions. She closed the door and took off. Which gives Greta the impression that she'll hear her neighbor's voice again singing his operas. She wishes fervently that it'll come true and that his death will have been nothing more than a nightmare. Did he die or was he killed? Why Gino, a harmless musician?

Camilo was ailing. He had wrenched his back. He was unable to move, poor thing. Greta found out because he sent the mailman to inform her. Foolishness, leaving the old man alone with the boy like that. She could lend him Zaíra for a week to clean house, wash, cook. Thanks to the Village representative she now had two free days, enough to respond to the emergency. The maid was responsible, she understood the problem. Greta visited him every afternoon.

"Give me someone's telephone number so I can make arrangements with your family . . ."

"No thanks, Greta. The time for Ivo's mother to visit is coming soon . . . I don't want them to put the boy away. He's very sensitive, he couldn't bear to be separated from me. He can't speak or walk, he's retarded, but he has feelings. And besides, I care about him. He's all that I have left in life. When he goes away I won't have a reason to go on living."

For an instant Greta considered asking him a question she had frequently rehearsed but always put off. First, however, she had to fill the hot water bottle.

"Doesn't your daughter care about him?" She adjusted the bottle under the old man's back.

"She cares. The problem is what the boy represents: failure, hers and the father's. Have you ever thought of what it means to look at Ivo every day? With the boy out of sight the sense of failure isn't so great. My son-in-law is a prominent figure. They have to entertain a lot, they give parties and dinners, his profession depends on personal success. Ivo would be an obstacle . . ."

"I understand. But the fact is, some day they're going to have to admit the existence of their son. Didn't they have any other children?"

"No. The disaster with the first child was a shattering blow. My daughter is a decent person, the ordeal has been hard on her, but nothing can be done. Besides, Ivo can't stand his mother. No one knows why. Which is very bad for their relationship."

Greta's eyes looked for the child: he was glued to the television. Maybe by chance, he looked at her with an expression of curiosity and affection. The affection of an animal, a cat.

"I think Ivo should have physiotherapy and training so he can adapt to the outside world."

The old man stirred in pain on the bed.

"I spoke with his mother. She promised she'd make arrangements with one of those associations for the handicapped where he could spend a few hours."

Ivo seemed to have been upset by the conversation because he hung his head sadly on his chest. Or was it a coincidence?

The doorbell rang. Greta went to the window to see who it was.

"Just a minute, Antônio," she shouted from above.

He was bringing magazines and newspapers for Camilo.

"How do you feel today, dear fellow?"

"Better. An angel is looking after me."

Greta looked down in embarrassment. The friends chatted about this and that until they got around to what was really bothering them: the Village representative.

"I don't understand what's going on. The man did a total about-face after he was elected. He stopped being polite. Just like that, he started having fits of anger; the other day he was actually disrespectful to Jane. He fired the maid for reasons that make no sense, claiming she was talking behind people's backs. Soares told me he went over to ask the most idiotic questions about me. He had the audacity to hint that if our dear dentist wanted to maintain relations with him, he must have nothing further to do with me. Can you believe it? He's also decided to change the order we put in for streetlights because according to him the design and the quantity don't meet the Village's needs. He's altered the plans, reestimated the number of lights, and distributed them differently. In my discussion with Soares I argued that artists are known for their vanity. Furthermore, I said that if he were able to convince the Electric Company to provide another location for the streetlights, or a greater number of them, and as long as the changes corresponded to the amount of our credit, the Village might even come out ahead. The important thing is that he not waste any time: the last time I went to the Electric Company I was informed the streetlamps would be put up in two months. And it's essential our streets be well lit, don't you agree? Soares, a very amusing fellow, came up with the idea that the artist is a madman who escaped from a mental hospital."

They all laughed. Ivo mimicked the adults. Greta wasn't sure if he laughed because of the conversation or the television.

"We've ended up with a real hothead," Camilo said, "but he came at the right time for Fortuna. Until we get our streetlights we'll continue being a haven for prostitutes. Have you noticed how busy their hangout on the Avenue has gotten? The other evening on the way home from shopping, this hussy tried everything she could to pick me up. At my age."

"It happened to my son Toninho, too. He was riding his bicycle and one of them was all over him, in broad daylight. The boy was speechless and he tore out of there as fast as he could. The woman started yelling and calling him a queer."

"The whole thing is awful," Greta exclaimed. "This estate used to be wonderful. Not anymore. My heart aches when I think about it."

"And how is Míriam's case coming along?" Antônio asked.

Greta told him what she knew.

"Getting her money back with monetary correction is an acceptable settlement. It's worth it even if they don't pay her interest on her investment."

"You're right. It's unfair, but . . . I do what I can to help."

"We know that, my dear," Camilo said. "We know you can only do so much. Don't be too hard on yourself."

"On my way over here I saw the representative going into the apartment building. He must be trying to put pressure on poor Míriam."

"Does anyone want coffee?" Greta offered. Zaíra, in a flurry, was fixing dinner and ironing clothes.

The last rays of sunlight struck the building. Greta had the fleeting impression that the concrete structure was moving. The trees were silhouetted in the distance, forming a kind of wall around the property.

Lovely. Then she saw an immense dark shadow cover the area. And she felt a shiver pass through her: the clock ticked monotonously.

♫   No one else would tell this story—that's the justification for going on. Or would they?

Reality is the pretext. The rest, imagination.

Carmen Miranda got more tanked than usual, and she's singing in the middle of the street, accompanied by a black guitar player. Serenade for a warm spring evening. The full moon illuminates the duo and the still trees: expectation or perplexity? The grass grows, the creeping vines unfold. The quiet night was ominous before the singing started. Why?

One in the morning. Carmen Miranda's tipsy voice cuts through the nocturnal silence. "An outlaw's woman never cries."

Greta feels a longing for something, but she doesn't know what. The emotional trap. Until now she hasn't touched on the subject of Breno. Those bland years of marriage are forgotten. She's been separated for three years and she still hasn't asked for a divorce. She would never miss Breno. When marriage is a mistake it leaves behind neither sorrow nor joy. An experience with no scars. Sometimes she doesn't even acknowledge that there was a marriage, that for eight years she lived under the same roof with a man. Dredging up that period of her life isn't worth the trouble. It meant nothing. Nothing, you understand? A dead space.

Luís was different. A passion with the flavor of ashes. Which was lost as well. That's why the letter is still sitting upright on the bureau, waiting to be sent. Sending the letter means she intends on staying in touch. But that has to do with Tina, not with Greta. Only neurotics harbor fantasies of eternity. They transfer to the other the affection they should feel for themselves. Tina attempted metamorphosis, the abstraction of her inner self. That is the reason for the imbalance.

Greta feels a longing for what, then? The feeling may be more one of oppression than of nostalgia. The house is empty: the door open. It's a question of going out and becoming part of the world. What world? The outside or the inside one? We are the world, she'd say if she had the courage. Anyway, this tone and these things emerging deserve to be thrown into the trash. Can she flee from her own stigma?

"An outlaw's woman never cries"—the samba tune, far away. Hopefully no one will make a fuss about Carmen Miranda's serenade. There are so many tiresome, impatient, and selfish people!

Greta is most definitely not having one of her more productive evenings. Loneliness dulls intelligence.

The moving van rolled up Palm Street and parked in front of Gino's house. This turn of events intrigued Greta, watering her lawn. The widow was going to move? Too bad.

Graziela, dressed in black, met the four men: when could she have returned without being noticed? An automobile Greta didn't recognize had been parked in the garage since yesterday. She thought it might belong to one of the children.

"Hi, Greta!" the widow shouted. "I'll talk to you in a bit."

In the afternoon, people coming and going like mad, a constant stream of furniture and boxes carried to the van. Greta thought of offering her neighbor some lunch, but no one answered the telephone. And in the end she forgot about the widow completely, as she was absorbed in repairing the arbor (the rain had done considerable damage to the latticework). The old carpenter carried on a conversation while he worked. Greta wasn't about to allow any harm to come to the jasmine vines or to the wooden benches, so she dawdled there to keep an eye on the work.

That Abdias is an unusual fellow. One can see by the fluid rhythm of his work that he loves his trade. His thick, wrinkled hands move with serene precision. Repeatedly he removes the wooden ruler from the back pocket of his dun-colored pants, measures the lattice, makes a pencil mark where he will cut, and immediately saws off a strip of pine, which in a few moments is nailed on to replace the damaged section. To strengthen the supports, he uses varnished eucalyptus posts. Finally the detached jasmine shoots are trained on the trellis. A job done by a craftsman who loves his work. Years ago old Abdias had repaired the roof, the parquet floors, the doors, and the windows: he restored the house, which otherwise would have been uninhabitable.

At four o'clock on the dot, the carpenter stopped his work,

wrapped the leftovers from his lunch pail in a newspaper—"nobody cooks like my wife"—put away his tools, and advised Greta to clean up the basement to make sure the rain damage wasn't too severe.

"See you tomorrow, Abdias."

Graziela was heading her way.

"I can't come in, Greta. The van's about to leave. They make it so easy nowadays, my dear. I didn't even have to remove the clothes from the closets. They took care of everything. I just told them what to throw out. Gino's clothing I gave to the men from the moving company. No one else would want it, would they?"

Greta noticed her face seemed to be in repose, almost happy.

"Life goes on, my dear girl. I'll be in Italy with my brothers and sisters a week from now. Maybe for good."

"We're going to miss you. What about the house?"

"My children will decide that. It's impossible to sell without the title deed. Renting it out wouldn't be a bad idea . . . It doesn't matter to me. I hated living here."

"Yes, so you've told me. I thought you'd gotten used to it."

"The only thing I really cared about was listening to Gino sing at night. If he lived in an apartment, that would've been impossible, wouldn't it?"

Greta agreed, but she was thinking about something else, about the question, "Why did he kill himself?" If the other woman wished . . .

The moving van's horn sounded. For an instant she thought the widow was about to discuss the matter. Her face revealed a certain yearning, or was it doubt?

Graziela kissed her neighbor and walked back to her house. Apparently she didn't go in because her car left right behind the truck.

Greta returned downcast, regretting her failure to ask the question. But she also acknowledged the widow's right to keep things in the dark. Not everything has an explanation in this miserable life. Let Gino's death remain a mystery. Why pry into insignificant secrets in the face of the irretrievable act?

♤ Theatre. She hadn't gone out for months. Going to a play seemed to her a courageous gesture. The next thing she knew she was seated there, waiting for the show to start. Without even asking what was playing, she entered and sat down. The small auditorium might once have been a warehouse. Instead of chairs, concrete risers with cushions. The open stage had no curtain, exposing the set: illuminated black boxes and dark walls. Maybe a scrim would be lowered from the ceiling. Maybe. Greta checked her watch. Nine-fifteen. In the audi-ence—she counted—thirty people. Could they be waiting for more spectators? Or were they going to cancel the performance? That thought was all it took for the house lights to dim. A stage light focused on one of the boxes, on which a woman is seated—when did she enter?—wearing a shawl over her shoulders, pretending to sew. She's a character of indeterminate age with large dark eyes. The panto-mime—inserting the needle in the imaginary cloth, pulling and cut-ting the thread—is perfect. Music by Mahler. The woman stops her movement, looks out at the small audience, and asks in a warm, strong voice: "Anybody got the time?" No one answers. The woman shrugs her shoulders: "As far as I'm concerned, every day is night." Her ex-pression conveys something sick, worn out. An upstage light comes up on a young couple engaged in conversation, whose voices cannot be heard. They're holding hands. The woman continues her mono-logue and her sewing. The young people in the isolated upstage area begin a simple dialogue about a volleyball game. Greta pays no atten-tion to what they say. At that moment she observes the audience: four teenagers chewing gum. That's a pleasure she's unfamiliar with: gum. She tried a few times but wasn't able to appreciate it. She found it repulsive, like a horse chomping. The teenagers' hair is kinky, frizzled; in the case of one girl, completely masking her features. Across the way, a hybrid creature, wearing lipstick and earrings, dressed like a man. Male or female? She tries to think what the figure's name might be, and the first thing that occurs to her is Darcy. On stage, the young people, holding each other closely, dance a bolero from the fifties. The woman, as she sews, continues talking to herself in a monotone, her voice disconnected and lifeless. "Yes, like everyone else, I had my time." The young people turn their backs to the audience, undress, and change into different clothing they take from a movable rack, while the woman loses her train of thought and speaks disjointed, senseless phrases. Gounod's Ave Maria. Dressed as bride and groom, the young couple kneels. The wedding. "Papa was so elegant. He looked just like a prince . . . (Change of tone) Damn. I don't know why I'm remembering him today. Must be old age." The young people con-tinue the ceremony, ring on the finger, etcetera. A hooded man comes on stage. The woman tamely lowers her shawl to receive an injection in the arm. Her body stiffens and shivers, as if she were going to die. Head hanging dejectedly. Voices: a party. The young people greet in-visible guests. The woman again utters a stream of non sequiturs. "Once I saw a talking flower. Its name was Violet. The chameleon changes its skin, did you know that? My father loved to hunt. He was always polishing his shotgun, and he treated his weapon better than he did my mother." Idiotic laughter.

Greta finally got involved in the play. All at once she forgot where she was. The young people relive the sick woman's story; the character recreates her own life. The very same scenes are repeated in nearly identical fashion; only a few details are corrected or added, which is rather odd. Memory sorting out information. The simple story of an ordinary woman, unable to change, to intervene in her own destiny, until one day she turns fifty and she chooses her only option: while her relatives celebrate her birthday, she sets fire to the house, killing the entire family. One can't tell from the play exactly where she ends up, whether in an insane asylum or in prison.

Greta found the story compelling and the production simple and unpretentious. She was sorry to see the house lights go up. She had spent an hour emotionally glued to the play; she wished it had lasted longer. In any case, she applauded enthusiastically. The rest of the audience clapped dully.

Pleased, Greta went back to the Village. From now on she'd go out more. She was tired of her loneliness, of the crazy isolation in which she had shut her life. Blood still ran through her veins after all.

Δ Tancredi went from door to door seeking support for the petition to alter the Electric Company project. Only twelve residents had agreed; the others would agree only if Antônio signed first.

The insurance broker had no other alternative but to go see the former representative. He sat fussily in the living room, pretending to be on a routine visit.

Jane hurried to make coffee, and her husband, somewhat irritated, turned down the volume of the television; at least he could watch a bit during breaks in the conversation. If there was one thing he appreciated it was soccer. He never missed a game on TV. Everyone in the Village knew about his passion for the sport, except, apparently, for Tancredi.

"I hope you'll pardon me, my friend, but I can't miss the game. You don't mind, do you?"

"Not at all, my dear fellow. I stopped by because I'm asking people to sign the petition to modify the plan for streetlights."

"I see. Do you have the plan with you?"

"It's attached to the petition. Do you want to see it?"

Antônio quickly examined the drawing and the specifications.

"The alterations are minimal," he said as he counted the small circles indicating the lights. "Only the number has been decreased, and there've been a few minor changes here and there."

"Alexandre says now the streetlamps are symmetrical in a way that will beautify the street. The eight inches he increased the distance between each one meant eliminating two of them."

"I notice, unfortunately, that the person most affected will be Greta, since her lot is the biggest and that section of the street won't be as well lit. Is she aware of that?"

"Not yet. I intend to go over there tomorrow . . . She'll be the most affected?"

"Look." He was distracted for a moment by the television when someone almost scored a goal. "Compare the drawings: according to the previous plan there were two points of light between Sônia's house and Gino's."

Tancredi studied the drawing.

"The other lamppost must have been removed from, let's see, oh yes, from here." He pointed. "At the end of the street, in front of Dilermando Canudos's house. Which is outrageous. That area is dark and unprotected."

Tancredi had trouble reading the blueprint. He didn't understand what a ground plan was.

"Where's my house?"

"Here." Antônio pointed but offered no further explanation. "I'll sign only because I don't want to give the impression I'm boycotting my successor. But to tell you the truth, my good man, the alterations are so insignificant they're not worth the bother. Eliminating a few lampposts won't have any importance one way or the other for the community, and a few trivial changes could delay installation. He'd be better off concentrating his efforts on repairing the drainage system to take care of the rainwater."

The insurance agent betrayed his concern.

"I'm almost regretting I got involved with him. He seemed so polite and courteous, but in fact the fellow is impossible. He won't accept the slightest suggestion or disagreement. He starts climbing the walls. He even picked a fight with the baker, complaining about the bread and threatening to cancel delivery if . . ."

Antônio waved his hand to interrupt the insurance man. A goal was about to be scored on the television screen. Rivelino faked out two players on the other team and took a powerful shot.

"Goooaaal! Oh, baby, you never disappoint me." He rubbed his hands together in satisfaction.

Jane came into the living room smiling.

"Was I gone long? I don't know what's wrong with the gas. The water takes so long to boil . . . Do you have that problem at your house, Tancredi?"

"The good woman's always complaining about . . ."

"Sugar or artificial sweetener?"

"Sugar, please. Life is bitter enough." He smiled.

He's always had a thing for clichés, the former representative thought, and he turned up the volume on the TV to hear the announcer's remarks.

Tancredi felt out of place. He took out his pen and asked Antônio to sign the document. His neighbor, feeling very good about the goal, bade him a pleasant farewell.

"Drop by anytime, my friend. Your visit has given me great pleasure. My regards to your family."

And he settled in comfortably to watch, at last, the second half of the game.

♤ A person's first trip abroad is truly important. There's a sense of eager anticipation . . . Sônia and Elisa bustle about. Every day they go out and return loaded down with packages.

"If I were you, I'd start out with my suitcases empty so I could fill them in Europe," Greta suggested.

"We're going to spend several days on the ship. And our wardrobe is so old. Plus we get off in Spain. Until we know where we'll be going . . ." was Elisa's excuse.

"When are you leaving?"

"In twenty days. Oh, how I've longed for this trip, Greta!" She let out a sigh. "Do you have any friends you want to send something to? Don't hesitate to ask."

"Watch out. I might take you up on your offer. Everybody has some request or other. Anyway, I may ask you to mail a letter for me."

"I'll be happy to, Greta."

"Sônia, did you know Graziela's going on a trip, too?"

"Yes, I did. The other day at Fortuna we also found out the house will be rented, although according to the deed it's prohibited."

Greta examined her neighbor sympathetically. She wore a finely tailored gray suit and a white blouse with a high collar and lacy ruffles. She seemed quite animated. That afternoon she would have said Sônia was pretty, not for her features, which had always been distinct and delicate, but because she had the look of a blossom opening up to life.

"Very fair of them to allow the rental," Elisa said. "The appraisal can take years. My dear, are you really going to visit that woman with the dreams?"

"Very soon, Mama. I want to tell Greta about the drawings of the circus we saw hanging on the Company's walls. Did you know about that?"

Greta, irritated, shifted in her chair.

"No. That means Fortuna bought the crazy idea. I'm going over there this week."

"The Village representative was coming out of a meeting with Dr. Alceu. By the look on his face everything's apparently peachy keen."

Elisa interrupted her daughter.

"As we've been saying, we women won't allow them to get away with this."

Sônia got up.

"As long as you don't act like Lysistrata!"

"Who is that?"

"Lysistrata is the first feminist in history. She convinced the women of her city to declare a sexual strike so their husbands wouldn't go off to war."

The blank stare on her mother's face made Sônia smile.

"Bye. I have to go. Where's the vase?"

"In the car, my dear. Will you be back late?"

"At dinner time. Enjoy your tea. Now that you have power of attorney, Greta, don't let mother get involved in the Village's problems."

"Don't worry about a thing."

Sônia studied the neighbor woman.

"You should wear only gay colors, Greta. That light-colored blouse makes your eyes bluer."

"Thank you, but I prefer dark colors. I think the reason is my clothes don't get so dirty and I don't have to waste time in the morning trying to figure out what to wear."

Sônia opened the door.

"Here come Jane and Clotilde."

The two women stood up to greet their friends.

♤ The names Dilermando and Clotilde Canudos are included on the list of the Village's first residents. They bought their ready-built house on the same day the advertisement appeared for the sale of the model home. The lingerie factory was fifteen minutes away, which would give the husband time to devote to his hobby: ham radio operating. The location: perfect. From a distance you could see the tower that had been installed on the back of the property, where he kept his apparatus. He performed a wide variety of services which he kept to himself—he felt strongly they were no one else's business. He spoke five languages fluently.

Dilermando and Clotilde had no children—to their everlasting sorrow. One day she brought up the issue: her husband's sperm was too weak to fertilize. After fifteen years of marriage they separated for ten years, but they started living together again in that very same house on Palm Street. No one knows the details of their years of separation.

A little more than six months ago Clotilde studied the possibility of turning the factory into an employee-owned business, with the condition of course that she continue to manage it, since she'd die of boredom if she stopped working. The factory belonged to her family, whose members had run it for four generations. Since she had no children or siblings, she decided on the cooperative. That was her way of contributing to society. Her mind was made up. As a rule Clotilde allowed the Village women to purchase her products at cost, which put her to some degree in a position of leadership. And she was strongly against the proposed streetlight reduction. Of course, she'd be among the most affected. So she went knocking on doors asking people not to sign the petition. She got what she wanted. The petition didn't go beyond Antônio's signature. The representative would have to wait for another opportunity to be creative. What right did he have to tamper with something that had been put together by the entire community, after exhaustive analysis? Clotilde paid a visit to the Electric Company as well: in two weeks the lampposts would be installed—that was the news she was bringing to the neighbor ladies at that afternoon's tea.

△   The black automobile parked in front of a house with a false brick façade located in São Paulo's Alto de Pinheiros district. It was obviously being renovated. Could this be the right address? She was looking for the piece of paper in her purse when she saw Alice carrying out an enormous wastebasket.

"Hi, Sônia. Come on in. The garbage man'll be by in a little while. Excuse the mess, but we're adding on a floor . . ."

"I brought this vase of flowers my mother arranged for you."

"Thanks so much. Come in through here, through the garage. Thank goodness this floor is finished. You can't imagine the mess there was with the roof off."

It was so dark that when Sônia entered the living room she could barely see.

"I close everything up because of the dust." She turned on the lights and opened the curtains.

An art-nouveau lamp shone on the round table, which was visually separated from the rest of the space by a wooden bookcase: on its shelves a colored glass collection, each piece more vibrant than the next. The walls, covered with paintings of all sizes, arranged geometrically. A delicious perfume in the air. Incense? Sônia sat on a sofa covered with antique silk. She had often read descriptions of particular settings, trying to imagine them. Occasionally she would come across descriptions of unusual objects, and she would then go to the library to find books with illustrations of them. That living room looked like a stage set: it was more exquisite than anything in her wildest dreams. But she was bothered by the absence of books. Not a single one in sight.

"I'm so glad you dropped by," Alice said. "Would you like a liqueur or would you prefer a glass of port?"

"Port. I prefer port."

Alice's departure allowed Sônia to look closely at some of the valuable objects exhibited. An image from the eighteenth century, beneath a Venetian mirror. She thought, the people who live here are happy. She sensed their inner harmony. Three cats appeared from nowhere and nestled comfortably. Each one in a different position and a specific place. The calico cat chose the sofa, the white one a basket full of magazines, and the black one a small chest. Alice returned with the glasses filled.

"I hope Tiago gets back soon. He's dying to meet you, the girl in the ads."

A young man with a beard came into the living room.

"Sônia, this is my son."

"Did you or Father take my guitar?"

"It wasn't me, Francisco. It wasn't your father either. Why would he take it?"

"Well, darn it, it's gone."

Alice smiles at Sônia.

"My husband's a model maker. Today he and Mateus went to look at a small farm we're thinking of buying together. Would you like to see Tiago's studio?"

Yes, she would. They crossed the yard and went into a large studio. A huge maquette occupied the entire central area. A scale model of a golf course. Even the holes were visible. An open building, the future country club, revealed partitions for party rooms, offices, and bathrooms. A swimming pool made of acrylic or painted glass. It was craftsmanship worthy of a goldsmith. Or of a madman, Sônia realized when she saw the miniature furniture.

"He builds all the pieces himself. Take a look at this."

The drawers are filled with tiny pieces of wood and glass in the shape of roof tiles, doors and windows, furniture, closets, and paintings. Everything meticulously arranged.

"Fascinating," Sônia exclaimed. "What's the grass for the maquette made of?"

"Glue and sawdust. Then he spray-paints it green. It's perfect, isn't it? I spend hours here watching him work. Sometimes I help. But I have big, thick hands. They're useless for this type of work."

"That's not true," Tiago said as he came in. "You're always a great help to me."

Alice introduced her friend.

"Where's Mateus?"

"He's chatting with the limousine driver. He'll be here in a minute. He's a classic car buff, you know."

"Shall we get back to our port wine?" Alice proposed.

Next to his wife, Tiago appeared short and thin, with a long neck and stooped shoulders.

"Cheers. Here's to our visitor," he said, "who looks like Ingrid Bergman. Not the Ingrid of today, naturally. The one who made *Casablanca*."

They all laughed. At this moment, Mateus entered. He greeted Sônia politely and sat in a rocking chair. She told them about her travel plans; she had come to say good-bye and to see if there was anything she could bring back for them.

Mateus seemed dejected, with dark circles under his eyes. It was odd, but she didn't have the courage to ask him why he hadn't been at his apartment at the appointed time. Nor could she bring herself to thank him for the translation she hadn't gotten around to reading yet, in spite of the fact that he had brought it over several days ago.

"Are you going straight home from here?" he asked Sônia.

"Yes, I am."

"Could you give me a ride to River Drive?"

"It's OK, Mateus. I have to pick up some medicine at the pharmacy; I can take you," Tiago said as he stood up. "Darn! I almost forgot; I told Pedro I was going to fix his son's model airplane."

Alice followed her husband out, asking about the farm. Mateus had the look of someone self-absorbed, lost in his thoughts. Sônia realized she was inexplicably attracted to him, as if . . . The idea was purposely cut off. The more you live the more you learn. This fluttering in my heart is ridiculous at my age . . . Oblivious, Mateus smoked a cigarette. She waited for him to say something to her. The silence left her ill at ease; she petted the cat lying beside her on the sofa. Despite the calico cat's loud purring, she could hear, if it were possible, Tiago inhaling his cigarette smoke. She took another sip of port. Should she start a conversation? Mateus, his legs crossed, rocked in the chair, creak, creak, creak, creak, his jaws clenched tightly. The mobile made from whale fins turned soundlessly. Mateus's eyelids slowly drooped and he fastened his gaze (provocatively?) on Sônia for a few seconds. The penetrating look of someone trying to unveil secrets. She returned his look against her will, sensing something strange about herself. Within her, a disturbing feeling: a premonition that she was swelling, swelling, swelling. What could that be? My god! All at once, the feeling of strangeness exploded in a wet throbbing. There, in that room, on the eve of her thirtieth birthday, her body was exploding in solitary love.

"Excuse me, Sônia. I went to put on a wrap because I was getting cold . . . It looks like the two of you haven't even opened your mouths. Mateus, such a character. What are you thinking about?"

"About the farm," he answered. "About the giant avocados I saw but didn't pick." Again his gaze rested on Sônia.

She was speechless, her face a deep red. Could he be speaking in metaphors?

"It's time to go, Alice. Mama's waiting for me."

It's strange how a person's appearance can be changed by the clothes she wears. The first time they met, Alice wore black and gave the impression that she was thinner; a short while ago she looked chubby in blue jeans and sandals; and now, with that wool tunic and high-heeled boots, wearing makeup, she looked slender again.

"Just a minute, Sônia. I want to give you a memento."

With her back to Mateus, Sônia went over to a painting and took off her glasses to make out the signature, but wasn't able to: illegible. A drawing, the portrait of the lady of the house, quite accurate. Alice brought out a beautiful cameo, which she pinned to the lapel of Sônia's coat.

"For good luck. If you should happen to pass by a store that sells products for animals, ask if they have birdbaths. For years I've wanted one of those glass ones so I could see my little birds wash themselves. The plastic kind they sell around here is junk. You can't see a thing."

Sônia promised she wouldn't forget the request. She'd do her best.

"Give your husband a hug for me. I'll pick up some miniatures if I come across any. What about you, Mateus, do you want something, too?"

"No thank you."

That night in bed Sônia surrenders to lingering caresses. Why not take advantage of the years she has left? This trip . . .

Discouraged and depressed, Greta lays her head on the table. It's so hard to tell the story you want to. Or how about—to tell the story you mean? Every day an enigma. A whole onion she was peeling layer by layer. Until she would find—what? That is the question. A precarious quest. Or flight. But she is unable to stop. Nothing else can be done until she finishes. And so, Sônia is going to Spain in Tina's place. Tomorrow she'll ask permission to borrow Sônia's books while she's away.

A dense, still night. The last lights go out and silence hovers over the Village; Greta leans out the window to close the shutters. No rustling of leaves. An air of expectation. Lost crickets produce the sound of . . . What sound could that be? An idiotic definition: the sound of hollow castanets. Correction: not an air of expectation, but one of foreboding.

 Camilo and Ivo are doing physical therapy these days. The daughter comes by or has them picked up twice a week. The old man is happy. He hired Zaíra for the days freed up when Ribeiro let her go. Now the only day she has open is Monday. She lives in a shack behind the cemetery. She's the mother of five children. Her husband, a grave digger, is training the first-born for the profession, because he has to help with the family budget and the education of the younger children. They walk to school in a pack, nearly a mile each way. If the Village had been successful, those children, four, seven, eight, nine, and eleven years old, wouldn't have such a burden thrust upon them: they'd go to our school. Zaíra complains about the worn-out soles of their shoes. Poor kids. They watch cars in the cemetery on weekends. In November, on the Day of the Dead, they earn a little extra.

Fantasy occasionally clashes with reality.

♤ A commotion in the Village: a prostitute, near death, was discovered by Carmen Miranda in the turnaround. The part of Palm Street located on the right side of the Avenue—the other part ends at the lake—is a cul-de-sac. The end of the street is rounded, like a large pocket, so that cars can turn around without complicated maneuvers. It opens out in the shape of a horseshoe where Dilermando Canudos's property begins, and it narrows on the other side, near Míriam's building. But the tractor left in front of the building has blocked traffic. Dilermando can't drive straight up to his house; he has to go around the pocket to reach his garage head-on. Another inconvenience: the cul-de-sac has turned into a perfect bed for the prostitutes. Protected by the tractor and the natural vegetation, they opened a narrow path through the empty lots, behind Dilermando's property, and nobody was the wiser. Before the tractor came, the turnaround hadn't been discovered and the residents had no complaints. The prostitutes could be seen only on the Avenue, leaning against tree trunks or walking along like any other pedestrian. What gave them away were their extremely short miniskirts; or what often happened was that a resident would unexpectedly come upon one of them opening her coat to exhibit her naked body. How else could they attract customers—usually taxi and truck drivers—except by displaying their wares?

One afternoon Zaíra mentioned that most of those girls lived in shacks over in the *favela* and that many of them weren't women. Which gave rise to constant fights: damn tough competition. The transvestites now controlled the area around the cemetery. They allowed a single exception: Pablita. Tall, thin, straight hair like an Indian's, flat chest, she would attract anyone's attention. She served as a decoy for the site. She's real pretty, Miss Greta. They say she became a prostitute to get back at her father, who raped her when she was twelve. Her mother, out of her mind with rage, killed her husband and is still in prison. Pablita lives alone and never speaks with her neighbors in the *favela*. It's whispered that she plies her trade in the flower bed where her father was buried. Can you imagine? What courage.

Two years ago there was no prostitution on the Avenue. It began recently, maybe because the nation's economic problems have become more severe and São Paulo's unemployment rate is increasing daily. Gossip has it that Fortuna purposely provided a haunt for the hookers. Greta doesn't believe it. Who would do such a thing?

Carmen Miranda was on her way home about eleven o'clock when she heard a moan. As soon as she found the girl she called the police, who arrived with their usual fanfare, siren blasting, causing an uproar. Nevertheless, not a single Village resident ventured out. Getting mixed up with the police is a hassle. It becomes impossible to work because they're forever calling witnesses to testify. People found out what was going on simply by calling Clotilde. The woman had been stabbed. Hopefully she would survive. Would it be better if she died? One never knows.

🔔 "That Alexandre Ribeiro is a sorry excuse for a human being," Soares exclaimed angrily. "I've never seen anyone so vain. If he doesn't have cancer of the soul, he will. I know what I'm talking about."

"Now what happened?"

"Greta, you won't believe this, but City Hall has shelved our request to change the numbering system for the street. Seems our Village representative failed to show up for a meeting he'd been summoned to."

"Why do you think he did that?"

"He could care less about Antônio's requisition, and he wanted to get back at all those people who refused to sign his Electric Company petition."

"That's terrible!"

"Isn't it? I found out because my brother-in-law works for City Hall. I asked him if he could get the wheels turning . . ."

"We've got to put this issue on the agenda for the next homeowners association meeting. And the tractor, too. It doesn't make any sense, that machine just sitting there blocking traffic. Yesterday I went over to Fortuna and I couldn't find a single director. They're all in Brasilia trying to get financing for something or other."

"Did you see all the commotion at Alexandre's house? The people from the circus came to look over the area."

"That's all we needed. Looks like we're going to be thrown out of here. My vote is only one against ten for the Company."

"Greta, I'm only telling you this to get it off my chest. Tancredi won't show his face because he's in up to his neck with Ribeiro. I just don't know. The detectives came by to question me about the stabbing. Did they talk to you?"

"If they stopped by they didn't find me. Well, I have to go. I want to stretch my legs and take a look at the lake. See you soon, Soares."

The dentist lingered in the garden for a few moments. Greta shouldn't go out walking alone in that area.

But Greta needed to relax. After crossing the Avenue, she heard the pleasant sound of her footsteps on the dry leaves. Her head, filled with anxiety over her involvement with . . . Sônia was getting over her withdrawal from the world; Míriam was preparing to return to Santa Catarina. One of these days everything was going to work out. In some ways, the two women and Tina could be a single character, if it weren't for the individual characteristics that differentiated them. Each one with her past and her sorrows.

A black bird flew up, startled. Greta began to enjoy herself. What a long tail. At that hour, the wall surrounding the Cemetery of the Flowers was tinged with pink. The landscape, still. In the late afternoon the Village is a paradise; she sighed. Imagine the chaos it will turn into if the plans for the circus and the amusement park are carried out. Why didn't they think about putting them next to the lake? Because it's too close to the cemetery, of course. Fun and death don't mix.

Oh, the lake. What an atmosphere of peace and magic. You can almost hear the elves, for when it was abandoned it gained an air of enchantment and mystery. The rocks, which were new and lifeless in the beginning, are covered with dark green moss. The statue of a nude woman hiding her breasts with a tunic carelessly draped over her body has also aged. Tina's grandfather had had the statue sculpted in marble when the estate was still operating. Who knows, maybe he had been preparing a mausoleum, because that's what the woman suggests as she sits on a rock, clutching the tunic with her right hand while her left holds a feeding goat. The face and the hairstyle are reminiscent of Tina's grandmother in an old photograph. A homage to love? Greta slides her hand over the marble shoulder and shivers. The willows are just beginning to bud after the winter drought, but the native trees are covered with vines, while the eucalyptus trees shade the lake, which had once been much larger; aquatic plants have reduced the space considerably. But they sparkle in the sunlight falling on leaves and bushes, reflected in the water.

Greta sat on a rock. That was the atmosphere she breathed in the Village: a somber atmosphere, with rare moments of respite and light. Like Gino's voice singing his arias. Too bad she hadn't brought paper and pencil. A compulsion to make note of small details, the crooked toadstools, the tenuous darkness. Good gracious, this has become an obsession, a kind of self-encounter. While she approached others in this return to childhood, with this skewed outlook, she was really groping for her own identity. But she was still bothered by an inability to express herself. She would experiment with a phrase over and over until it sounded something like what she wanted to say. Between thought and writing, there was an endless series of veils, blocks, incompetence. For example, finding a way to reproduce the sensation she gets from the lake at this moment, the shiver she felt when she touched the statue's shoulder, as if she were caressing her own grandmother, who, in spite of the still, petrified gaze, revealed an infinite sadness. Might she have been unhappy? On certain occasions, seized by an idea, her hand swept across the page as if she were in a trance, so fluidly did the words pour out. On the other hand, there were nights when her head and nerves would freeze up and all attempts were futile, not a whisper came forth. During those periods she considers digging into her deepest pain but she always ends up running away, letting her mind wander, or getting sidetracked by the arrival of some person or some opportune event. The fact is, she has yet to face her most fundamental experiences. But she will, she will. She must approach them cautiously. Like someone putting a bandage on a wound that might hemorrhage.

A fat toad hops and lands at Greta's feet. Slowly it raises its nearsighted eyes, attentive to the slightest sound, and jumps again, this time into the lake.

Greta tries to follow its movements and realizes it has gotten dark. She must hurry, or else . . . It won't be long before the church bells begin to toll.

Bitten hearts. What to do with the scars?

The visit to Fortuna was discouraging. The chronicle of the circus and the amusement park was beginning to unfold. In fact, a new drawing was hung on the wall beside the previous ones: the parking lot. The Company holds the property and intends to rent it out, without spending money on leveling the ground. Arguments against the project were rejected by those petty directors, who were sensitive only to profit, to the chance of earning commissions on easy sales in a housing project (to be built on a client's property, not on theirs). Fortuna's job would be to build and sell the apartments. Alexandre's scheme fit perfectly with theirs, because the Village was a thorn in everyone's side. A failure no one could admit to. Greta had the misfortune of running into Ribeiro when she arrived. The louse actually kissed her hand and laid the flattery on thick. Once she shook off the unpleasant experience—what a sneaky character—she went firmly ahead with what she had set out to do. Míriam's problem, the night watchman—the stabbing of the woman was more than ample proof of the need for protection—cleaning out the sewer pipes for rainwater drainage.

Barbosa, one of the directors, presented Míriam an offer: an apartment with living room and bedrooms on Major Diogo Street in the Bela Vista district. Either she accepted or Fortuna had a perfect right to wash its hands of the whole affair. The apartment was empty and the papers could be drawn up in a few days. Greta was satisfied with the offer. She knew Barbosa liked her more than the others did. This was not a good time to complain about the circus.

"See you, Barbosa. I'll call and give you an answer tomorrow. Get that hideous machine out of there, OK?"

Barbosa promised to comply if she'd join his family for lunch on Saturday.

♤ An idea out of the blue: have the letter hand delivered to Luís. He and Sônia would get along famously. A voracious reader of books, someone to talk to, a woman like that doesn't come along every day. And a playwright might be excellent company for Sônia; Greta smiled. A happy ending? If loving means desiring the other person's happiness, the idea really was a gesture of love. Not selfish, overbearing, possessive love, but the generous love of a friend. Animals don't experience jealousy. Sônia and Mateus would never work out. Bringing the two of them together would confirm her own skepticism. Míriam and Gricha were cursed by incest, by fate, by the dark secret. But happiness exists, by God. It has to.

Sônia goes up to the registration desk of a small hotel in Madrid. While she waits for the clerk to call Luís, she examines the tortuous design of the building: some disciple of Gaudi? Luís appears in blue jeans and a heavy sweater, his beard grown out. Sônia delivers the letter and chats about the Village. She'll give her version of Palm Street. She'll say that Greta never goes out, that she is writing. She'll ask him what to do and see. Luís will politely offer to accompany her to this or that place. Their first few times together they'll be reserved. Sônia will take her mother along. Until Elisa decides to go to bed early: her excuse, a headache. Then Sônia will go out alone. And in those lonely hearts curiosity will awaken. Elisa will go to Switzerland on the appointed day. The daughter will catch up with her later. The first step toward severing the bonds. Luís and Sônia, alone, will go on a grand tour of the city, they'll go to a bullfight, but the sights of the city will mean little to her. The important thing is the feeling that will explode inside her. At the slightest touch, a thrill of pleasure will spread through her body. She'll fly right through the damn traffic in flats (so as not to be taller than he). When they say good night, she'll have an empty feeling in her stomach, even if she's just had dinner, and she'll look happily at her reflection in the mirror. She'll brush her hair in bold strokes and try out different hairstyles. Lipstick, never used before, will be applied, and blue eyeliner. Satisfied, she'll sleep with her insides slightly swollen and bobby pins in her hair. Luís will sit in his own room, tense, wondering whether he should dial the phone, just to hear her voice. He'll ask her to say something, anything, while remaining silent at his end of the line. He'll ponder whether he can afford to fall in love again. But he'll already be falling under the spell of Sônia's burgeoning passion, that total availability for love, that—why not?—naïveté. Culture not experienced is merely ornamental. Sônia has read, not lived, a great deal. One day he'll take her delicately and tenderly to bed, he'll touch that body tremulous with emotion, he'll shelter her virgin breasts in his cupped hands, and his kisses will linger over the smooth down, he'll taste the tumescent flower, which will contract when it swallows his own tumescence, he'll fall back exhausted and sated, angel upon angel, at peace with life.

The moment of parting will be carefully concealed. Sônia will go to Switzerland, and the promise of a meeting in Paris will alleviate the pain of separation. He'll probably forego his dinner in order to surprise her with late-night calls at her cousins'. Two weeks later in Paris the spell will remain unbroken. They'll walk hand in hand and visit museums, go to the theater, which he finds mostly disappointing; she hardly minds, it could be any play, her attention is fixed exclusively and obsessively on him, and the two will go to small bistros and talk for hours on end, and she'll ask him to take her to some of the places she's read about; she'll cross the Luxembourg Gardens on a Sunday afternoon and see the French people carrying their chairs to sit in the weak November sun, and so much else to see, it's impossible to imagine everything; a record cold spell is forecast, so she'll go into a store and buy a wool coat with fur collar and cuffs, and a cashmere scarf for him, spending a small fortune, and afterwards they'll go to the pleasant hotel on the Rue Jacob, and suddenly it's time to return home without having gone to London, to Amsterdam, which is of no importance, and they'll part with a sob stuck in the throat, and he'll promise to come very soon, possibly in March. And Elisa? She'll go ahead with the plans to see her cousins, take a tour around Lake Geneva, weekends in the mountains, she'll tell the cousins about her fern plants and astonish them with descriptions of their size, and she'll heave brief sighs of longing or happiness, who knows which, and she'll buy watches for herself, her daughter, and her brother, chocolates for her nieces and nephews, and on the date set she'll board the plane with Sônia at her side, a woman she'll no longer recognize.

Greta smiled. How gushy can you get.

◊ Dylan Thomas's nocturnal writings: "In my craft or sullen art/ Exercised in the still night."

◊ After watering the plants Greta decided to take a bath and dress, because Míriam had asked her to look at the apartment in Bela Vista with her.

Hot summer day, blue sky; she took out a pair of white slacks and a red cotton blouse. The transference of Sônia's spirit? Maybe. Míriam was also dressed in light clothing: a peasant skirt with a floral print, a silk shawl worn over her shoulders. Her bare feet in a pair of raw leather sandals. Her hair hung down her back in a long braid.

"You look great, Míriam."

"Thanks." She took a handkerchief out of her bag and blew her nose. "I've caught a cold, I'm afraid. Horácio and Elizabeth had better be careful. Every time I get sick they catch it, too."

"I see."

The old gray building looked sad from the outside. But when you examined it less critically, you noticed a doorway in a distinctive art-deco style. Three floors. The cross-eyed concierge looked in a drawer for the key to apartment 301, and complained about Fortuna. A broad staircase, well cared for, solid wood banister.

"What do you think?" Míriam asked as soon as they had looked through all the rooms.

"Accept it. Immediately. With a coat of paint the apartment will be quite pleasant. It's got decent-sized living and bedrooms. You just rent it out and take off for Santa Catarina. Or you could turn it over to one of those real estate agencies that manage apartment buildings and take care of leases, collect the rent, etc."

"Then let's go over to Fortuna. I want to get this over with as soon as possible."

The deed would be drawn up as soon as all the paperwork was ready. A real estate broker would deal with the matter on a priority basis. Fortuna couldn't bear the pressure any longer, the endless lawsuits postponing the demolition of the apartment building. It was in the Company's interest to break the deadlock.

Greta and Míriam celebrated the news with some delicious ice cream topped with nuts. Míriam mentioned government financing available for planting crops, but Gricha had opted for raising thorough-bred Manga-Larga horses.

"He's crazy about horses, Greta. I can't believe I'm really going to Santa Catarina!"

It was four in the afternoon when the small station wagon entered Palm Street. A black cloud promised rain. In front of Gino's house, a moving van. Whose could it be? Greta had to wait for the men to maneuver a double bed (odd, the mattress cover was purple) before she could enter the yard.

♩ They found the prostitute's assailant: her husband. Her name is Regina; she didn't die, she only ended up covered with stitches. Agenor, a doorman who works nights for a bar, was unaware of the kind of work the mother of his children was engaged in. By chance he switched his weekly night off with a co-worker. He saw his wife on the Avenue. He hid behind a tree. She was displaying her body, naked under her raincoat. A taxi stopped. The enraged husband waited a few minutes before he ran down the path to the cul-de-sac. No one knows what happened to the other man, how he managed to get out of there at that time of night. Unless he plunged into the dense vegetation.

After the attempted murder, the doorman took the children and disappeared. In the shanty, clothing covered with blood.

The newspapers published a photograph of Regina crying in the hospital. She emphatically defended her activities and said that Agenor, whom she loved, didn't earn enough to support her and the children. A profession, like any other, since during the day she had to stay home. Who would take care of the children? There was no day-care in the *favela*. The newspaper article concluded by reporting that Regina refused to press charges and that she wanted her husband back.

"Greta, you should have seen Zaíra; her blood was boiling. If it had been her she would've taken the guy apart. You're always hearing on the radio about cases where women are killed by their husbands and lovers, just like that. It's like we're a pest or vermin. That's what she said. Does it make any sense? Miz Jane, she said, couldn't Agenor just leave his wife? Do you think he needed to stab her?"

Greta and Jane smiled.

"And my mother-in-law, boy, my mother-in-law. She was scared out of her wits. She actually wants us to move away from here. Things were getting dangerous as it is, but those incidents in the Village were very, very disturbing."

"I agree," Greta concluded. "Unfortunately."

The two women looked at each other without a word. As if each knew what the other was thinking.

♩ Amelita Baltar's voice filled the living room. Greta, seated on the sofa, put her book aside to listen to that powerful and expressive voice, which she had heard so many times before. Could singing be more fulfilling than writing or painting?

The howling wind was a sign of a change in the weather; she tripped over a pile of books she had borrowed last week from Sônia's library, and turned up the volume on the record player. Amelita really does sing from the heart, she's pure emotion.

Someone's knocking at the door. Greta checks her watch. Ten o'clock. A visitor, in this windstorm?

A couple: the new neighbors. They'd come over to see if they could use the telephone because theirs hadn't been hooked up yet. The woman, so fair as to be nearly transparent, is a medical doctor. A fragile creature. The husband apologized for the late hour and introduced them: Sofia and Leonardo Mendes.

"Sofia has a critically ill patient at the hospital."

"Please make yourselves at home. The phone's here in the hallway." She turned on the light.

"Won't you have a seat?"

Out of the corner of her eye Greta studied the calm, elegant, self-possessed man.

"Mind if I smoke?"

"Not at all. In fact, I find it pleasant." With her foot Greta pushed aside the books on the floor. He offered to pick them up. "Leave them there, they're not in the way."

"We interrupted your reading."

"No problem. A little conversation is welcome any time. There's not much to do here in the Village for people like me who live alone but don't care for television." She looked directly at him for the first time and smiled.

He looked away to pack the tobacco in his pipe. He closed the leather pouch and drew on the pipe several times. The sound of the needle on the record made Greta realize the music had ended some moments ago.

"Excuse me." She lifted the arm from the turntable. "Is there anything you'd like to hear or . . ."

"If you want to play the other side, that'd be fine. To tell you the truth, it was your music that gave us the courage to ask to use the phone. We were certain someone was awake."

Greta lowered the volume and then took out a bottle of wine and three glasses.

"It's all I have to drink."

"I'll have some, but Sofia doesn't drink alcohol."

"Really?"

Greta sat facing the visitor.

"How do you like Palm Street? Cheers."

"Cheers. A week isn't enough to form an opinion. We leave early and come back at night."

"And why did you decide to live so far from downtown?"

"Oh, it's not far, ma'am."

"Please, call me Greta. OK if I call you Leonardo?"

His eyes appraised her briefly.

"The difference between thirty and sixty years old is irrelevant."

He gives the impression he's thinking over what he's just said as he relights his pipe. Greta notices he's graying at the temples.

"As I was saying, it's easier to get from here to the clinic than it is from my house in the Sumaré district. If you take River Drive you can get there very quickly."

"Are you a doctor, too?"

"A psychoanalyst."

Sofia comes into the room.

"I really appreciate your kindness." A soft, reedy voice. "My patient's responding well to treatment. I won't have to go to the hospital tonight."

"Would you like some juice or coffee?"

"No thank you. Your house is lovely . . . Have you lived here long?"

"This was the first house built back when it was still a plantation and progress hadn't made it this far. Land values went up and the family decided to subdivide. You see these wide boards? They're from the turn of the century."

"They're marvelous. We must be off, Leonardo."

The door facing the street swung open violently. Greta ran to close it, and at that very moment the lights went out.

"Just a minute. Here are the candles." She took a candlestick off the bureau. "Do you have a light?"

The psychoanalyst lit a match, and the candle flame flickered unsteadily.

"These things happen on windy days. Would you like a little more wine?"

Leonardo accepted. His wife declined politely. Would he mind hurrying up? She had to get to sleep early tonight, tomorrow's her shift at the hospital, she won't even get back home.

"How often do you have these shifts?"

"Once a week. We have a personnel shortage."

The conversation turned to the problems faced by doctors in poorly equipped hospitals, precarious sanitary conditions, lousy pay. Why, you often hear about people who come in to have their tonsils taken out and leave with hepatitis. Greta experienced an odd feeling of uneasiness as the woman talked. Maybe it was because of the dim light or the calm, silent husband, aware the whole time of his own gestures, relighting his pipe—the ashtray was overflowing with burnt matches—crossing and uncrossing his legs. Twice she had detected an almost imperceptible spark in his eyes, as if he were absorbing, devouring her like a cannibal, a sharp contrast to Sofia, with her cold, steady voice. And what about Greta, how did they see her? A sticky snail trying to hide in its shell?

"I'd like to know where that bell is, or maybe bells, I heard ringing yesterday afternoon," Sofia inquired.

"In the Village church. They rang yesterday afternoon? I didn't hear them. Oh, I know. I went out with Míriam, our neighbor who lives in the apartment building and . . . ."

"Alexandre told me they're going to tear it down. They're just waiting for her to move out."

"Are you acquainted with the Village representative?"

"As soon as we moved in he came over to welcome us. He's so charming and intelligent. Leonardo didn't think too much of him."

Her husband stirred in his chair, visibly displeased. In the candlelight the color seemed to wash from their faces and dark circles appeared under their eyes.

"I wouldn't go that far," he disagreed. "I simply don't share your enthusiasm."

"He gave us lots of friendly advice. We shouldn't buy from the Village baker, or hire a cleaning woman, let's see . . . I forget her name, a terrible gossip. And he invited us to the next homeowners meeting. He warned us we might not be accepted by our neighbors because you're not supposed to rent out the houses here, and a lot of other stuff."

"That's nonsense," Greta interjected. "Everyone recognizes the widow's right to rent out her house until the appraisal's completed. At any rate, it's a good idea to attend the meeting so you can get to know everyone. We used to meet only once a year, but now there's so much new happening we meet every month."

Greta refrained from commenting on the other matters. Let her find out for herself if what she was saying was true. It's unbelievable Ribeiro would make trouble for a nice old man who takes such pride in baking his own bread.

"Leonardo, don't you just love his idea to hold an exhibition of drawings and paintings in the cemetery?"

"Where?"

"In the cemetery. He joked that it was the busiest place in town. He's certain the funeral chapel is the one place the pictures will be seen." She laughed. "An arts center in the cemetery!" She stood up. "Apparently the Company directors thought it was a great idea and they've asked him to run the gallery and to invite other artists after he's shown his own work."

That's all we needed. Greta shook her head. A circus, an amusement park, and now an art gallery, she thought but didn't say.

"See you around, Greta. Thanks again."

"It was nice to meet you. Drop by any time. You're welcome to use the telephone whenever you want." She placed the candlestick in the shelter of the hallway so the wind wouldn't blow out the flame.

The moment she opened the door the lights went back on, shattering, perhaps, the intimate mood they had shared.

"Greta, look, the paper on that table's flying all over the place."

She excused herself for not seeing them out and went to pick up the sheets of paper scattered on the floor. Amelita's voice once again filled the room. But Greta was no longer paying attention. Her thoughts were focused on the visitors.

🔔 The handwritten, xeroxed invitation was delivered to every home. A pretentious invitation, in spite of the poor graphics, announcing the opening of the exhibition and the new arts center—the Gallery of Fame—in the Cemetery of the Flowers administration building, sponsored by Fortuna, a company in the service of Brazilian art.

The first one to react: Camilo.

"Greta, this is a desecration."

Ivo tried to clap his hands so his favorite neighbor could see what he had learned in therapy.

"If you think about it, why not? Art can be shown anywhere, Camilo."

"That's correct, my dear. However, cemeteries aren't meant for parties."

"Who said he's going to serve drinks and stuff like that? The invitation says nothing about cocktails or grand openings. It just mentions a simple opening: Saturday at noon.

"I must be getting senile. I don't understand anything anymore."

She thought for a moment before responding.

"Senile? Hardly. It's just that the fellow's very creative."

Ivo finally managed a perfect clap. Greta congratulated him effusively. The boy then attempted a whistle.

"The kid's doing beautifully in school. It hasn't been a month yet but you can clearly see the progress he's made. He loves the exercises. When he's in class I do physiotherapy for my back."

"Great."

"Yes, my dear. You can adjust to anything, floods, earthquakes. But this business about using the cemetery as an exhibition hall is too much. I'm going to sell my plot and ask Mirna to have me cremated. At least then I won't be a part of this human degradation."

"Don't think that way, Camilo."

"Listen, Greta. You don't get away with fooling around with the dead. If there's an afterlife their spirits will react. Imagine how Ananias must be writhing in anger; he was so religious. He'd never accept the idea of a funeral chapel, which one assumes is a place to express grief in privacy, being used to show painting and sculpture. Bright-colored pictures in a place like that? No, my dear, I will never be able to understand it, much less accept it."

Ivo continued his effort to whistle.

"Bright colors aren't necessarily meant to cheer you up."

"Be that as it may, I called Soares, Dilermando, and Antônio and asked them to come over. I want to find out what others think." He got up slowly and went to fetch a tray of cookies he kept in the cupboard.

Camilo's posture was getting worse every day. For a long time now he's been unable to push his grandson's wheelchair along Palm Street. He goes out only with the chauffeur or when his daughter comes to pick him up. The upstairs bedrooms are no longer used.

"I can't climb stairs much anymore. That's why I moved the library upstairs. Ivo and I always sleep together; we don't need two bedrooms. To tell you the truth, I'm not suffering from anything specific. My illness, Greta, is old age."

"What about the bathroom?"

"Ah, my dear, you know how these developers are. They advertised a house with three bedrooms and three bathrooms so they could up the price. So next to the library they put in a sink and shower. That's how they hoodwink the buyer. But we were lucky. All I had to buy was an electric shower head."

Ivo gave up on whistling and resumed his clapping. Greta wanted to tell him he shouldn't worry, she didn't know how to whistle either, it was perfectly normal. But the boy wouldn't understand.

"Have you heard any news about the circus and the amusement park?"

"Not a thing. I saw the blueprints hanging on the wall at Fortuna." Greta checked her watch. "I have to go."

"Can I ask you a favor? Could you lend me some books, my dear? I know all of mine by heart."

"What are you interested in? Still like detective stories?"

"No. See if you can find me some books on history."

"I'll bring them over tomorrow." She kissed Ivo and left.

As she crossed the street she saw Gricha going into the apartment building. Míriam will be happy. At least you can say that about one person in the Village.

The exhibition opened on a sunny, hot Saturday, with only ten residents from Palm Street in attendance. The people from Fortuna showed up in force, with the exception of Barbosa who had invited Greta over for lunch. A simple reception. There was no other choice, since a body lay in the funeral chapel on the left. The painting and sculpture exhibit had been set up the previous afternoon when no corpses were present. That's a detail needing further study. No one sets a date for dying. True, the cemetery administration is consulted beforehand. Nevertheless, it was impossible to cancel a wake because of an art show. On Friday the rooms were empty and all of a sudden someone keels over and dies and . . .

It must be said that contrary to Camilo's allegation the gallery did not interfere with funerals and wakes. The old man was needlessly upset. The building had plenty of space to move around in and rooms for different purposes, as well as another level reached by six steps that led to a coffee shop. In the center of the space was a garden with a continuous stone bench around it where people could rest. The walls in the main lobby, the stairways, and the second level were perfect for exhibits.

Alexandre Ribeiro placed three sculptures on a garden bench—including a globe he'd kept in his house—and others on white wooden boxes in the main lobby. And on the walls off to the side he hung framed drawings. Not a single painting done in colors. Only drawings in pencil or ink. No one could complain about an exhibit like that. A closer look might lead one to question whether that was the proper place to display one of the sculptures, a female nude. But it was so delicate . . . No, the fellow had achieved just the right balance. And the drawings—landscapes and human figures in candid street scenes—were quite good. Fortuna ought to be pleased. Would other artists be so discreet? That remained to be seen.

A few reporters and social columnists invited to the opening took pictures, a bit of a nuisance for the family grieving its dearly departed. You could actually hear moaning and crying while viewing the exhibit. But what did the visitors expect, background music? If an artist wants to show his work in the Gallery of Fame he'll have to accept the ambient sound. Pleasant or not.

Antônio and Jane entered the gallery before four o'clock, a bit earlier than the burial procession. Some of the relatives and friends admired the pictures as they waited for the soul of the deceased to be commended.

"What a pretty drawing, Antônio. Do you know how much it costs?"

"There's a price tag right next to it," the husband answered curtly.

"Maybe you could give me one for Christmas."

"Don't go changing your mind, Jane. Didn't you want a tape recorder?"

Grief-stricken crying: the burial procession was about to begin. A hysterical woman was making a scene.

"Don't go away, my darling. What will I do without you? How could you leave me alone like this. No," she shouted, "don't close the coffin. Oh, my God, why didn't you take me instead of him? Why?"

Antônio rushed his wife outside nervously.

That night during the poker game he exclaimed to Soares, "I can't forget that woman's voice at the wake. It was awful!"

♀ Missing the clinic. Could Tina be coming back?

"The news that Sofia is a doctor has spread like wildfire. The poor woman hasn't had a minute's rest for three days, Greta. Do you mind if I call the hospital to tell them she'll be a few minutes late?"

"Of course not, Leonardo. You know how to find the telephone." Greta recovered from the shock of seeing the psychoanalyst alone. Cheeks slightly flushed.

People were bound to find out soon enough how good a doctor she was. One of Zaíra's children, the oldest, gashed his foot with a scythe. According to his mother, he was cutting the grass in the cemetery and was daydreaming as usual when he took a hell of a chunk out of his heel. Greta advised the maid to go find the doctor, since the boy was bleeding to death. Sofia gladly attended to his wound, put in a few stitches, gave him a tetanus shot, bandaged him, and the boy was soon working in the noonday sun. She made a serious miscalculation by not charging for her services. That was all it took for the sick people from the *favela* to go see the generous doctor. They actually lined up on Palm Street.

"I don't know how this business is going to turn out. It'd be a crime to send those people away. Sofia can't bring herself to do it."

"Why don't you advise her to open a small clinic in the *favela*? That way no one would bother you at home. Especially on a Sunday."

"You see, the problem is she has neither the time nor the equipment."

"Would you like a coffee? I just made some."

Leonardo examined Greta's desk while she readied the tray. A half-filled sheet of paper in the typewriter. Beside it, a pile of manuscripts covered with scribbling. Dictionaries. A grammar.

"What is it, a research project?" He turned toward her as she brought in the coffee.

"So to speak. Notes on the Village."

"Do you let people read it?"

"No. It's just a way to pass the time." Her hand trembling, she handed him the cup.

He wore gray slacks and a black shirt.

"Writing was never just a way to pass the time."

"I agree. But I don't want to seem pretentious. I still don't know if it's good enough to be published. It's a long way from intention to completion. In my lowly opinion, everybody's born an artist."

"I wouldn't go that far."

"Life, education, the environment, they all inhibit the development of artistic sensibility. Or do you think that being an artist is a privilege reserved only for the few?"

"Perhaps . . ."

"The difference, if you admit everyone has the same opportunity, is the obsession."

The psychoanalyst seemed distant. What could he be thinking about?

"A friend of mine stopped writing to avoid turning into a schizophrenic. He lived with ghosts all around him. Maybe that's what's going to happen to me."

Leonardo gave an ironic laugh. Greta was concerned she was getting in over her head. After all . . .

"What are your plans for today?" He looked her straight in the eye.

"No special plans." She felt ridiculously available.

"How about taking a walk? You could show me the Village."

"Be glad to. But there's not much to see. Have you been to the lake?"

"No."

"What about the cemetery?"

"Negative again."

"Then give me a minute to change shoes."

Leonardo noticed that one could see his living room window from her desk. He approached to get a closer look at the garden. The arbor was enchanting with the wooden bench and all those plants.

Greta blushed again.

"From here you can see your living room, and from that window you can see Sônia and Elisa's, they're our neighbors who are in Europe—incidentally, I have to unlock the place and air it out a bit—and from the kitchen I can keep an eye on Camilo."

"You're dangerous. Aren't you ashamed to be prying into other people's lives?" He smiled.

A frank smile, Greta observed, that begins in his eyes and ends at his mouth, without crinkling his skin.

He picked up the tobacco pouch and the key ring that were on the sofa.

"It depends what you mean by prying. I'm not a gossip. It'd be more accurate to say I'm researching others' lives for the sake of curiosity. Somebody else could record humorously the same scenes that I portray in my own way. And without the slightest sense of humor, I assure you. Shall we go? You first. I'm the only one who can get this door closed; the lock doesn't work right."

"Who are these neighbor women?"

Later, when she was alone, Greta was very distressed. The walk had been wonderful. Leonardo turned out to be pleasant company, interested in everything and everyone. At the lake they unintentionally came close to one another. Was this unanticipated? The dampness of the rocks, the vapor rising from the lake, the dream-like atmosphere they let themselves slip into, speaking softly so as not to break the spell, and as a result the intimate faces lightly brushing, hands almost touching; could all of this have lured them toward an expectation that might never be fulfilled? A fleeting intimacy that wasn't repeated the rest of the afternoon . . . Unless . . . Come on, Greta, admit it, what about the lunch in the kitchen? He made the salad while you carefully prepared the pasta. The two of you had some fine moments. He laughed and laughed when you told him about why you stopped going to the clinic, about your relationship with Dr. Oswaldo, about your decision to find yourself without anyone's help. How affectionately he listened. You were mysteriously extroverted (an effect of the wine?), revealing secrets even you were unaware of. How serious he became when you talked about Tina, about the way you hid her away and abandoned her: why? Don't you believe in people anymore, in their ability to recover by adopting a new set of values? And so on and so forth. The red wine made your face bright as a child's, and your eyes shone with excitement, or perhaps you were moved. You washed the dishes and let him dry them, and your receptive fingers rubbed against his, a pleasant coldness in the pit of your stomach. Then you made filtered coffee and the two of you even finished off the bottle of wine, relaxed and smiling, as if that encounter would never end.

And all at once the emotion was cruelly interrupted and you felt humiliation and regret for having revealed so much. Unaccustomed as you are to that outward display of feelings, you must have really played the fool; or maybe it was just the opposite and you played exactly the role he wanted, the repressed woman in need of affection, you think, looking for support. What the hell, whether you like it or not, recognize that other self, the true self you've been out of touch with and that today came intoxicatingly and uncontrollably to the surface. Stop checking his house every fifteen minutes; he's married. Period. Forget this fantasy you're stubbornly fostering. His wife is so gracious, and they must love each other very much. They've been married for years, they've been through thick and thin together; who are you to get in the way of their relationship? A single day of pleasant company means nothing, just that, pleasant company. He's not to blame for your anxieties; he was the first man to appear in the Village who took you, craving, by surprise because he had nothing better to do on a Sunday. The other day while describing a love scene you must have realized it's been a long time since you've been involved in one yourself and that must have influenced your sudden permissive attitude and exacerbated your emotional state; but really, it's not his fault, the man is a delightful companion—did you just see him walk through the living room?—he's alone, his wife won't be sleeping at home, just imagine, and if you were to behave shamelessly and invite him over for dinner? No, he would never understand, and compromising the integrity of others is hardly the right thing to do. If it were your husband, would you like it if another woman took advantage of your absence and tried to seduce him or offered herself to him? No. Therefore, respect the dignity of a married couple and go to bed and get some sleep, think about the card you got from Sônia telling you how happy she is, their tour of Toledo, the kiss they both sent you. Sometimes you think you're some sort of visionary. Or could you be an enchantress?

♌ Dilermando Canudos was on his way home from shopping, complaining about the heat. He bumped into Soares fixing his gate, who with screwdriver in hand was trying to tighten a screw. Each lit a cigarette. After a while, Dilermando mentioned that Alexandre Ribeiro had been seen frequently with Pablita.

"Imagine what a couple they'd make, Soares. Him short and skinny with that woman who must be six foot six." His body shook with laughter.

"It's not funny, Dilermando. It's tragic. This guy brings the girl home right in front of God and everybody as if it were the most natural thing in the world. From my window I could see her naked inside his house."

The ham radio operator thought about suggesting to his neighbor that if he saw anything it was because he wanted to, but he didn't say anything. He attempted to soothe his friend's anger.

"Alexandre's an artist; he must be using the girl as a model, Soares. That's all there is to it. If anything else were going on he wouldn't make a public display of it like that."

"He told Tancredi he was screwing her."

"Well, she is a professional."

"Then he's showing his contempt for the Village."

Sitting on the curb with the package from his shopping trip on his lap, Dilermando brought the discussion to a close with a few words about the difficulties he faced because of the cul-de-sac.

Alexandre Ribeiro opened the door of his house and crossed the street.

"So how's the famous radio operator? And how are you doing, Soares?"

The Village representative wore a white suit and a tie and carried a briefcase.

"You two are really lucky. You don't have to go downtown in this heat. I'm dealing with the matter of the circus bids. Did you know that we have several candidates?"

"Has anyone approved the project?"

"Fortuna. The lease for the land is temporary. We'll do a test run first."

"And where does the homeowners association stand?"

"Most of the members are in favor of the plan. Only about twenty residents are opposed. Antônio's friends."

"That's not true. And anyway, aren't you worried about our unspoiled environment becoming a complete mess?" Soares asked the question in a threatening tone.

"If you had examined the blueprints carefully you would have noticed that we won't be disturbed. The tent will be raised over half a mile from here, in that area." He pointed. "We will be quite protected."

"What about the animal wagons?" Dilermando picked up his package. Without waiting for an answer he threw another question at him. "My friend, how much are you earning from this project?"

Alexandre was a bit taken aback, but he answered that it was less than he needed to live on and less than he could earn with another company were he not the Village representative.

"And what chance would you have had to cook up a scheme like this?" Soares tried to put him on the spot.

"My friends, I admit I might not have come up with such a brilliant idea, but when my dear uncle died opportunities opened up for me here. That's why Antônio must be burning with envy and resentment. He had the same chance and he failed to take advantage of it."

"How dare you talk that way about a loyal, devoted, and considerate friend?" Soares shouted, seized with rage.

"He would have solved my problem with the cul-de-sac by now," Dilermando interjected.

Soares ignored him.

"Pardon my frankness, but you'd have to be insane to think ill of Antônio. He'd never criticize anything just because he was the previous representative. There is no way in the world he would harbor feelings of envy or any other form of pettiness. He's a superior human being, a man of integrity. If I were you I'd enlist his support and listen to his advice."

"Nice to see you. I have to be going. We'll continue this conversation some other time." The Village representative abruptly took his leave.

But inside he was boiling with rage. Who do those two mediocre characters think they are? They have no idea who they're up against or what I'm capable of. They'll see, I'll have them groveling at my feet; he signaled for a taxi. He's been considering a political career for years and now he's about to obtain the necessary means. If he personally takes charge of the grand opening of the circus and the amusement park . . . The *favela* ought to be good for about five thousand votes. At least that's a start. A banner stretched across the Avenue: The People's Circus—Fun for Everyone. And he'll send Tancredi to drum up support in the *favela*. An undertaking by Alexandre Ribeiro, local artist, friend of the poor. Do slum dwellers have money to go to the circus? A free night. That's something he needed to arrange. Whoever accepted the proposal would win the bidding. Fortuna was impressed with his efficiency. The Company wasn't about to turn down someone willing to help them maximize their real estate profits, to change laws . . . Any self-respecting company should have a city councilman behind it. If I can gain the confidence of the directors . . . The exhibition, a success. Some newspaper commentators made fun of the arts center, but when all was said and done Fortuna capitalized on the P.R. The Cemetery of the Flowers was frequently mentioned in the press, plot sales went up; he sat up straight. Thanks to me, to my magnificent efforts. I can't get that doctor out of my mind, that lovely woman who's come to the Village. She could have some influence in the *favela*. And unless he was mistaken, she's been giving him those come-hither looks; he grinned smugly.

As he climbed the stairs to the meeting at Fortuna, Alexandre Ribeiro felt the euphoria of a self-confidence he had never experienced.

"Eat your hearts out, all of you."

🔔 Greta caught a bad cold. A week in bed, with a fever and unbearable headaches. Sofia paid a visit to see if she needed any help. Zaíra, who had asked her to come, opened the door to let her in.

"This way, doctor."

Sofia entered the semi-darkened bedroom. An inhaler was turned on.

"This is awful, Sofia. I haven't had such a bad sinusitis attack for years."

"Are you taking anything besides the inhalant?"

"Antibiotics and allergy medicine. Don't worry, I'm taking care of those staph germs."

"When the worst of the attack is over, it would be a good idea to be vaccinated." She took her hand. "Your skin feels cool."

"The fever gets worse in the late afternoon . . . How are things going?"

"So so. I found a shack to set up an office in. My god, I must have seen thirty patients from the *favela* yesterday."

Greta looked on the doctor with tenderness. She wore jeans and a white blouse. Petite. She felt an urge to cry. She was betraying that kind and gentle woman as she secretly dreamed about . . .

"You need to get better in time for Clotilde's birthday party."

"Yeah. The way I'm feeling I'm not sure I'll be able to go."

"You'll be over it by Saturday. What's this stuff on the plate?"

"Slices of raw potato. It's Zaíra's idea. She says it helps headaches."

Sofia laughed. And she looks ugly when she laughs, Greta noted. Her face gets all wrinkled. Without question, that is something the doctor should never, ever do, at least not that unrestrained laughter.

"Leonardo said to give you a hug for him. He couldn't come; he had to go see a patient in a serious state of depression. Poor thing. It's a sad case, a masculine identity problem. He's quite nervous because he's been taking care of the man for over five years. The hell of it is, psychoanalysis doesn't cure anyone. I can write a prescription for sinusitis. But the most a psychoanalyst can do is make the patient aware of his limitations and help him deal with his conflicts to the point where he can muck through life. If he's lucky."

Greta felt a twinge of envy.

"Do you talk about these things a lot?"

"No, he doesn't like to. I know about this case because the problem has reached a critical stage. But getting back to the subject of your sinusitis, I brought some anti-inflammatory pills for you. They may help. My only recommendation is that you take them with milk or with meals, because they tend to irritate your stomach." She stood up and went to the window. "Take three a day."

Greta, disconcerted, fidgeted in the bed.

"This is fantastic, from here you can see everything that happens in my house. All the more since the curtains aren't up." The doctor turned to the sick woman. "Seeing you in profile like this reminds me of something Leonardo said, that you are the prettiest and most intelligent woman he's ever met. Pretty both inside and out."

"Me?"

"Exactly. You were ideal company for him last Sunday. And he swears you're an excellent cook."

"Very kind of him," Greta said, uncomfortable and a bit disappointed. If he discussed it that freely with his wife it's because that day had been insignificant or . . . She turned her head slowly on the pillow. Did she have to feel so guilty?

Sofia sat on the edge of the bed to give her a kiss.

"Bye. Take the pills and cheer up. Oh, our telephone will be installed Monday. Isn't that great? Anytime you need some help, just give a yell."

Sofia left. The maid brought something to eat and a glass of milk before she also went out. Soon Greta was in a deep sleep.

♧ She woke up the next morning feeling very little pain, but she clearly remembered an erotic dream from the night before. She had been trying to seduce—of all people—Camilo. After a strange intellectual dialogue, she, naked, affectionately kissed his face and neck, as if she were his daughter, and finally decided on his lips. A long, smothering kiss.

She took another pill and went back to bed. She'd look at back issues of the newspapers. When you're sick, light reading is all you can handle.

She fell back to sleep and opened her eyes again at one in the afternoon. Her head still felt heavy. A hangover from the pain. The crisis had passed.

A hot shower and clean clothes improved her mood. It's cloudy today, she noticed, and sat on the sofa. Weak in the knees, she needed some food. The moment she finished eating someone knocked on the door. It was Míriam.

"I'm glad it's you."

"You're so pale. Were you expecting someone else?"

"No. I mean . . . who knows what I was thinking. That's why I look so surprised. I've been laid up in bed; I'm foggy from all the medicine, that must be it. Sit down and tell me what's new."

"Gricha hated the apartment."

"Oh no. For god's sake don't back out."

"Of course not. Everything's settled. I signed a contract with a rental company. But I suddenly felt so sad about leaving the Village."

Greta was touched by this.

"In spite of all the bad things that have happened, I've grown accustomed to this street." She gave her friend a pained look. Deep circles under her eyes darkened the cameo-like face.

"I'll miss you."

"Would you come visit us in Santa Catarina? Clotilde promised me she would. Gricha plans to install a ham radio at the farm. He thinks it's absolutely necessary to sell the horses when the time comes."

"Are you going to take your furniture?"

"No. I'm leaving all that junk behind. I don't have anything decent, just that armoire my aunt gave me. Would you accept it as a gift?"

"Why don't you have it shipped?"

"It's not worth it. I don't even know what the house looks like. And the farm is fifty miles from the nearest city. You could put that round jacaranda table with the four chairs on the veranda. The bed, the mattress, the two old armchairs, the kitchen cabinets, the stove, all that stuff, maybe . . ."

"Give it to Zaíra."

"To tell you the truth, I'd rather give it to Carmen Miranda; she's getting married."

"Well, either way it's a good idea."

"A voodoo priest is going to conduct the wedding ceremony. Isn't that funny? He's a samba composer and he sells bottled gas in the *favela*. He earns a pittance."

Greta felt too weak to offer coffee or tea.

"How silly of me. Let me fix something for you."

Míriam declined; she'd just had some French toast. They didn't chat for long. Greta was still feeling tired and listless. Míriam left, promising to come back later. Must be a side effect of the medicine. Nothing serious.

♧ Palm Street finally got its lights. People home at the time, Soares and Dilermando, as well as the women and children, were overjoyed when the streetlamps were turned on. The one placed in the cul-de-sac ensured that from now on the people who had been using it as a hangout would have to take their business elsewhere. Greta wasn't home when the memorable event took place, but she found out through Camilo that Alexandre Ribeiro went around fishing for compliments, as if the success of the project were his.

"And several people congratulated the jerk. It's incredible. Even the doctor, she went out with him to celebrate Antônio's achievement."

"It's understandable, Camilo. She doesn't know the whole story."

"I want you to go over to Antônio's with us, Greta. He, and he alone, deserves our thanks."

"I'll be glad to. Who else is going?"

"I don't know."

"Wait a few minutes; I'll be right over." She hung up the telephone.

Antônio clearly deserved the tribute. And what about calling Míriam?

Days of silence. You don't even want to think about Clotilde's party. You don't want to or you can't? Both. Your face turns red at the slightest reminder of that night. No, no shame over drinking too much. Why then? Leonardo? Yes, well. But it doesn't amount to . . . Could it be? Come on, Greta, face it; otherwise you'll have no peace. Is Gino's suicide bothering you? The dead don't come back to life. Míriam and Gricha will seek fulfillment in Santa Catarina, safe from indiscretion and prejudice. They'll guard their secret on the farm, blessed by a curse (if it's possible to say such a thing). You know the meaning of shame, but have you ever asked yourself whether brothers and sisters or relatives should love each other more than outsiders? The call of the body, the reintegration of divided molecules, that's what turns someone into another Oedipus or Electra. The coming together of selves torn apart, you explained to yourself. The brother and sister certainly love each other and give each other more pleasure than mere mortals, right? Sônia and Elisa dream in Europe. Not all within you is lost. There is a shadow of hope. The faint signs of hope that led you to lean wearily on Leonardo and to allow him to embrace you, to demonstrate the consequences of reaching out to him; and you offered yourself, submissive and feminine; the scars of loneliness nearly gone at that moment when he showed you the effect your body, your voice, and your look had on him. At the same time, he did something that made you drop the mask of the failed woman with no vocation for love. You even forgot where you were—you looked around slowly—but no one seemed interested in anyone else. He noticed your concern and he smiled. All of a sudden you saw, near the curtain, Alexandre Ribeiro and Sofia kissing full on the mouth. That hurt you. The woman had no right to behave that way in front of everybody, even if she was doing precisely what you would like to do: kiss Leonardo. The revelation of the two of them, grotesquely irresponsible and shameless, wounded you deeply. As if Alexandre and Sofia were reflecting the foolish and improper image of your romantic feelings for Leonardo. You felt such shame and indignation you almost broke down. And then, to keep him from noticing, you led her mate to the other side of the living room and out to the veranda. No, you didn't want the husband to see his wife in that intimate situation, since it was obvious he would be upset and . . . You couldn't bear it if he . . . you don't even know what, do you? You invited him to have a bite to eat and the two of you sat at one of the tables outside—the party decorations were so lively and gay—in the midst of Clotilde's friends, who had come out from the city. Leonardo—he hadn't seen his wife—thought the invitation meant you wanted to be alone with him and he tried to hold your hand under the table, but you ever so delicately moved away; the spell was broken, at least for that night; you sighed, feeling sorry for yourself. Leonardo thought maybe you were being overly modest; he lit his pipe and began talking about the patient he had lost a few days back, a homosexual patient who had unfortunately committed suicide; he told you how much he, Leonardo, had suffered from a feeling of medical impotence about the case and how he had even felt like leaving the profession. So psychoanalysts experience despair too? You looked at him again and once more were overwhelmed by an avalanche of contradictory feelings; it was your turn to take his hand, and the direct contact created a bond between you, a separate link. He put away his pipe and got up. Come, he said, and you followed after him without asking a thing—and for what reason? He crossed the garden, you were in high heels, your white dress caught on a fat woman's purse; he ran over to pull off the offending thread. You amiably said excuse me and ran after Leonardo, who was now at the door—and if someone were to appear? No one appeared and he went up to your front door, opened it, and told you to go in, and your heart beat wildly with emotion. He whispered, don't turn on the light, where's that candlestick? He sat on the couch and pulled you close to him; you felt awkward and nervous as a schoolgirl, he put his arm around you affectionately and made you lay your head on his shoulder: *now we can finally feel at ease.* The two of you, side by side, safe from prying eyes, you relaxed and let yourself be soothed by his silence, his breathing, his hand playing softly along your arm. You felt glorious then, still and cozy. He turned his head and gave you a lingering kiss, and you reciprocated and abandoned yourself fully and without guilt to the physical sensation, delighting in the pleasure of being caressed, touched. And then he took you into the bedroom.

Several times that night you felt the joy of being a woman, but you would rather have no memory of it. Because that is where your torment began. The torment of being alone, of wanting him to be yours and yours alone. You go to the window a thousand times a day, you nervously pace the floor, you wish he'd hurry up and get in touch, if only for a few moments, because unexpected feelings have emerged: insecurity, he treated you like an object and had no more use for you; guilt, his wife caught you *in flagrante* and felt betrayed; her husband wasn't there when she got home and she waited for him to account for his absence, how humiliating; and the main thing is the feeling of being abandoned, because if he didn't share your desire to be together, wouldn't that mean fantasy is blinding you to reality? Well, wouldn't it?

You've begun to live in the commonplace hell of passion. It's a sign you're still alive. And is there no such thing as passion's heaven, you ask yourself as you wander about the deserted room, along the deserted street, in the deserted Village. It's five o'clock in the morning and you're still trying to get to sleep, crazy with missing him. Change keys. Imagine what might have happened that night with Alexandre and Sofia. You can't? Of course you can. He took her home and told her about his political plans and espoused the idea that the intellectual should play a role in society, that it is essential he come down from his ivory tower and seek ways to work with the community, and so forth; Sofia listened indifferently. But she thrilled with hope when he jokingly defended free love and spoke against the shackles of marriage, a mere social obligation that should be experienced without thwarting the individual's instincts, the important thing being that family unity be maintained regardless of extra-marital pleasures; a love affair didn't imply a commitment but was a pure manifestation of the senses, and it didn't threaten marital stability but in fact reinforced it. Sofia laughed and asked why he was single, and he answered that every time he gets interested in a woman she's married, and Sofia went so far as to suggest that maybe he chose people with commitments so he wouldn't have to be burdened with emotional attachments. He controlled the impulse to put her down—he was about to suggest that she sounded like a psychoanalyst—and tried instead to convince the doctor that she needed healthy lovemaking with no strings attached. And at that moment what she most desired was that very thing, an emotional release, and so she ended up in bed with him.

She returned home disappointed. Either he didn't know how to make love, because he was used to servile and hurried prostitutes, or she hadn't been able to achieve release in time. Out of kindness she didn't let on, but she promised herself that never again would she fall into a trap like . . . ; she tiptoed into the bedroom. Leonardo was sound asleep.

She was mistaken. The psychoanalyst realized he and his wife were slowly growing apart. It was obvious: if he was that distant from her, then she was feeling the same way. If he was that interested in Greta, it was natural for his wife to seek another man. He clearly saw her with Alexandre during the party and it didn't bother him. One of these days the marriage would come to an end. The trick was knowing how to handle it.

♤ And the garden? The mint, parsley, and tomato seedlings were thriving, but the bell pepper, watercress, and spinach seeds never sprouted. The lettuce in the wooden flats needed transplanting, so Greta prepared a bed by turning over the soil and mixing in fertilizer, the hoe so heavy and the sun so hot on her back. Then she took the green seedlings and, kneeling on the ground, planted them one at a time in a zigzag pattern, her old pants rolled up and a straw hat on her head. Suddenly, Leonardo showed up unannounced and stood there under the mango tree, laughter in his eyes, watching her in that lamentable state, flushed, the sweat pouring off her.

"Don't hurry, I'll wait."

"Just these three left," she answered in embarrassment, her head bowed. "I thought you'd be at your office this time of day."

He explained nothing and stood silently smoking.

Greta took off her gloves and picked up her tools; he offered to carry the hoe. She wiped her damp brow with the back of her hand— you'll get your clothes dirty. She gave in and let him help her because she really was tired. And she went in to take a quick shower.

She found him sitting on the sofa reading a book. A sensation she would not forget. All women in love understand the meaning of that image, the man relaxing in the living room.

Her hair washed and hanging lankly, her face clean, Greta flopped into the old leather easy chair and offered him a docile expression. She was content. Quite content.

"Did you buy a new table?" he asked.

"No. Míriam gave it to me when she moved to Santa Catarina. She suggested I put it on the veranda but I thought it looked better over in that corner. She also gave me an armoire, that one." She pointed.

"You mean they're going to tear down the apartment building?"

"I think so. I haven't been out this week or telephoned Fortuna. I miss Míriam. Speaking of the telephone, has yours been connected yet?"

"Monday."

The thought passed quickly through her mind that he could have . . .

"What time is it?" Greta interrupted her thought and chastised herself mentally.

"Five. Why?"

"I'm hungry! I thought it was later than that."

He smiled.

"Why don't you sit a little closer? Right here beside me."

Greta obeyed; she felt self-conscious because she smelled of soap. Leonardo put his arm on the back of the sofa without moving closer to her. Suspicious, Greta looked at him out the corner of her eye.

"You're so lovely when you look like a scared little girl."

"At my age?"

"How old are you?"

"Thirty-two. And you?"

"Forty."

An uncomfortable silence separated them. Which he broke.

"Tell me a little about yourself."

"Me?"

"You can start by telling me where you were born." He watched her circumspectly, as if that were the only reason he had come.

"How much time do I have, doctor?" She immediately regretted the question.

He ignored the provocation. He simply stroked her hair.

Greta gave an honest and objective account of her past, without embellishing or dramatizing. Leonardo paid close attention and showed understanding. At times his eyes smiled (but not his mouth)—tenderly? She shared specifics about herself as if she were describing a fictional character; she avoided making judgments and related everything that came to her mind. She stopped at age eighteen.

"And then?"

"My first love was a poet. The second, a journalist. The third, a doctor. The fourth, a painter. The fifth, a lawyer, whom I married. We lived together for eight years. I opened an art gallery in partnership with my sister-in-law. I sold my share to her when the marriage fell apart. And that's when I met Luís, a playwright. I've always chosen talented and complicated types. I've never been attracted to men who lack intelligence. Which is unfortunate. Perhaps I should have been less incompetent. Or more competent. Who knows. All my relationships have been tortured, difficult. You'll probably say that I picked complex men because I was limited to a certain environment. Maybe. Everyone develops her own expectations for the other. Maybe I received more than I gave. I'm not entirely convinced of that. The problem is I was romantic and childish: I believed in a single, eternal love. What motivated me to keep trying was the certainty that each love affair would be the last. Maybe being separated from my mother and father can explain this need for a bond to make me feel whole. Could be. Anyway, I didn't succeed and I ended up in the Village for good. Luís wanted to marry me, but my hopes for eternal love were dashed. What you see today is a woman approaching old age terrified of failing again and determined to remain out of harm's way. Thanks to my financial solvency and the fact that I live simply, I can afford not to work in the city. My only struggle is for emotional survival. I'm not one of those people who value only money and property. If I wanted to I could probably get rich: I'd invest in the stock market, in real estate, in gold, in whatever. I'd have good opportunities for sound investments."

"You have other values."

"Exactly. Period. The session is over."

Leonardo sat and looked at Greta for a few moments. As if he were about to reveal something.

"How long did your most recent love affair last?"

"A year and a half. No one was to blame for its failure. We just couldn't get along. I believe that love, and not life, is the opposite of death. Has anyone ever told you that before? It's the first time the idea has ever occurred to me."

He leaned over and kissed her.

"What do you expect from me?"

"Eternity."

♄ Dinner. Rice and vegetable salad. What else?

"I want to look in the refrigerator."

"There's some leftover roast beef."

"Perfect."

He offered to set the table while she carved the cold roast. Out of habit she looked toward Camilo's house, completely dark—odd.

As they sat facing each other in the kitchen, she realized that she needed very little to be happy. Love. Or did that mean needing a great deal?

Leonardo told her that he was from Rio and that he had originally wanted to be an orthopedic surgeon like his father. But his first wife,

Estela, had serious psychological problems and in the end he turned to psychoanalysis. After ten years of married life, they separated. She's since remarried and has six children. They've remained friends.

"Were you your wife's analyst?"

"I know what you're getting at. The answer is no. We're psychoanalysts in the office during our appointments. Then and only then. Personal involvement isn't a good thing. A gynecologist is a doctor in his office, but with his wife he's just like any other man. Otherwise . . ."

"Do you go through analysis?"

"Every five years. I've been rather lax because I'm so busy. One of these days . . ."

"And Sofia?"

"We've been together for seven years. Marriage currently on the rocks."

Greta wondered if she should go any further. She suggested papaya for dessert. He declined, looking at a collage on the wall: a still life. A tray with bloody human heads instead of fruit; seemingly out of place, a flower, a calla lily, blooms. The perspective of the walls is distorted. A composition made from clippings, bits and pieces of other pictures, forming a magical and intimate texture.

"I like that picture."

Greta went up and took it off the hook.

"It's yours."

"Who made it?"

"Tina." Her face reddened. "Want some wine?" She attempted to change the subject.

When all is said and done, it's impossible to get everything off one's chest in a single evening. It has to happen without rushing things, without anxiety, while enjoying the pleasure of giving oneself to and discovering another slowly, a spider spinning its web. A web of love. The emotional threads are delicate and fragile, so fine and tenuous that you have to weave the fabric patiently, carefully, she told herself.

Leonardo examined the picture closely, trying perhaps to decipher its imagery.

"Ivo's been nervous lately. I turn out the lights early to see if he'll calm down. You know, Greta, I don't sleep much. I'm afraid of dying in my sleep. Who will find me?"

Greta suggested Camilo hire a full-time maid, and that he shouldn't brood about these things.

"What's gotten into the kid?"

"It could be the therapy or something else. I'm finally going to have to admit I'm an old man, my dear. The impotence of old age." He laughed, not without an edge of irony. "Enough of this talk. Have you heard from Sônia and Elisa?"

"Just that postcard."

"Are you upset, Greta?"

"Me?" She blushed. "No. Why?"

"Your expression has changed."

During his long pause, she wonders if the old man has seen Leonardo in her house.

"What are your new neighbors like?"

Greta overcame her sudden embarrassment and praised the couple. The old man listened politely but made no comment. No right to interfere in other people's lives.

"They're going to tear down the apartment building tomorrow, aren't they?"

She hesitated before confirming. She was helpless, she thought, when it came to figuring out the true nature of Leonardo and Sofia's relationship. She went to the window: two men were attaching an enormous iron ball to the crane. A truck was being loaded with bricks, window frames, doors, and bathroom fixtures. At that moment Carmen Miranda was salvaging objects from the rubble, and with a man who was surely her boyfriend she was loading a cart rented to transport her finds. Greta knew the cart's owner, the same man who bought old newspapers and empty bottles. The old nag waited patiently. Once she'd been curious to know where he sold all that useless junk.

"The newspapers go to the butcher shop on the Avenue, the bottles go to a recycling center."

"Can you live off that?"

"Well, miss, I do other odd jobs like helping people in the *favela* move and paupers' burials."

"Of course," Greta realized. One knows so little about the world. Camilo interrupted her reverie.

"Poor horse," he exclaimed. "In this heat!"

They both laughed when Carmen Miranda nearly fell climbing into the cart.

"You think she's already loaded?"

Complaining about his back, Camilo decided to sit down.

"Some days I think a lot about my late wife. Today is one of them. The two of you would have been good friends."

Greta looked at the framed portrait and tried to think of a positive response.

"She had it taken when we were sweethearts," he explained. "She was almost twenty."

"I thought she was older. Women in your day started looking matronly at such a young age."

"That was the fashion. Girls made a point of looking older."

Greta accepted the explanation. Widowers always display photographs of wives in their youth.

"How old was she when she died?"

"Fifty-four."

"Then why the photo of her when she was young?"

"She was very pretty."

Greta nodded in agreement. She seemed well groomed, the fox fur draped around the shoulders of her silk suit, the small hat fitting tightly on her head and revealing only a few curls. Charming.

"Tell me, Camilo. When you think about your wife do you picture her as young or old?"

"Picture's not the word. I sense her presence, certain gestures; I remember particular events. But her face is dim in my memory. I can't reconstruct her features. For that I need to look at a photograph."

"Do you have any taken when she was older?"

"Open that closet door. Do you see a box with silver trim?"

She took it out and brought it to Camilo; he put on his glasses.

"Look, this is her with Mirna on her lap. The girl's birthday."

He continued rummaging through the box, putting aside several photos without showing them.

"My daughter's wedding. My wife must have been about forty."

Women at the altar, ridiculous hats. The 1950s? Men standing stiffly in tails. Camilo was a handsome fellow.

"In this photo she was about forty-eight. If I'm not mistaken it's the last picture of her."

Greta regarded the stout, smiling, healthy-looking woman, and compared her with the young woman of twenty. It was obviously the same person. But what a difference. It was easy to understand why Camilo chose that picture for framing. A gallant gesture; she handed back the photographs.

"What time does Ivo get home from therapy?"

"He should be back by now."

No sooner had he spoken than the car pulled in. Camilo got up. First the driver took out the wheelchair and then lifted Ivo out. The boy was clearly happy to see his grandfather.

It was time for Greta to leave. She had to close up Sônia's house. By this time Mário, the chauffeur, would have watered the garden. Leonardo wasn't back from the office yet—she crossed the street and closed up Sônia's house.

A few blue patches in the cloudy sky. The threat of rain was over. Tomorrow she'll go into town. She doesn't want to be around for the demolition and she couldn't bear waiting any longer for Leonardo to call on her. Maybe she'd go to the movies and get over that morbid tension. No question about it, love isn't worth the trouble. It causes more pain than . . .

She should've figured that out with Luís. The circumstances were different, the consequences identical: suffering. The agony of being apart is greater than the ecstasy of being together. Could that be true? She suddenly remembered the sensation of Leonardo's un- shaven face rubbing against hers and she shuddered. Damn. Couldn't she stop thinking about him?

The telephone was ringing. She ran to answer it: hello, she said, her voice unsure, excited, who is it?

At the other end of the line her uncle was asking her to attend a meeting the next morning.

"Is anything wrong, my dear?"

"No, uncle. I have a cold. My sinusitis . . ." She hung up, feeling wretched.

There are times she can't contain her exasperation. Not knowing the rules of the game is awful. Tonight, for example, there's no one home next door. Not Leonardo, not Sofia. How can you stay calm if you don't know what's going on? If he'd phone, give her a sign, tell her not to worry, Greta could relax and wait. A sudden urge to hire the psychoanalyst: how much does an hour of love cost? Play with fire and you get burned. She's tired of hearing that. Fate determined that Gino commit suicide and fate brought Leonardo to the Village. The snares of destiny (or illusion?), Greta. I'm going to go crazy, you say, and you throw open the window. What do you see?

Tina in the garden, dressed in her nightgown. In the black and starless night that fleeting white form has no fear; she sings in the darkness, wanders among the trees, spies on Leonardo's bedroom, returns, hovers in the air. A phantom. You hurry to shut the window and slip under the covers, your heart pounding.

The sound of the iron ball smashing against the walls of the building echoed along Palm Street on that hot and sunny day. The rubble on the ground would be hauled in wheelbarrows to be piled on the sidewalk and from there loaded on trucks. Twenty men worked nonstop. At lunch time they sat on the curb, lunch buckets on their laps, and some practiced a few samba rhythms while others stretched out for a nap. At five o'clock the company bus came to pick them up.

The lot was cleared in a week. The foundation was intact, leaving the impression the building would reemerge and rise up all by itself.

A letter from Sônia advising that she and her mother had extended their stay in Europe. Their attorney will arrange for bill payments. If Greta could get the bills together and turn them over to Mário and continue taking care of the house, she and Mother would appreciate it. Nothing in the way of personal or confidential news. Nor any mention of Luís. Only the phrase, "your newborn friend Sônia."

Early December. The circus tent has been raised. A green tent made of plastic and held together with steel struts. Various diesel trucks and house trailers surround the circus ring. Eucalyptus posts have been set in concrete for the lights. Hustle and bustle—Alexandre Ribeiro runs around like a chicken with its head cut off. The circus has hired people from the *favela* to clean up the lot next door, which will be used for parking. Tancredi apparently won't be in charge of the lot, since the circus owners have insisted its use be free. A high-class circus like this doesn't charge for parking. He felt betrayed by the Village representative. Ribeiro solved the problem by promising to arrange a position for him: manager of his campaign for city councilman. A matter of days. And as soon as the amusement park is in place . . . Anyone driving along the Avenue sees wooden arrows indicating the distance to the People's Circus, as well as a few posters and banners. The prostitutes are not at all happy with the increased police presence. In general, police patrols at the most notorious hangouts consist of enjoying the prostitutes' services and paying by winking at their activities. Now and then they haul everyone off to jail, only to release them twenty-four hours later. This happens when public complaints appear in the newspaper or on television or when there's a fight or a crime is committed. There isn't enough room in the police station to hold so many people. The situation is probably worse for the transvestites. Pablita, in fact, has disappeared and no one knows exactly why. There are those who say she's dancing in a strip-tease show. But for now that's purely conjecture.

Greta didn't mention it to anyone, but the other day she noticed Pablita going into the woods behind Alexandre's house. Appearances sometimes can be deceiving.

Besides, she had her own problems. The crisis between Leonardo and the woman doctor seemed endless. He was vacillating and he frankly questioned their relationship. They'd lived together happily for many years and under those circumstances it would be foolhardy to go any further. He loved Greta but he also loved his wife. Since the situation was so upsetting to her, it would be better if they stopped seeing each other for the time being.

"I fell in love with you," she confessed. "You should have thought of that when you got involved with me."

He looked at her sternly.

"I'm sorry, Greta. It's the responsibility of each of us to solve our own problems. No one forced anyone else. The involvement was mutual."

"I'm so miserable I can't sleep. I feel abandoned."

"Take a tranquilizer. I can't play this role you've chosen for me, the father who'll take care of his emotionally unstable daughter. You're charming, intelligent; you could make any man happy. Unfortunately, I'm not free."

Greta ensconced herself in her bedroom, prepared to die of a broken heart. She wallowed in self-pity and was incapable of lifting a finger for three days. She didn't even notice them putting up the circus tent. And the neighbor women's house, shuttered?—she got up. She was still suffering—the drawer is full of letters that will never be read—but she went back to taking care of the garden, to the meetings at Fortuna, to her visits with Camilo. Poor thing, he had been so dejected in recent days, yet in spite of that he was putting up his Christmas tree. Every year he decorates it differently. Last year's tree was so creative: silver balls attached to black threads hanging from the ceiling formed a suspended cone. The old man was clever, oh, that he was.

♌ The official opening of the circus was preceded by a free performance for the *favela*. Zaíra got very excited. She had never seen anything so sumptuous.

"Where I come from, the rain actually leaked into the tent at the circus I used to go to when I was a kid. I just loved the circus. Women and children got in free on weekdays. So you can bet I was always there. The funny part is we went to see plays, a new one every day. I remember one, it told the story of a lush. It was called *The Drunkard*. I always cried. But here it's different. The artists are all covered with sequins, even the animals are decked out, the monkeys do all those monkeyshines . . . The clowns, what a riot. What I liked most were the trapeze artists. They're incredible."

The Village representative chalked up a victory. People in the *fa-*

vela were talking about nothing else. But they were complaining about the fact that tickets for the regular season performances were so expensive. On the other hand, several youngsters got jobs watching cars, and a few women, mainly from Bahia, sold coconut and peanut candy on the Avenue. Everybody was ecstatic.

The circus failed to give rise to the much-feared disturbances, at least those first few days, and it wasn't going to stay longer than two months in the Village. Nothing serious, beyond music during performances, drum rolls, and applause.

Greta resolved to go for a stroll around the circus grounds, but she got no further than the chimpanzee's cage. When he noticed a visitor, he seized the opportunity to show off: he put on a knitted coat, took it off, hung it on a nail, cleaned his plate in a basin, brushed his teeth, swept the floor. He was over three feet tall. He wasn't young. She accompanied his movements with exclamations of approval and enthusiasm. Then she decided to say, "Bye, I have to go," and he let out a loud guffaw. Why? she asked herself, perplexed. The chimpanzee soon stopped laughing, approached the bars, and supporting himself on the backs of his hands gazed directly into her eyes. He seemed to be feeling her out, his look probing deep into her personality. Greta felt disoriented, frightened; breathing heavily, she turned her back on the chimp and headed toward home.

She would return again another day to look over the circus and figure out if that chimpanzee's lustful gaze was real or if it was mere suggestion. Wow. It had really unsettled her.

The church bells tolled, slow and melancholy. As soon as the pealing ceased, shrieking was heard throughout the Village, and above it was a kind of roaring sound followed in turn by a grunt of rage as if an elephant were about to attack. The animals were frightened and they reacted with strange cries and growls, astonishing the circus people.

"I just don't know what happened," the terrified keeper shouted. "All of a sudden the animals got nervous. If there had been a performance today . . . I never saw anything like it in my life, I swear."

The dwarf, driven from his trailer by the commotion, asked the keeper if the animals might not have been disturbed by the bells.

"What bells? I didn't hear any bells. Are you plastered?"

"They rang a little while ago."

The keeper thought maybe the dwarf was getting old or crazy in the head. And he headed for the office.

The dwarf tried to calm the sobbing, trembling chimpanzee. It pained him to see his partner so upset. If a chimpanzee could cry, this one would be shedding copious tears. The trainer watched the lion roar, its head down to make the sound louder. He knows there's a danger of attack when the beast is frightened. Puzzled, he turned to the keeper.

"Funny, I heard these weird bells. I thought they were from that church over there, but it's empty."

"So you've gone off the deep end too, eh? I've been here the whole time and I didn't hear a thing."

"Maybe you're deaf but I'm not."

The animals quieted down. The dwarf went back into his trailer to finish straightening up. He has done his own cleaning ever since he became a widower. He and his wife lived together for twenty years in that nomadic home. Pasquim began life in the big top with the Costinha Circus, which had been run by the same family for seven generations. As a boy he sold lollypops. He learned how to paint sets and posters, help raise the tent, and several other jobs. Francis the Clown taught him the art of making people laugh. When Francis got too old he left the circus and went to live with one of his daughters in Vila Ema, a working-class district on the outskirts of São Paulo. He gave the dwarf his own trailer as a gift. A circus artist without a trailer can't get work. That gave him a chance to show what he could do and he was in like a shot. Pasquim traveled all over Brazil. He met Raimunda in the northern state of Paraíba. It was his turn to teach the craft to a future partner. They acted in a melodrama for one, and only one, short season. It was called, *Heaven United Two Hearts.* The main actors came down with hepatitis, and there was no other way to keep the circus going. And so the two dwarves screwed up their courage and played the roles of the young couple whose parents forbade their love. At the end of the play the young lovers died and were framed in a red satin heart all lit up. Just beautiful. He cried with heartfelt emotion each time the play was performed. Only Maria would have given them such an opportunity: she was the best circus owner he ever met. No other group was interested in having the couple play dramatic roles. Dwarves are supposed to do comedy, not drama. The sad truth. But they worked out fine as clowns, and the children loved them. After Raimunda died, the chimpanzee became his partner. As Francis had done, he planned to leave the circus some day. With his wife gone, his heart was no longer in the circus life. But he didn't know where else to go. What would he do?

That night, Pasquim looked at their wedding picture—Raimunda was so dainty—and he got falling-down drunk. Those bells got under his skin. He had a nightmare. He dreamed that she was alive and pregnant. Then the child grew into a giant. Even standing up, he was too big for the circus. Pasquim woke up crying.

Passion takes a time-out, even if the body makes its demands twenty-four hours a day. The seed wants to grow till it bursts but it must be watered with affection and not with despair. The bottle of tranquilizers is half empty. Would this simple prescription succeed in checking the sensual irritation? Could that be the secret, the great wisdom? Aha. Our pills reduce the pains of passion. Try them.

A visit from Breno. That's all I needed, Greta thought when she saw him in the doorway huddled under his umbrella.

She asked the routine questions, how're your parents, brothers and sisters, cousins, nieces and nephews. He answered politely and asked similar questions. When the subject of family was exhausted, she offered him coffee and immediately regretted the faux pas. She had forgotten he suffered from an ulcer. He didn't drink coffee, soft drinks, or anything else.

Dressed in a suit and tie, her ex-husband was still an attractive man. He could be an advertising model selling fancy cigarettes or sports cars.

How must he see her? She didn't try to guess, she really wasn't interested, she could care less. A brief scene appeared vaguely in her mind, she didn't know why: she and Breno, naked and indifferent, reading in bed.

He talked about the office, about a complicated lawsuit dealing with an industrial design copyright. And the reason for his visit? He wanted a divorce.

"No problem. Have the required three years of separation passed already? My goodness. I lost track of the time."

"I've brought the papers to sign." He opened the briefcase.

"So, I'm going to be single again, eh?"

"No. A divorcée."

"Are you planning on getting married again?"

He was flustered but he finally admitted it.

"Who's the girl?"

"You and your indiscreet questions. She's a judge."

"That's nice. You work in the same field."

As soon as she asked the question she thought of Leonardo and Sofia and she was mortified.

The agreement was simple, more so than she would ever have imagined.

"OK if I sign it?"

The rain had stopped. Breno praised her yard, the magical atmosphere. He wouldn't be surprised if a witch suddenly appeared holding a broom.

Greta smiled.

"Do you want to see the garden I've planted in the back?"

Distant and impassive, they said their friendly good-byes and exchanged a ritual kiss.

At that precise moment Greta saw Leonardo at the window, watching them.

A robbery on Palm Street caused fear and consternation; everyone was up in arms. It happens thousands of times a day in the city, but it was a first for the Village. And it had tragic consequences: Tancredi and his wife were murdered. It's believed the crime took place in the early morning. Joaquim, who owns the tavern, said that his business had increased when the circus opened and that he closed his doors at two a.m. He vaguely remembers a suspicious-looking fellow with a wooden leg who was the last one to leave and who spent hours drinking at the bar and asking questions about the Village. He'd never seen the guy in his life. There were always people he didn't know drinking at his bar, so he couldn't go around raising the alarm left and right.

Clotilde complained indignantly to the Village representative about the hiring of a night watchman.

"I beg your pardon, madam, but Tancredi himself was opposed to the plan because he was in financial difficulty."

"What are the homeowners association funds being spent on? As far as I know, the six months you've been our representative, nothing . . ."

Alexandre Ribeiro cut her off and insisted he'd give a financial report at the year-end meeting. The bill for cleaning the sewer drains hadn't even been paid yet. Clotilde, furious, shot back that it was up to Fortuna to pay for that and not the association. Soares put an end to the argument.

"Fate, my dear neighbor. It can happen to anyone anywhere in this country. Unfortunately, it happened here this time; we're no longer safe. The only solution is to pick up and leave like Altair did."

The brutality of the murder—the bodies slashed and defiled—seemed more the work of a psychopath than a burglar. Soares regretted he'd seen nothing, considering their houses were so close. If not for the blood on the sidewalk the bodies would have decayed before anyone discovered the tragedy.

"There's no point in thinking about the matter," Dilermando said. "No matter how hard one tries to imagine the horror, we'll never know what happened here, or how much the couple suffered."

Greta huddled in her chair and didn't say a word to anyone. Dilermando was right. No one would ever really understand the tragedy. And she took her mind off it by examining Altair.

She'd heard nothing from him for a long time. Altair had never actually lived in the Village. His house, number 506, a kind of chalet, is located at the back of the property and is hidden by a thick hedge which he had planted to completely surround the yard. Its three lots, each with ten thousand square feet, make it one of the largest properties on the street. The house is shuttered because Altair takes care of an orphanage. He used to come occasionally on holidays but he would hide out, and no one ever so much as laid eyes on him. At first there was a great deal of curiosity about that eccentric character. However, gossip stopped when the source for news dried up. Altair was smart enough to behave discreetly and maintain his distance, so people soon got used to him.

In 1967, '68, or thereabouts, Altair faced serious problems because two young people accused of terrorism were caught right in his house. At that time the subdivision was in full swing and most of the houses were under construction. The streets were clean, the lots marked out and numbers fixed on the concrete posts, the lake clear, a vision of paradise palpable in the beauty of the old estate. Potential buyers were delighted by the old family home. Fortuna had its temporary offices there while construction of the three-story building was being completed, although the old house was still not ready for occupancy due to problems with the water pipes and deterioration of the tile roof and parquet floor, devastated by termites.

Altair built the chalet in the late sixties as a refuge from a hostile world unwilling to accept the fact that he was openly homosexual. He would come to the Village accompanied by his mother, a tiny, distinguished-looking woman. There was a clear view of his property then, and whoever wanted to could see Altair in a silk dress, made up, wearing a necklace and bracelets, sitting calmly on the veranda chatting or drinking tea with his mother. Two girlfriends getting a bit of fresh air in the yard. A governess took care of everything. Her name was Frida. A tall and uncommunicative German woman who wore her hair in a bun. Altair had always been fat. In the orphanage he dressed in a shapeless uniform, a white shirt perhaps, with beltless black trousers—held up by a piece of cord? It was common for people to address him as Miss Altair, which made him puff up with pride. The orphanage, a model of efficiency, had been founded by Miss Augusta in 1940, after she lost her husband in the war. Because she had no children of her own she adopted Altair, a ward of the Juvenile Court. Two years old. She was very concerned about the problem of abandoned children and since she couldn't adopt them all she decided to found an orphanage and became its director. Thirty children, no more than that. As soon as the first group turned fourteen, she placed them in jobs to open up space for other children. The orphans left her establishment having completed primary school and vocational training to be electricians, hair dressers, plumbers. Not everything, however, came up roses. She had to confront all sorts of obstacles, and the orphanage consumed her fortune. So as not to have to close it down, she was forced to ask for government support—malicious gossip has it that the house on Palm Street was built with the money, but this appears to be nothing more than a smear campaign. The old woman went through many bitter experiences. Some orphans never returned, not even to pay her a visit, and a few of them became criminals. She hated to talk about that. But there were examples of gratitude and affection. Six of her wards stayed right there working in the garden, in the kitchen, or helping to care for the children. Miss Augusta was the only woman in the orphanage. Although in a certain way so was Altair, who showed a special preference for the newborn, an astonishing maternal vocation.

The terrorists arrested on Palm Street had been orphans: one was an auto worker and the other was doing his military service. Both were under twenty years of age. Wanted by the military police, they used their friendship with Altair to borrow the house for a few days, without mentioning that they were in deep water politically. He knew that the young men had joined the struggle for radical social change, that they participated in the movement opposing U.S. imperialism, and so on. They wrote slogans on walls demanding agrarian reform, the end of repatriation of profits by foreign companies, reestablishment of relations with China. Youthful ideological concerns. Altair failed to understand how they could have picked up all that stuff so quickly, but he did support them. After all, those were his children courageously upholding the idea of change to create a more just society with fewer special privileges.

And he cries when he thinks of the boys, who have disappeared forever. He searched for them everywhere with no luck. The police chief of São Paulo's Santo Amaro district, who occasionally sent him babies found in the street to be cared for by the orphanage until their situation could be clarified, interceded on Altair's behalf and thus saved him from serious trouble with the police. He could do nothing, however, to find the boys.

The Village residents contribute donations to the orphanage. In addition Clotilde employs or finds work for those who have to leave. The one who collected the annual donations had been Tancredi. That accounts for Altair's presence at the funeral, black dress, suede purse. When Miss Augusta died, he took her place in the orphanage and adopted feminine dress for good. Unfortunately he is going bald, which forces him to wear a wig. But it is discreet, with short hair and bangs. Those who are unaware Altair is not a woman suspect nothing.

He hadn't shown his face in the Village for a year. Greta had all but forgotten him.

"Well now, Altair, it appears you want nothing more to do with your old friends."

"Honestly." He adjusted the bracelets on his wrist. "The orphanage takes up all my time. It's no use keeping the house any longer. I'm going to sell it."

After the funeral, which took place in the city rather than in the Cemetery of the Flowers, Altair asked Clotilde to collect donations in the Village.

"Things don't look good, and I probably won't be able to accept a single child this year. The government hasn't paid last year's stipend yet. The situation is getting worse all the time," he lamented. "Isn't it shameful?"

Clotilde promised to go all out at the next Christmas fundraiser and she urged the poor soul not to lose hope. Some day his good works and dedication would be rewarded.

The Village of the Bells is deteriorating both in terms of the people and the environment, Greta complained during a Fortuna meeting.

The tragic death of the Tancredis temporarily made her forget her sorrows. Leonardo and Sofia hadn't attended the funeral. Perhaps they were away on a trip.

"If you don't take drastic steps, I guarantee you'll regret it," she continued sternly.

Barbosa took the floor and tried to calm her. If a night watchman is hired, the firm will pay half the cost.

"Then talk to the representative and order him to hire one immediately. I have no intention of leaving even if I have to live there by myself. I know that my safety is nobody's problem but my own. But if the homeowners sue, I wonder how Fortuna will be able to pay up."

"A lawsuit like that could drag on for years."

"I wouldn't be so sure about that if I were you," she argued, seated at the table. "You're taking a huge risk. One line in the newspapers and Fortuna will be discredited. And you can kiss any future public bids or projects good-bye."

The arguing continued. Fortuna was right at the point of closing several deals to finance ventures both inside and outside of São Paulo. Moreover, the Chamber of Deputies was considering a zoning law that would allow the firm to put up taller buildings in the Village. If the legislation passed, the area on the left or lake side of the Avenue would immediately be sold or incorporated, thus attracting new investment. Fortuna was leery of Clotilde, a strong-willed and knowledgeable woman. If she gave the signal, everybody would follow her lead.

"Altair needs to sell the house. The orphanage is deeply in debt. I advise you not to create obstacles."

Greta felt she'd scored a bull's-eye by threatening to expose Fortuna in the press. No one in attendance at the meeting dared to disagree. She left, satisfied with her small victory.

The moment she was out of the room Barbosa smiled slyly.

"Alceu, why don't you make a little visit to the orphanage? Bring along a check, a donation for those needy children. Greta will be none the wiser. Be tactful but make it clear that for the time being no one in the Village is allowed to sell, OK? Soon, very soon, everything'll be settled once and for all."

🔔 Soares stopped shuffling the cards.

"What's Christmas going to be like this year?"

Antônio scratched his head, moved his glass of beer, and crossed his legs.

"I don't know. We should pay our respects to Tancredi by not planning anything. He was after all our Santa Claus. And another thing, Soares, there aren't any children left in the Village young enough to appreciate that sort of thing. Do you realize that in the last two years not a single child has been born here?"

"That's true."

"Jane and Clotilde will organize the annual fundraiser so Altair will have money to buy presents for the orphans. But that's about it."

Too bad. Christmas in the Village had always been so much fun. Tancredi would put on the red suit, stick a pillow inside it, patiently glue on cotton for the beard and mustache, and go from house to house delivering presents which the parents had wrapped out of sight of the children. On the twenty-fourth everyone was stationed in the yard awaiting his arrival, the trees trimmed and other decorations, put up especially for the occasion, ablaze with light.

There will be no festivities in the Village of the Bells this year.

🔔 Greta and Tina—who is who?

🔔 In life we come into contact with interesting people who disappear from our lives without warning, as if by magic. No sooner do they appear than they are gone for good. Mateus, Alice, and Tiago, such exciting folks! How does one get back in touch with them? Sônia was the connection during her dream-buying period. The experiment, testing a fictional theme in real life, came to nothing. Sônia was in a transition phase and she showed herself capable of change, rather than being a static element in an omniscient narrative structure. She still had a future to look forward to. And she tried to break away. It remains to be seen how she'll develop. If in fact she doesn't settle in Europe, selfishly. Greta misses Sônia and her sleep-walking look, which voracious readers always have. And what about Luís? No news from him for a long time. Will he disappear, too? Hopefully not.

Celebrating Christmas wasn't the same without Santa Claus. Neighbors who were close friends visited each other's homes the afternoon of the twenty-fourth. Greta joined Camilo and Ivo as they waited for a ride to their relatives'. Camilo wore a silk ascot and a white linen suit. They exchanged presents: she received a boar's-tooth and silver necklace, the old man a lamp for reading in bed, and Ivo a flute. Greta played a few notes to show him how it worked; the boy loved it.

Late in the afternoon Antônio and Jane dropped by to invite their friend to dinner. Greta declined their gracious offer and lied, saying she was having dinner with her uncle and aunt. You have to indulge your relatives at least once a year, isn't that so? They exchanged small gifts, she served them a Scotch, and Jane commented on the success of the fundraiser, which took in a goodly sum.

At seven o'clock Greta stopped by the home of Clotilde and Dilermando Canudos, just back from the orphanage. Clotilde was in charge of the presents this year because Altair had his leg in a cast and was supposed to keep off his feet. A minor sprain, a short period of rest. He was cheered by the fact that the orphanage would stay open another year, the money from the subsidy in the bank at last.

Soares called from the beach, where he was taking care of his grandchildren, his wife still in a state of shock over the death of the Tancredis. When they got back they planned to pull up stakes. No matter how much they stood to lose. Their mental health was what counted. Merry Christmas, dear friends.

As soon as Soares hung up, the phone rang again. Greta hoped it was Leonardo. It was Míriam calling from Laguna, telling her excitedly about the ranch and the horses. She insisted Greta take a few days off to relax in Santa Catarina and she sent warmest greetings to one and all.

At ten o'clock Greta set the table, took the bottle of Chablis from the refrigerator, turned on the record player—Horowitz—and sat by herself. Her only pleasure would be Leonardo's presence; he could show up at any moment. Then . . .

Vain hope.

🔔 "Think of it as a test," Tina said.

Greta gave her a skeptical look.

"I'm serious. Love demands sacrifice. No one loves without paying a price."

"I've heard you say something like that before. Aren't you repeating yourself?"

"Don't be mean. You chose to be alone. How about doing yourself a favor, a little kindness?"

Greta realized she was clenching her teeth; she moved her jaw around.

"Give us a smile. The ham is delicious. The lemon custard is excellent. Savor your food, caress it. Eating is one of the best things in life. The other is drinking. Both are essential when you're unhappy in love."

"At least they're necessary. Love . . ."

"You're crazy about this sweet-sour taste. A little wine? Liszt played by Horowitz hits the spot," Greta recognized, glad she'd put the turntable on automatic so it would play continuously.

Tina, with her drifting, romantic, secretive air, hesitated to criticize Greta for forgetting her . . . She'd been out of circulation longer than she deserved. But it was Christmas Day. They should be easy on each other. The rejection, however, was unfair, yes indeed.

"Funny. The other night you were floating above the yard and over Leonardo's house; you almost had an attack of sentimentality."

"What's wrong with you is you deny normal human emotion. People cry, dammit, they suffer, laugh, torture themselves, shout with happiness, feel despair. For no reason. The so-called cheap emotions are the most common and believable. You need to loosen up and let the tears flow. You want to project an image of the mature, civilized adult. Come on, girl, accept the fact that crying purifies the soul."

Greta, her fists tightly clenched, sensed that her eyes had reddened and felt her jaw tremble. A lump in her throat—she got up and closed all the shutters in the house. She wasn't about to let anyone see her fragile and emotional. Not even Tina. Not this Christmas or any other.

Tina smiled.

"It's up to you. The way things are going now, it makes no difference. What do you think about the Village?"

"The whole thing has fallen completely apart. Uncle Alceu was well-intentioned. He tried to copy real estate developments in other countries. He wanted to sell the idea of a return to a simpler and healthier lifestyle in housing units more suitable for human beings, because people have always preferred natural settings and peace and quiet. The fact is, at the time he could have sold the whole estate outright for a fortune. In his own screwy way he was a romantic, too."

"Oh, don't give me that nonsense. We both know he was in a tight spot. What about the fact that he put the estate up as collateral for a loan? He wasn't supposed to subdivide. It's against the law. If he'd paid the homeowners back the original investment, with interest . . ."

"A lot of people don't want that, and the time isn't ripe for that kind of honesty. (Fortuna lost its shirt on some of its projects and hasn't recovered yet.) Another thing in his defense: he's not the sole owner. There's a whole pack of heirs, uncles and aunts and cousins, and they're not about to lose a cent if they can help it. As for myself, I didn't find out about the problems until after the subdivision had been sold. Does it do any good to go to meetings, demand improvements, and try to find ways to make the mistake of the original purchase less painful for the residents? If the project had worked out, we'd have paid off the debt and we'd be swimming in money. The Village of the Bells would be a model of how to make a decent profit for other real estate investors to follow. If Uncle Alceu could do it all over again he'd sell the estate outright. You have to recognize that."

"If I didn't recognize it I'd spit in all their faces."

"So whether you like it or not, you're an accomplice to this farce."

"Oh no, I don't agree. If I'm to blame for anything it's for considering the project viable in the first place. I'd be proud and happy to live in a prime area developed in good taste, ten miles outside of São Paulo, where people believe in friendship and community. I swear, we were on the way to achieving that here. The new representative upset our way of doing things to some extent; he set us against each other and did Fortuna's bidding instead of working exclusively to alleviate our troubles. A circus, an amusement park! Have you ever heard of such a thing? It won't be long before the park is put in, and Fortuna will make hardly anything on the rent. It's an affront to the people who live here, don't you agree?"

Tina paused to create an ironic climate of suspense. As if she knew what was coming and Greta were merely lost in supposition.

"Am I way off the mark?"

"You're just passionate."

"I'm going to do something about this passion tomorrow."

◬ Twenty-sixth of December. Greta received an unexpected call from Sofia, an invitation for tea the next afternoon.

They agreed to meet at four at Brunella's Restaurant, in the Moema district. Greta pondered the worst-case scenario; her agony was pitiable. What if Sofia asked her point-blank if her husband . . . She considered calling Leonardo: what should I say? How much does she know? A childish attitude. It was up to her and her alone to use her perception, intelligence, and common sense to judge the situation, which she would do at the proper time.

If only her head would stop spinning! She couldn't sit still or concentrate. She decided to take a walk around the Village.

It was a lovely day. A summer day. She ended up at the circus. At that hour, eleven in the morning, nothing stirred. She approached the chimpanzee's cage; sitting down, he was looking for fleas or lice on his legs. The animal looked up, raised his eyebrows, but paid no attention to Greta. As if he hadn't even seen her. She walked on. The lion was snoring. Where were the artists holed up? The trailers shut tight.

Pasquim, who had been sweeping the dirt floor, leaned on the broom; pots and pans were drying in the sun.

"Looking for someone, Miss?"

"No. I live over on Palm Street and I came to see the circus caravan, you know, what goes on behind the scenes."

"Why?"

"Curiosity."

"Better satisfy it quick, because we're moving on. We're thinking about cutting our season here short."

"You don't say. Bad audiences?"

"Terrible. We're losing a lot of money."

"What do you know. I thought the bigger circuses . . ."

"That's baloney, Miss. We try one place, it don't work, we go someplace else."

Greta compared the dwarf and the chimpanzee physically—they looked like brothers.

"Besides the small audiences," Pasquim went on, "everybody's feeling low and complaining about being sick. Even the animals have been in a bad mood. I just don't know. If I believed in witchcraft . . . Having a circus next to a cemetery brings bad luck."

The dwarf pulled a miniature bottle from his pocket and took a swig.

"Want some? It's good booze."

"No thanks."

The dwarf shrugged his shoulders and drank again.

"So what happens when a particular place doesn't work out?"

"We pack up and leave. Want to take a load off, Miss? I made some corn bread." He bowed toward the steps leading to his trailer. "That'll give you an idea how we live. Got some trailers around here for rich folks, like the trapeze artists for example. Mine's a poor man's. It was a present. You don't look a gift horse in the mouth, right? Those trapeze artists are rolling in dough, that's for sure! And they don't even live with us; they sleep somewhere else."

Greta entered the combination bedroom-kitchen with a stove near the doorway. A curtain in a floral pattern served as a divider to create a sleeping area. Two plastic armchairs. One could see where the legs of the furniture and the stove had been sawed off. A vase of flowers decorated the china cabinet.

"Where will the circus go after it leaves here?"

"We're thinking of going down to the coast, to Guarujá. That's what I heard. Everyone's ticked off, nobody talks, they just whisper. Lordy!" He crossed himself.

Greta wondered whether or not she should ask any more questions. What if the dwarf were offended? She took a bite and praised his baking. Pasquim acted as if he hadn't heard her and tossed the plates into a washbasin.

Greta stood up, her head nearly touching the ceiling.

"Thank you for your hospitality: your trailer's very cozy, and I hope you can visit me, too." She put out her hand.

The dwarf squinted, a saucy look on his face, adjusted his trousers, and unbuttoned his checkered shirt.

"Want to fool around? The bed is clean and Pops here is a real artist." He winked.

Greta felt panicked. Her face was visibly flushed with indignation. She quickly tried to regain her self-control and not show she was offended, mortified.

"See you, Pasquim. I have to go." She placed a foot on the stairs.

The animal tamer appeared at that moment. He looked the visitor over from head to toe.

She hurried back to Palm Street. A blazing sun. Her head hot. She should never have gone to that place. Never.

She walked into her yard, exhausted, when she heard someone calling her. Who could it be? She had never seen the woman before.

"My name is Ângela. I'm Alexandre Ribeiro's sister."

"Oh, glad to meet you. Come on in."

"I apologize for dropping by unannounced, but my husband's car was available because he's in Araraquara today. And I wanted to talk to you about the Village. Since my uncle died, well . . ."

"Sit down. I was very fond of old Ananias."

"I know." She looked up. "How much is his house worth?"

"I couldn't tell you. I have no idea."

"It must be worth a bundle."

"Your brother might know. After all, he lives there."

"That's just the problem. Uncle Ananias left it to both of us. He moved in and he's never paid me rent or anything else. And he's not planning to leave . . ."

"Oh!"

"We're facing serious difficulties. My husband is an economist and he hasn't been able to find a job since he graduated and quit the bank where he was working. A client made a commitment to him but at the last minute . . ."

"Those things happen."

"Until now I haven't minded Alexandre staying here, because the assessment wasn't completed. But I went to ask Fortuna about it and they said that selling it would be very complicated and that I should work things out with my brother. Why is it so complicated?"

"All the residents have an agreement regarding buying and selling. No one has a clear title. If you can find a buyer who'll accept the same conditions, I see no problem at all. In case you're interested, Fortuna is counting on the approval of a zoning ordinance that would allow the construction of apartment buildings in the Village, on the other side of the Avenue. If that actually happens, anybody who wants to will be able to exchange his house or lot for an apartment. I'm pretty sure you and your brother could ask for two small apartments."

Ângela had a distant look on her face. Tall, dark, with lustrous flowing black hair, about thirty, attractive.

"Live in the same building with him? God help me. Alexandre has been nothing but trouble for us. He's short-tempered. He's always ordering people around, he has to have his way. He's unbearable. I'm prepared to get this house business over once and for all, no matter what. Can you believe he doesn't have a single friend in Araraquara?

163

Not one. Can't you tell what kind of a person he is? I don't know where he got this crazy idea to run for city council. He's barking up the wrong tree. Who would vote for him? The artists? I doubt it."

". . ."

"The only thing I'm worried about is he could go deeply into debt. An election campaign costs a ton of money. The property is all we have. My father owns a neighborhood grocery store and he barely gets by."

Greta offered her guest a glass of passion fruit juice.

"I picked the fruit in the garden early this morning. It's so hot out . . ."

"What do you think I should do?"

"Wait another month. By that time the situation with Fortuna will be clear."

The two women, quiet, sipped the juice.

"Won't your brother give you and your husband any help at all?"

Ângela finished the rest of her juice in one swallow.

"Help? Are you kidding? He's always been peculiar. Since he was a kid. When he was in high school I was going steady with his best friend. They used to study together. Every month they'd take turns being number one. They challenged each other. I mean, Juca was the challenge. My brother had to do better than his friend; that was the most important thing. Even if it meant cheating. Juca's best subject was Portuguese. Alex's was geometry. For one of the final exams, my brother purposely taught Juca the wrong way to draw perspective. Juca knew all the rules, but he couldn't find the point of convergence. It was such an important exam, and Alex screwed his own friend so he would get only a B while Alex himself made sure he got an A. It was Juca who told me about my brother's dirty tricks."

Greta laughed. Strange; as an adult he appears to be following the same behavior patterns. He wants to be better than Antônio, even though he's completely out of the picture; more than just being a good representative, he wants to outshine his predecessor, as if he represented a challenge.

"Later on, when he opened a painting studio," Ângela continued, "there were two other artists who gave him a lot of assistance; they shared the rent and bought canvases, paint, and brushes together. The first chance he got he double-crossed them by holding an exhibition of just his own paintings. He called his fellow painters mediocre and worse behind their backs. No one could ever understand his need to drag others down to make himself look good. I think the people he admires the most are those he wants to destroy. I don't know a damned thing about psychoanalysis, but I assume there must be some meaning . . . The other artists are doing great, they live in Rio. One of them, Ari, is married to a cousin of mine. He won the National Salon Prize this year! Alex must have been beside himself! That's probably why he's decided to run for office, so he can gain power and look just as important as his old friend. If he couldn't have it as an artist, he'll try to find another way."

"If he worked at it, Alexandre could be a fine artist. He has talent."

"There was a time when I cared about that. I even bought one of his paintings at an exhibition. You know what he did? After I had the thing framed, he asked to borrow it one day, and he sold it without saying a word. A year later he admitted it. Anyway, enough of that. I need to resolve this matter of the house. Thanks for your advice. It won't hurt to be patient and wait another month."

Greta was sorry to see Ângela leave. She seemed like an intelligent person. She walked her to the gate.

"Do you work?"

"I'm a teacher. This year I'm going to work on my Master's thesis. Oh my, it's nearly one o'clock. Bye."

The neighbors' chauffeur was watering the garden, the black car shining in the driveway. Greta approached him.

"Before you go, Mário, can I give you some bills to deliver to the lawyer?"

"No problem."

"Have you heard from them?"

"Their lawyer thinks they won't be back until next month. Sônia's mother is sick, some problem with her heart."

"Really?"

"Yes, ma'am. They took her to the hospital."

"That's too bad."

News Greta hadn't been expecting. Elisa had gotten sick in Switzerland.

The afternoon was unproductive. No matter how hard she tried Greta was unable to concentrate. Total panic over tomorrow's meeting. On the one hand fear and on the other hope. The emotional seesaw. The whistle of a far-off train in her memory. Why? A fast train.

When all is said and done, what does Leonardo mean to her? They hadn't established any bonds. A few pleasant times together. Nothing more. A calm, fulfilled man, tied to married life. And what about her? A love-starved woman who was foolish enough to place her happiness in his hands. An absolutely irrational act. The future passed her by. It was yesterday, don't you see, Tina? At this very moment Leonardo and Sofia are probably locked in an embrace of mutual trust and forgiveness. Greta's heart beats faster, ashamed to think she may have interfered in their union, coming between them like a selfish and random probability. What audacity to create a climate of romance . . . If she weren't involved she would feel neither jealous nor hurt. Jealous of their shadow glimpsed in the distance, walking arm in arm down the city streets. Smiling, together again.

Greta rubs her sore neck with a damp cloth and looks in the mirror: what does she see? The wrinkles of passion, insomnia, loneliness. The wrinkles of folly. Today she'll need a tranquilizer. An overwhelming need to sleep, to forget everything, to plunge into the void, into the world's hollow center. Not to have a head or trunk or limbs. Not to be; the pill stuck in her throat. She took another swallow of water.

The living room in darkness? She hadn't noticed that night had fallen; she turned on the lights. Had she fallen asleep? Her stomach ached with hunger. Eight o'clock. She hadn't even eaten lunch. Her nerves were frayed: her circus experience, the visit from Alexandre's sister, the news from Switzerland, fear. She tried not to think about what new lunacy tomorrow will bring; she picked up an apple and ate it without washing it.

Night whispers in the kitchen. Leaves rustle. The wind murmurs softly. Nocturnal verbs, what preciousness. Has anyone ever tried to listen to the night? Ah, you will say, hark the sound of the stars. Of course, the poets. The poets listen. You can easily get your fill of silly clichés, right Tina?—Greta laughed out loud. And her laughter echoed through the Village like a scream. The circus animals became restless again. And the church bells tolled ominously. At this hour?—she looked toward Camilo's house. The old man was closing his window. Naturally he had a foreboding of something alien. The bells never rang at night.

🔔 Brunella's Restaurant was nearly empty. On the other hand, the adjacent ice cream and pastry shop had long lines of young people with colorful clothing and souped-up motorcycles. Greta chose a table for two against the wall in the glass-enclosed dining room. Four o'clock. Sofia appeared, dressed completely in hospital white, her face without a speck of make-up. Greta dried her sweating hands on the napkin before greeting her affectionately.

"I'm sorry I had to make you come all the way into the city."

Greta gave her a concerned look. Or was it dramatic? The anxiety visible in her air of expectancy. Sofia, however, seemed unexpectedly calm.

"I called you because I've had no time to go to the Village. Besides, I haven't the slightest desire to set foot there. I'm very confused."

The waiter approached: Sofia insisted on having tea and Greta ordered a large sundae.

"Well," Sofia went on, "Leonardo and I have been going through a period of crisis, as you know. And we haven't been able to resolve it. At the moment he's on a trip; he went to see his family. I've been staying at the hospital or at Mama's house. After I heard the horrible news about that Tancredi, good heavens, I'm not about to spend a single minute alone in the house. I'm terrified of being robbed. I don't know how you . . ."

A couple came into the dining area. The girl couldn't make up her mind: where should we sit? The boy led her to the back of the room.

"I'm going to be totally frank and I want you to be, too, Greta. I know all about your affair with Leonardo. He told me. We're honest with each other. For my part, I confessed my extra-marital fling . . ."

"What was his reaction?"

"Obviously, he was upset. But he understood. If he could fall in love with you he recognized that I also might be capable of becoming involved with someone else. He was, however, unhappy about my choice, a surgeon, a colleague of mine."

"I thought you and Ribeiro . . ."

A detail Greta had failed to notice, the doctor had a nervous tic: she continually blinked her left eye. Maybe because she was under a great deal of strain.

"What? That was out of pure despair. I was trying to get over my affair with the surgeon. Alexandre is such a vain fellow. He sometimes tries to act like a rabbit, but he does a lousy job of it. He's not even worth discussing."

Greta's innermost feeling about the revelations was shock. She could never be so brazen herself.

"You must be dying to know why I'm telling you all this, right?"

She took a huge bite of the ice cream to avoid answering.

"It's important you understand that Leonardo and I have had a wonderful life together. Our marriage suddenly began falling apart. Out of boredom, monotony, several factors, I can't even recall what they were, but problems intrinsic to the institution of marriage, I think. Just like I became involved with another man, he became involved with one of his patients a few years ago. Both times we managed to get past the mistake because we were able to admit that we had let things slip emotionally. Neither of us is possessive like most people."

Sofia slowly spread jelly on her toast.

"You don't own the other person, do you?" she continued.

"That depends." Greta nearly choked. "It's not a question of owning. It's a matter of keeping what you want for yourself."

"Maybe. At any rate, things got very complicated this time around. We lost our mutual trust. We're touchy, easily irritated. We tried a week at the beach to see if we could find a way to be compatible again, but it was a disaster. We argued over the silliest things. Which means either we're still connected or . . ."

"The exact opposite? I'm more inclined to believe in the first hypothesis."

An uneasy pause. Sofia propped her head on her left hand, took a sip of tea, and looked at Greta inquisitively.

"Do you love him?"

The other woman, blushing down to the roots of her hair, breathed deeply and then concurred; Sofia seemed to be analyzing Greta, as if she distrusted her response.

"Funny. I thought you were so detached from the world you'd never fall in love."

"I wish your impression were true. I wouldn't feel so unhappy."

"What do you intend to do? Stay with him at all cost?"

"No, Sofia. I'm obsessive, I fall head over heels, but . . . After the obsession I do an about-face and accept defeat. I give up. Right now I'm wavering between a terrible sense of guilt and the certainty of failure."

"I know the feeling."

"Leonardo stated explicitly that he had no intention of seeking a separation, that he was confident he could resolve the crisis."

"He said that the last time you were together? There's been a lot of water over the dam . . ." Her statement faded.

Sofia chewed her toast in silence. For a brief moment her spirit was far away and only her body was there at Brunella's.

"Can I ask you a favor, Greta?"

"Whatever you want."

"First, I'm going to be a bit indiscreet so you'll understand the reason for my request. Leonardo told me that of all the women in his life you're the one he's been happiest with sexually."

Greta was shocked by the confession. He went too far. How absurd.

"And that's a very important point, especially for men. He swears that it isn't," she checked Greta's reaction, "but I know it is. Just as it is for women. We've gotten along so beautifully in the past, as I've told you, and that's why I'd like some credit for our relationship. I've broken up with the surgeon and chosen Leonardo. I'm waiting for him to come back so I can inform him of my decision."

"What's the favor?"

"Not to see Leonardo while we're putting our marriage back together."

"Relax, Sofia. He won't even try to see me."

She knew in her heart that Sofia had a right to make such a request. It was a gesture of humility, an attempt to . . .

"He may want to talk to you to reach an understanding. But a conversation I had with my surgeon almost drove me back into his arms for good. Situations like that are touchy; they really get to you. Especially when you're as infatuated as I am."

"Then . . ."

"As I told you, Greta, it's not right to end a relationship sense-lessly. Leonardo and I have a chance to be happy."

"I understand. You don't want to give up a sure thing for some-thing so uncertain."

"It's not that. It's a matter of common sense. I care about him.

The fact that I fell in love with my colleague means nothing; it changes nothing."

Greta thought about how she could never comprehend such an attitude. If you're capable of feeling passion for someone else, it means you're free and clear when it comes to love. She couldn't see the distinction. Love exists, or . . . She must be a narrow-minded bumpkin.

"Do you agree with my request?"

She did.

"You're not very convincing."

Greta smiled.

"You can trust me."

"I know I can. Thank you."

"What about the house?"

"I'm going to cancel the lease, pay the penalties . . ."

"Your office in the *favela* . . ."

"I'll keep it open. I can't abandon those people. But if I had to, I'd find someone to replace me."

She attempted to pour more tea.

"The pot's empty. It's time to go. Is there anything you want to say to me?"

"No."

The two women stood up. The waiter brought the check, which Sofia insisted on paying. Once in the street they went in opposite directions. Sofia felt serene after her direct approach. Greta returned to the Village dejected and uncertain about what she should do in the light of their conversation. The doctor's frankness, her straightforward approach, somehow hurt and offended her. As if Sofia were master of two puppets, she and Leonardo, and had decided to take them out of the shop window to comb their hair and dress them. They had no will of their own. Dummies sitting on the lap of the all-powerful ventriloquist, who exposed them to open view, allowing them no secrets, no inner life.

🔔 The twenty-ninth day of December. The circus was dismantled. In a few hours, all that was left of the tent and the caravan were tracks on the ground, which the next rain would wash away. Unless the space were rented out again—anything is possible—anyone passing by on the Avenue would think the circus merely the result of an overwrought imagination. Meanwhile, everybody is aware of its brief but indelible presence in the Village of the Bells. Especially the circus people, who will not soon forget the experience.

Pasquim came happily over to Palm Street. Not to say good-bye to Greta but to bid farewell to Suzi, Antônio's daughter, his young friend. She vowed to the dwarf that she would become a circus artist. No matter what.

"That's fine, Suzi, but you'd be better off in theater, music, or the movies. Anything. The circus isn't worth it."

She embraced him with tears in her eyes. The circus was a revelation to that sensitive ten-year-old girl.

Last night of the year. Greta is preparing dinner. Her heart heavy and sad. Why? Even the strongest can be shaken on sentimental occasions. New Year's Eve is one of them; she smooths out the openwork tablecloth, reserved for festivities. Even if she has to dine alone, it's essential to maintain the ritual. Under her skin, Greta could feel the loneliness, exposed by the banal sound of silverware and dishes echoing in the room. And if she were to turn on the television? She would hear human voices; she set the table carefully. A place for her, another for Leonardo. Physically absent, present in her imagination. She turned on the set. An American musical on the tube. In the kitchen she tended to the roast pork baking in the oven. Celery and shrimp salad. Rice with cooked vegetables. Hungry, her stomach rumbles. Now all she needed to do was to dress; she went to the bedroom.

At eleven o'clock she sat at the table. Nude.

"How can you dress sadness?"

Tina, pressed against the window, peeks at the canvas Hopper would love to have painted. Pink linen tablecloth, transparent glass china, purple begonias in the vase. Body white and naked, blond hair undone, flower behind her ear. Dream-like atmosphere. On the white wall behind Greta, a dramatic collage and the partially opened blinds completed the painting.

"Sometimes you can be sufficient unto yourself. Even if you have to turn on the television."

The musical's climax. The singer, in spite of attempts to make her glamorous, in spite of her false teeth, was insipid, artificial, and although she stayed in tune, her singing was lousy. Patience. Nothing's perfect.

All at once Greta's mood lightened. The roast was delicious, the Beaujolais sublime. Living in the here-and-now is more important than digging up old memories or fantasizing about the future. I have a name, whether I like it or not. I am somebody.

"Happy New Year, Greta Cristina de Almeida."

♤ A telegram from Switzerland. "Sorrowfully regret announce Mama passed away 2nd stop Sônia." Greta folded the telegram, grief-stricken. And she went to share the news with their friends.

Camilo started to formulate an idea he didn't finish: old people have no options left. Something like that.

Late in the afternoon they all gathered at Elisa's for a symbolic memorial. Antônio suggested to the group of friends that they hold a seventh-day mass. Maybe Clotilde could make arrangements with the Village representative. The homeowners association would officially sponsor the mass. If he rejects the idea we'll contribute on our own . . .

"I haven't seen Alexandre around here for two weeks. He vanished after the circus packed up and left," Clotilde said.

"He's an odd fellow. New Year's he wasn't in the Village, but yesterday I saw him coming out of his house. He was looking behind him suspiciously to check and see if he was being followed," Camilo remarked. "I offered him a ride but he declined. By the way, when will the homeowners association meeting be?"

"Let me find out. Altair wants to sell his house. He's already asked me about the meeting two or three times." Greta took a deep breath. "Wait a few days. I overheard someone at Fortuna say the deed problem will be straightened out in a few days. Unfortunately, a few of us are missing, what with Soares at the beach and Sônia in Europe."

"On the other hand," Clotilde sat up straighter, "a lot more people are upset. That foreign family was incensed over Tancredi's death. The couple and their children have overcome their apathy and they're ready to fight. They wrote the representative a letter demanding that a night watchman be hired."

The residents who never wanted to get involved will soon be up in arms. You can bet on it.

"Fortuna has authorized the hiring and will cover half the expenses. But Ribeiro has failed to take the necessary steps."

Dilermando Canudos looked around.

"Do you think Sônia will stay on here, now that she's alone?"

Painful silence. No one ventured a guess, perhaps fearing the worst.

After they had all left, Greta shuttered the house. As if there were a living human being inside. At least that is what she felt.

♧ An exhibition in the Gallery of Fame. A collective showing of primitive artists from the town of Embu, famous for its arts and crafts. The theme: wakes and funerals. Greta smiled: an amusing idea; she threw away the invitation. Intelligent black humor.

♧ A frenzied longing for Leonardo. Total defeat?

The dead converse in dreams with the living. Last night Greta spoke for a long time with Elisa. She laid her head in her lap and cried.

♧ A meeting at Fortuna. The municipal zoning law was approved only in part. The Village of the Bells wouldn't get any assistance. So much money and time spent to no avail. Now the situation is very serious. The note matures in March. Either they pay up or they lose the land. The financial officer is tense. Maybe it's possible to get an extension. The moment the home-owning families find out and start making demands all hell will break loose. They may even have the directors put in jail.

"We must at all cost avoid a scandal so we can protect our other investments," Barbosa argued.

Pimenta, the financial officer, mumbled to Greta out of earshot of the others.

"Why don't we offer the owners those apartments in the Perdizes district?"

"That large building?"

"That's the one. The building's been up for sale for years. The market is terrible and we haven't made many sales. That building is worth a lot more per square foot than the Village, but we shouldn't be so greedy that we ruin the Company's reputation."

Greta screwed up her courage and asked for silence.

"After speaking with our very capable financial officer, I believe he has a suggestion to make, which has my backing."

Now that he had Greta's support, Almeida cleared his throat, sat up straight, and, stammering, explained the idea. He was aware of the other members' positions regarding the firm's recent experience with real estate.

"We may lose some money. Even so, it's better than being arrested or losing our credibility," Greta completed the proposal forcefully, facing the directors. "Not even the Cemetery of the Flowers could stand up to public scrutiny."

The president straightened his tie, a typical gesture when he's dealing with an important matter.

"I agree in principle, Greta. We have to prepare an economic and financial plan to study the feasibility of . . ."

"If you wish I can consult with the association members. Many people dislike the Village representative. I could act as intermediary. That would be my contribution to Fortuna."

The directors looked at her in disbelief. *Is it possible she's coming over to our side?*

"It doesn't mean I'm moving out. Right now there's not the slightest chance of that. I'll act as intermediary because I feel responsible for the Village residents. I know how much those people sacrificed to buy their property and to what degree they were deceived by the advertising and by the firm. With few exceptions, maybe half a dozen, most of them are people struggling to make ends meet. They've had to give up so much just to make the monthly payments. By the way, Pimenta, they're all up to date, aren't they?"

The financial officer concurred.

"The last few who were behind in their payments got caught up in December."

"Isn't it obvious Fortuna has to clarify its position?" Greta looked sternly at those in attendance. "What has cousin Oscar been up to now that he no longer comes to the meetings?"

No one knew. His participation was needed for final approval. Without his consent—he was an attorney—no decision could be made.

"We'll ask Oscar's opinion at the proper time."

Greta stopped by the building in Perdizes before returning to Palm Street. She checked out an apartment. Yes, it was good enough to offer in exchange. The construction was of indisputable quality. The view in both directions from all four wings of the building was delightful—on smogless days, it goes without saying. Only eighty of the two hundred and twenty two-bedroom apartments were occupied. The Village homeowners would do quite well.

Traffic was flowing normally. Why couldn't it always be that way? It was a breeze to drive in São Paulo during the holidays, what with more than a million people having left the city. She would be home in less than half an hour. The light turned red, allowing Greta to look for a radio station to her liking. Her eyes were burning. The way things were going, the residents of São Paulo would soon have to wear gas masks when they went out. The light turned yellow. She looked in the rearview mirror and caught a glimpse of Leonardo in the car behind her. Her heart leapt in her breast. She wasn't sure whether she should let him see her or pretend . . . She shifted gears and drove on without giving it a second thought. Leonardo passed right by her and turned at the corner.

It took some time to recover emotionally. So, he was in the city. An infinite sadness came over her. They would have no further opportunity for explanations, for understanding. All those mental conversations, rehearsed and modified, came crashing down. How discouraging.

She turned into Palm Street, feeling miserable, and failed to notice Ângela coming out of Alexandre's house. She missed the apartment building. It was ugly but it was part of the landscape, and besides, that was where Míriam lived.

Suddenly she remembered a dream from the previous night. Míriam was waving to her from her apartment window and showing off her dolls, now grown. The three of them were oddly adult yet dressed in the same clothing, and they were also waving excitedly. They looked like actors about to go on stage: Daisy, the peasant girl, with her braided hood; Elizabeth, the English lady from 1800; and Horácio with his velvet suit. They were greeting each other affectionately when all at once Greta noticed a gigantic machine, a steamroller, heading for the building. She gesticulated desperately to Míriam to try to tell her to take cover, but she just laughed, unaware of the danger. The church bells tolled nervously. Greta ran out her door to warn her friend. Through the gate, she saw the steamroller had disappeared. Where the building had stood, a field of daisies swayed in the wind.

🔔 If it weren't for her, would the Village of the Bells exist? She looked indecisively at the stack of paper. She wasn't satisfied with the way the story was going. She could after all go back and disguise the truth and come up with another version—so many had occurred to her! The overwhelming certainty that at this point everything was irrevocably determined. In the beginning her approach was that of a photographer who is about to make her prints without being sure how the pictures will turn out. The image slowly appeared, began to take form, became absolutely clear. Impossible not to be true to the facts. She did after all go from one reality to another—perhaps that suggests total madness. In a certain way the Village was part of a real-life system. That's it. She couldn't triumph by deception. That would be implausible. The Village is stuck with the limitations of its geographical location. As are the inhabitants. Unfortunately. She turned out the light, determined to sleep.

And if she were to try?

♤ Greta was awake all night. In the morning she watered the garden and picked some lettuce for lunch. Then she decided to sunbathe on the veranda. She hadn't done that for so long, allow herself the pleasure of sitting around, enjoying a Sunday off . . . If possible, lie there without thinking, her head empty, in limbo. How about some pleasant recollection? What would it be? Mother. The sweet sound of her voice. Her smiling blue eyes. The smell of vaseline on her hands. Her porcelain complexion. No, the image wouldn't come. Instead Greta remembered the preposterous letter Ribeiro sent to the Village residents, informing them that the streetlights had been put in, "thanks to the efforts of Fortuna Construction and Real Estate, a company deeply concerned about the welfare of the community." Unbelievable. Didn't he realize everyone was aware of Clotilde Canudos' influence and Antônio's struggle—for over two years—to get the lights? Why would he lie and say it was his accomplishment? Or Fortuna's? It was most senseless effrontery and at best made him look ridiculous. Not only was he claiming others' accomplishments as his own, he was kissing Fortuna's behind. Too much; Greta turned over on her back. Why bother to remember unimportant things? What she should do was indulge in the pleasure of sunbathing on a quiet Sunday. Blessedly quiet.

A figure floats into her mind: Pablita. The last time she asked Zaíra about her, the maid said she had disappeared and her shanty was empty. Was another character going to escape just like that? Absolutely not. She'll take a walk in the cemetery in the afternoon. The folks over there will have more recent news. And since she'll be in the neighborhood she can take in the new exhibition. Could Pablita still be posing for Alexandre Ribeiro? There's another one who hasn't shown his face for a while. Was he embarrassed about the failure of the circus? Had Tancredi's death affected him more than it did his neighbors? You never know. Or maybe the reason . . . Of course, he was just avoiding calling a meeting of the homeowners association because he was afraid people would blame him for Tancredi's death— he had failed to hire a night watchman. Poor fellow. He's not to blame. No one dies before his time. Any home could have been robbed. Any of them. If Tancredi's was singled out . . .

The doorbell interrupted her thoughts. Greta wrapped herself in a towel. It was the newspaper boy asking if she wanted to renew her subscription.

After lunch Greta put on a white tunic and went for a walk. It was a clear Sunday, not a cloud in the sky. Camilo and Ivo—the house was shuttered—doubtless had gone out with Mirna. Leonardo's garage was filled with dry leaves. The foreigners, sitting on their veranda, waved to her and she returned their greeting. Antônio was taking his nap on the lawn. Where might Jane and the children be?

Greta, perspiring, entered the gallery. Damn, it was hot! Some of the pictures were of the commercial variety, done by people who had studied painting but had only learned to copy the recipe mechanically; nevertheless, most of the works were interesting. The primitive artists, in their depictions of wakes and funerals, showed humor and a certain euphoria in the colors. Only one painter, Egas or Egon, she couldn't read it clearly, used heavy, dark tones, revealing an expressionist tendency: a woman, covered by a gray shroud, lying in a black coffin; deformed, empty chairs; beside the casket, a cross-eyed, ragged child. Greta asked the receptionist for the price and requested that it be delivered as soon as the exhibition was over.

"You'll receive the picture at the end of the month, ma'am. You see how well we're doing? Just yesterday I sold three pictures. We've also had six funerals."

The guard sat placidly on the stairs smoking.

"Working in the afternoon, Sebastião?"

"I ain't on duty. But the good woman's gone out and I didn't have nothing to do at home . . . It's a lot more fun hanging around here than in the *favela*. Joca's on duty now. He's the one with the cart. Wanna talk to him?"

"No thank you. I wanted to find out about Pablita."

The guard spat and adjusted the uniform cap on his head. Greta noticed that his deep wrinkles were lined with black dust. Even if he washed his face, that dust could never be removed. The same dark tracks were visible on his dry, cracked hands.

"I heard she wound up with some guy runs a numbers game and owns a night club near downtown São Paulo. She does a strip act. One of the boys said she was doing real good. And you know, ma'am, she deserves it. She's a swell person."

"Has she been able to find something for any of her friends?"

"Yeah, for Constantino, the blond guy; he was real tight with her. Everybody else is jealous as all get out."

Greta wondered if the old man was beginning to adopt the gestures of a transvestite, which didn't suit him at all. She thanked him for the information and said good-bye.

She ran into the representative when she got to Palm Street. Alexandre Ribeiro gave her a defiant look.

"How's it going? I've just seen the exhibition."

"In the end, my ideas always work out," he sneered.

She considered asking him what he meant by "in the end," but he didn't give her time.

"I'm tired of people undermining my plans. Were you the one who interfered with the amusement park contract?"

"Me? Of course not."

"After you went to Fortuna, they suspended all my projects. Either you or somebody else tried to block me."

Really, the fellow must be crazy. So much fuss over nothing.

"Fortuna has dozens of undertakings. The Village of the Bells is rather insignificant . . ."

"I hear you've been going around trying to convince people to exchange their property for an apartment in Perdizes . . ."

"That's true. Speaking of which, I looked for you yesterday. I'm only checking to see if people are interested."

"Who gave you the authority to do that? I seem to recall I'm the Village representative."

Greta laughed tolerantly.

"You are our representative. But that doesn't mean you're the owner . . ."

He started to make an angry gesture but thought better of it.

"Don't think I'm going to consent to this. I like it here and I have no plans to move."

Greta responded disdainfully to the representative's hostility.

"Be that as it may, your sister did show enthusiasm."

Alexandre Ribeiro was livid with rage. Could he be unaware of the fact that the two women speak with each other? In any case, he'd never let on.

"I'll be the one to work things out with my sister."

"Great. If everything works out the way we hope, no one will lose any money and there'll be a fair return on the investment."

Greta sensed the representative was unaware of what was going on. Was it possible that not a single kind soul had informed him of the dispute over the title deeds?

Ribeiro realized that she was talking about something he had no knowledge of, and decided to end the conversation.

Greta went into her house and sprawled on the sofa. Jesus, she's not as young as she used to be. A simple little walk and she comes back huffing and puffing.

Tonight she finished reading *The Unicorn*. Too bad. It's so rare you come across a good book. Iris Murdoch is one of her favorite authors. She'll have to ask Sônia to bring back other titles for her. Few have been published in Brazil. She'll address the letter to the attorney and have him forward it. And at the same time she can explain the exchange. Now that her mother is dead, would Sônia want to continue living in the Village? Unlikely. Who would take care of the garden?

 Empty days. The meeting at Fortuna was postponed: the feasibility study wasn't completed yet.

Clotilde and Dilermando Canudos bought a small farm in Ibiúna, thirty miles from São Paulo.

"The Village just brings us misfortune, Greta. So many friends absent or dead. Violence, uncertainty. One accident we can put up with, more than one . . ."

"What if the apartment idea works out?"

"We can rent it out. I would never live in the city." Clotilde blew her nose. "I'm allergic to pollution; I hate the traffic. I've worked so hard, I deserve a little rest. I have an agreement with the factory to come twice a week. It's best not to fool around at age sixty, don't you think?"

"Sixty? You look much younger."

"I know where my shoe pinches."

"So when are you planning on moving?"

"The end of the month. We're having the house painted. I haven't felt so excited in years, Greta. Not since we came to the Village. The farm is lovely."

"We're all going to miss you."

"Ibiúna isn't far away. I'll always come back to visit. What about you, are you intent on staying here?"

"What choice do I have? Besides, I like Palm Street."

Clotilde felt a surge of affection as she contemplated her friend. Greta looked dejected. Maybe she felt down about the stampede out of the Village. But everybody had to watch out for himself.

Camilo and Ivo were coming back from their physical therapy session, which gave Greta an excuse to take her leave.

But she would not go see them. She was tired and extremely discouraged. Clotilde and Dilermando, what a loss. The Village had deteriorated much faster than she had imagined.

△ Greta, wrapped in a blanket, felt an urge to take stock of her life. As if looking back would erase the scars from her memory. But they can't be erased. No one is reborn. The simple act of recognizing the wounds changes nothing. Destiny mapped out since conception. Family history engraved in stone. She would never be an autonomous, complete being; only a part of the whole. Thus the conflicts. When this first dawned on her: revolt, criticism, insecurity. Later, more mature: acceptance. Would she have been different with another genetic background? Her mind wandered, lost in conjecture. Could this question in fact be the motive for her neurotic search for identity? It wasn't. She was merely trying to avoid thinking about Leonardo, about the rejection she felt, about her shattered self-image. An uncontrollable desire to put off her feelings, the consequence of anger, shame, sorrow. A man and a woman in need of love, briefly joined. Wasn't that explanation sufficient? Why this insistence on a happy ending? It was good while it lasted, period. She wanted more, much more. That was the basis of her suffering. She was insatiable.

I'm going to forget everything for a few days, Greta promised herself. The Village and its insoluble dramas, the world drowning in a sea of troubles, and she, sitting there in her warm and cozy living room, foundering in matters of little importance. Does it make any sense?

△ February. Greta went to extreme lengths to set up the meeting at Fortuna. She had made a commitment to the residents, and Barbosa stated categorically that as soon as the feasibility studies were approved he would let her know. No use putting the cart before the horse. She tried to argue that Ribeiro was going from house to house and insidiously trying to talk the residents out of the exchange and making outrageous promises. Barbosa, at the other end of the line, chuckled in satisfaction. Which Greta noticed. Could the representative be scheming with Fortuna? In what way? Or to what end?

Greta had a dream about Mateus. A peculiar dream. She saw him living in a kind of cellar, with a child on his lap—his son? He was sitting in a rocking chair feeding the child with a false rubber breast made from the tip of a nursing bottle. She woke up in the middle of the night and wrote a long short story. A novelette? She's not certain yet. A story that poured out, tortured, confused. Some day she'll do something with it. She filled several writing tablets. As if it weren't she but Mateus writing through her hands. A first-person narrative. The point of view of a man overcoming the frustrations of his feminine side through a maternal experience.

Dreams and fantasies are so enigmatic. For days and nights— interspersed with short periods of sleep—a man took her place. But the question is this: did he, Mateus, want to be a woman, or did she want to be a man?

If she doesn't stop thinking and trying to find an explanation for everything fiction can suggest, she'll get sick. Just like Tina.

Clotilde and Dilermando Canudos' send-off was a noisy one. All the women on Palm Street showed up at the farewell party. Clotilde promised to keep selling products from her factory at cost and participating in the homeowners association meetings as long as the question of the deeds went on.

The next day, Sunday morning, Sônia returned from Europe in the company of a Swiss friend. Doris, an odd sort. At first one couldn't tell if she was a man or a woman. Skinny, with her hair cropped. And she wouldn't look anyone in the eye. Shy, perhaps.

Sônia was also thinner; Greta looked her friend over as she sat next to the foreign woman on the couch. She couldn't explain why, but Sônia seemed harder and her conversation somewhat scornful. She spoke matter-of-factly of her mother's illness, as if her death had been a relief. She turned frequently to Doris, who understood but didn't speak Portuguese. Looks exchanged revealed intimacy. She talked about the joys of traveling to Holland—the country she most admired—where she had met her friend, and about their subsequent trips to Germany and Austria.

Greta hesitated asking about Luís, since Sônia herself didn't mention him. But she screwed up her courage.

"Luís? He got married. To a French journalist. He's living in Paris now."

And she tried to change the subject, after she checked to see if the Swiss woman had reacted in any way. Doris chain smoked. One cigarette after another, her teeth yellow with nicotine stains. An expressive, tense face.

"Doris is a choreographer. We're hoping she can find work in Brazil. She has quite a background. In any case, whether or not she finds anything I've promised to produce a show for her." She winked affectionately. "And how are things going in the Village?"

Greta gave her the news, good and bad. Sônia was sorry she hadn't received the letter requesting the books and informing her of the exchange offered by Fortuna.

"We could never live here in the Village, could we, Doris?"

The other woman shrugged her shoulders.

"Don't mind her. She's a little unfriendly when you first meet her. I don't know what I would have done without her. She's a wonderful person."

Greta indicated she understood and offered a glass of wine. Doris accepted by nodding her head. Greta went to get things ready. Where was the corkscrew? She looked in the kitchen. My god—her sigh was prolonged—what a grim scene. Why so nervous? Just as she returned to serve the wine she saw Sônia and Doris locked in an embrace. One with her head on the other's shoulder. For a moment she was unsure if she should walk in on them or . . . Sônia sensed her presence and went out to meet her, searching for something in her purse. She dumped the contents on the chest of drawers. A small black box rolled on the floor.

"Here it is," she bent down, "just what I was looking for. You've been a generous friend, taking care of my house like that. I'm very grateful."

Greta accepted the box, served the glasses of wine, and after the welcoming toasts she opened the present: a gold coin, and on it were stamped the images of Pope Pius XII and the Vatican. Date, 1958.

"Fabulous."

"About five ounces. I bought it from an uncle of mine who lives in a perpetual state of panic; he's terrified of war and thinks a Russian invasion is imminent. He invests all he can in gold. Isn't that insane? He's eighty years old."

Greta smiled and thanked her effusively for the gift.

♧ An exercise in concentration. The images emerge, they are selected, noted down. Besides the story of the man (Mateus) and the child, another one was suggested by Sônia and Doris. Greta is overcome by a feeling that there is something indecent about going to the window and invading the privacy of the neighbor women. A sudden feeling. Why?

Heavy downpour. Summer rain. The church bells tolled tragically. As if they were playing a pavan.

"Have you seen old Camilo lately, Miss Greta?"

"Of course, Zaíra. At least once a week. His schedule has changed because of the physical therapy. Sometimes he's away for quite a while. Why do you ask?"

"He was real depressed yesterday. He could barely walk."

"Really? It's a good thing you told me. I'll drop by in the afternoon."

The cleaning woman was dusting the living room.

"You can leave the table alone because I clean it myself."

Greta paced back and forth while she waited for the maid to finish cleaning.

"Tell me something, Zaíra. Is Doctor Sofia still running her clinic in the poor neighborhood?"

The domestic stuck the feather duster under her arm.

"She comes every other day. She's been bringing a male doctor recently, and they divide up the patients. Dr. Castro. He's one of them doctors do operations. Nice fellow."

"Do they charge much?"

"Hardly nothing. Just enough to buy stuff they need for the office. They even give away medicine for free. Dr. Castro's real cute. And a real good doctor. He operated on my Junior's hernia."

"I see."

Camilo was sitting in a chair and reading when Greta arrived.

"How's everything, Ivo?"

The boy drooled happily and clapped his hands. She took a piece of chocolate out of her purse and gave it to him.

"Are you ill, Camilo?"

"No, I'm getting old. I tire so easily. I get queasy riding in a car. Mirna rented a cottage for us near her home."

Greta said nothing. She had hoped that one day that would happen. It would be much better for the old man.

"I don't know if I should feel happy or sad," he went on. "I've lived in the Village for ten years. I've gotten used to the quiet here. But . . . I think everybody will get out eventually, don't you? At least our friends. Antônio came over to see me yesterday. You can't imagine how distressed he is. His mattress factory is in difficulty."

"I didn't think he had any financial problems."

"Everybody does, Greta, with Brazil's inflationary spiral. Mirna chose to rent a house because the boy . . . going up and down in an elevator with the wheelchair . . . It would be a hardship. The apartment wouldn't do Antônio any good either. It's too small for all his kids. The factory is only fifteen minutes from here, but it would be all the way across the city from the apartment. What a mess. However, if all those people move away, in what kind of a position does that put those who stay?"

"You're right. I'll have to talk to him. Maybe it's time for him, and for the others, to hire a good lawyer. If nothing else to put pressure on Fortuna."

"I wouldn't like to be in your shoes, Greta. I know how unpleasant all of this must be for you."

Greta smiled; unpleasant indeed!

"You know who came over asking for a job?"

"..."

"Carmen Miranda. She's been unemployed since Clotilde left."

"Poor woman."

Camilo rose slowly and, dragging his right foot, went over to the rear window which commanded a view of the foothills bordering the Village.

"I'll never see this countryside again."

Blue mountains backlit on the horizon. Springtime shook the garden's pink flowers. From that perspective, the vegetation covering the Village streets created a patchwork of several shades of green. Birds swooped over the nearest clumps of bushes and flew up to the church belfry. Black and gray birds.

Greta leaned over the windowsill and looked for the Avenue. She had the distinct impression she saw a Ferris wheel turning. There are times fantasy can create miracles.

Camilo asked her to close the blinds. It wouldn't be long before the bells began to toll.

What the old man needed was a lady friend. To rediscover the joy of living.

March. Incensed, Greta walked out of Fortuna's offices. They were a long way from resolving the internal feuding over the excessive profits some of the heirs were earning. The solution was a lawsuit rather than the apartment exchange. But the wheels of justice turn slowly, there were allegations of corrupt judges, and so forth. No one can resist the temptation of money, one of the cousins argued. There are plaintiffs whose cases have dragged on in the courts for fifteen years because the defendants pay to have the verdict postponed. The person who pays the most wins. Let the Village residents be the ones to institute proceedings.

"I'm an attorney. I'll take care of the family property," cousin Oscar blustered. "If the old man had let me see the original charter for the housing project, we wouldn't be in this situation."

"You never paid any attention to Fortuna."

"They wouldn't let me."

Greta used the argument that there would be a scandal if the newspapers published any reports on the matter.

"Scandals in the press are very short-lived and they have little or no impact. Brazilians don't read newspapers. Compare the circulation of our newspapers with that of any American publication."

"What about television?"

"No one makes accusations on TV because you have a right to equal time. Besides, my dear cousin Greta, don't forget that we spend a lot of money on advertising."

Everyone around the table laughed. The Village's problem would be put off. For the umpteenth time.

Greta felt powerless to continue the struggle. She would communicate her opinion personally to the homeowners. Each one would have to do what he thought best. If power corrupts, alienation is equally destructive. Alexandre Ribeiro and his followers, whether lacking scruples or fearful of demanding their rights, would find in Fortuna full support and illusion. Let the conscientious residents unite or act individually. As long as ignorance, cowardice, and venality held sway, real estate companies would continue exploiting good faith, the dream of owning a house, the sacrifices made by naïve individuals, people easily tricked by clever ploys. Once she had fulfilled her duty by sounding the alarm, Greta would withdraw from the fray. Perhaps she, too, would desert the Village.

Those were her thoughts as she drove home. It was the first time she had considered leaving. Which no longer seemed like a tragedy. She had paid so little attention that . . . Her heart speeded up: the lights were on in Leonardo's house.

🔔 My god, at last. She went into her bedroom but left the light off so as not to call attention to her presence. Quickly she combed her hair, checked her clothing, yes, no, she wouldn't change, it's OK; she put on some perfume, went to the living room, turned on a lamp near an old leather chair, and sat down to wait for the doorbell to ring.

Can a minute last an eternity? She sighed. No, it lasts exactly one minute, sixty seconds. No more, no less. Oh, the temptation to get up and look over at the house next door. She would stand there listening to the wind. Camilo once said he no longer noticed the hours or even the days, only the years. She wished she knew if it was worth the trouble . . . Banal questions receive even more banal answers. She gave up. The hands of the clock never stopped moving. One of the shutters began banging desperately against the wall. No, she wouldn't shut it. Let it bang until it broke. Could that noise be what was causing this feeling of anguish? Of course not. Her distress came from the inside out. Alarm, anxiety, hope. Once again a chaotic mix of jumbled up emotions. Untranslatable. She rehearsed so many monologues, so many dialogues, and yet if Leonardo, or her father, were to walk in she wouldn't have a single word to say, her mind blank, shattered, confused. What would Tina do under these circumstances? She doesn't know. Nor does it matter. She, Greta herself, was standing there, standing with all her might, thinking, rationalizing, trying to justify herself. In the age of reason, of human respect, of common sense. This is the honest-to-god truth. She was a sensible person. An adult. There was a time when . . . Was there really? Memory makes everything so distant and inexpressive. Obsession, acts of courage, selfishness . . . What time is it? Five to a short time from now, to nothing or to everything. The anguish is fading. Breathe deeply, try to relax, that's it.

Now, look through the window. The storm has passed. Go and close the window. Quickly. Did you see? Your imagination tricked you. There's no one home next door. Give up this dreaming. Or this suffering in vain.

🔔 "How are you, Soares?" Antônio answered the telephone, a glass of Scotch in his hand. "Are you in São Paulo? . . . You don't say. A what? A residence hotel? Ah . . . Go ahead, I'm listening . . . That sounds fine, room and laundry service, telephone . . . Too bad the apartments are so small . . . Yes, you're right. Later on when the kids are bigger . . . Who knows. It's not going well in the Village. Camilo and the boy are moving this week . . . That's right. The old man was more enthusiastic than anyone . . . No, the exchange business is kind of up in the air. For now things are at a standstill. Greta said that both Alceu and Barbosa are hedging . . . We're back where we started with the deeds. I hired a lawyer, a former judge. He assured me it's a lengthy procedure but there's no question as to our rights . . . If you want I can give you his address . . . We've decided to rent out our house, too . . . Fortuna promised not to create any obstacles. Of course, Gino's widow set the precedent . . . Have you let them know you're going to rent yours out? . . . Good . . . Jane found something in the Alto da Boa Vista district. We're going to make the final arrangements tomorrow with a rental agency. As far as I'm concerned, this is a bad time because of the recession. But what can you do? . . . No, it's not far from the factory. An extra fifteen minutes . . . No, there's no way we can stay here. Even Greta's thinking about throwing in the towel . . . Really!" He took a sip as his friend spoke. He placed the glass on the table and immediately regretted it; he tried to dry the wet spot with his shirt cuff. ". . . Ribeiro? Please, my friend, don't mention his name; it brings bad luck." He knocked three times on the table. "He managed to get the usual cowards involved. We're sick and tired of the way those people react. Not even after Tancredi's death . . . The foreign couple has been talking to Greta. If I'm not mistaken, Schmidt wrote to the homeowners association requesting an urgent meeting . . . We could wait till hell freezes over! . . . Zaíra told me the banner announcing his election campaign has disappeared from the *favela*. Maybe he's dropped out of the race . . . Who knows . . . What's your telephone number? . . . I've got it, Soares. As soon as everything's settled . . . Nor did I. I thought I'd be the last one to leave the Village . . . That's the way it goes . . . Well then, my dear fellow, I'll call you one of these days. I want to beat you the next time we play canasta . . . See you soon." Antônio, gloomy, hung up the phone and remained seated. It was truly unbelievable what had happened. The Village was part of him, his younger children were born there; he swirled the ice in his glass.

"Daddy, Gugu's hittin' me." His smallest child, dressed in pajamas, clung to his legs.

"Where's your mother?"

"Sleepin'."

Antônio broke up the fight, put the children to bed, and went back to his nocturnal Scotch. If it doesn't kill you, it'll make you fat.

♤ Everyday verbs. Someone is always coming or going. A labyrinth that leads all gestures back to the starting point. Sit down, stand up. Open, close. Turn on, turn off. Is there no other way to express movement?

♤ April. Jane walked along Palm Street. So many friends gone. Among the dead and wounded, a survivor, Greta, whom she was on her way to visit, with a cutting from her coffee plant. An ancient promise not yet fulfilled. Signs of desolation reading "for rent" or "for sale." In the once clear turnaround tufts of grass and plants cover the cobblestones on the outer edge of the asphalt, which awaits repaving. Once upon a time Clotilde had managed to get the yearly repairs done, with the help of her brother-in-law, a city official. Never before had the street fallen into such disrepair. Never. Not even the garbage truck has been coming by regularly, a reprisal for the lack of a Christmas bonus; Ribeiro had refused to present it on the community's behalf. Plastic bags have spilled out on the sidewalk. If the residents had known about the refusal, they would have given the bonus on their own. Without question. She found out about it only when she informed the garbage man they were going away for good.

"Darn it, Miz Jane, things are gonna get real bad around here. Everybody's leaving!"

Jane counted mentally: of the first fifty residents, including those in the apartment building, twenty no longer lived in the Village; she rang her friend's doorbell. She noticed there was still no sign in front of Sônia's house.

Greta waved her in from the window. What a surprise.

"Isn't Sônia going to rent out her house?" She pointed.

"I don't know. Doris, her Swiss friend, wasn't too crazy about me. She called to say good-bye. The house is still set up for occupancy. She only took a little furniture and her clothes. Maybe she's coming back."

"I brought your cutting."

"How nice. I always wanted a coffee plant in my yard."

"I planted one at the new house. They say it brings good luck. And that's something we could really use. Antônio is still having trouble with the factory and with moving . . . He's got a nervous stomach and he's been running to the bathroom all day. An awful case of diarrhea."

Greta offered her tea, and as she was preparing it Jane thought about how attractive she looked that afternoon, her hair shiny, her eyes moist. It was beyond Jane how she could live alone the way she did. Greta seemed to read her friend's mind.

"You know, I'll be the one leaving soon." She put down the tray.

"I hope so. The Village doesn't deserve to have you stay."

"When I finish the work I'm doing—I'm almost done—that stack of paper over there, I'll decide."

"What's that picture?"

"A collage I did a few years ago. Like it?"

"A lot."

"Then it's yours. I wasn't sure if I should fill in those white spaces or not. If you think it's good then it's finished."

"I'm glad, Greta."

"I love collages. Written ones and visual ones. A gift for your new home." She handed Jane the sheet of pasteboard. "Do you want me to have it framed?"

"No. My brother, I mean my niece—he gave her the money so I always think it's his—has a frame shop, don't you remember?"

"Vaguely. Where is it?"

"In the Moema district. On the square."

Jane studied the collage.

"This is an imaginary place, isn't it?"

"Yes. It's an inner landscape."

"The toy train you drew in the background . . ."

"I didn't draw it. Those are pieces of paper cut out and glued."

"Where do you find the patience to do that?"

Greta smiled. An exercise in persistence, in self-control. If Jane only knew the emotional state she had been in when she began. The night when she imagined Leonardo had returned. She had been in a bad way when she sat down to take her mind off her troubles, and it had been so long since she last used the instruments . . . Better change the subject.

"And the children, have they adjusted to the new neighborhood?"

♭ "Everything is a novelty to them. The biggest improvement is that now the school bus picks them up in front of the house. That's why I've come to visit. I don't have to hurry off at a particular time. Talking about what time it is, the bells haven't rung today."

"I don't know if it's because I'm getting absent-minded, but I haven't heard them for days."

"Before old Ananias died—remember?—we didn't hear the bells for a month. And all at once, bang, they started up again."

Greta failed to catch the meaning of the observation.

"In the Alto da Boa Vista district there aren't any churches nearby. I don't hear bells anymore. I thought I'd hear them in the Village . . ." She stood up. "It didn't work out."

Soon it would be completely dark. Greta walked her friend to her car. Lights or stars were twinkling in the distance. Frogs were croaking loudly. A dull, far-away murmur of traffic reached the Village, muffled. They both became aware of a strange smell, like a rat or something else decomposing, but they pretended not to notice.

♭ Weeks with nothing stirring. The abandoned houses stand empty. For how long? Camilo and Ivo have settled in on Ingleses Street. They have a nurse. Camilo maintains that his longing for the Village will be the death of him.

♭ Alexandre Ribeiro flew into a rage. A group of homeowners, his friends to be precise, went to Fortuna to complain about the filthy street and the rotten smell that had begun to invade their houses. No one could figure out where the stench was coming from. From the bodies in the cemetery? Ridiculous. A former priest, whom Greta disliked, led a protest rally in front of the representative's house, blaming the prostitutes on the Avenue. This was the smell of sin.

Alexandre Ribeiro is apparently unused to criticism. Nor does he know how to deal with it. He exploded and began shouting at the moralistic villager and tried to drive him off. He screamed the most vile insults, his emotional instability apparent to all. Did he actually think that because he controlled a few homeowners he was immune to criticism? Those who saw him foaming at the mouth were shocked. The fellow looked like an escapee from an insane asylum. That's what they said.

◊ Further astounding testimony. A few months before, Ribeiro submitted a proposal to Fortuna that called for painting the side walls of the buildings already up, as well as those under construction, in a way that would make them identifiable from a great distance. The project included a geometric design that would vary according to color from building to building. He proposed purchase of the idea itself, as well as payment for each color survey, which depended on the neighborhood and the angle from which the building was viewed. Fortuna put off the decision regarding approval with its usual procrastination. Every week the Village representative made a visit to the office, bowing and scraping, his brownnosing unrestrained, and hinted that he was negotiating with a rival firm, an obvious ploy. He didn't want to show Fortuna that he was desperate to have the idea approved immediately, so he occasionally mentioned the amusement park, inquired about whether or not the land would be available for leasing, and set up appointments for the forthcoming exhibition in the Gallery of Fame.

And lo and behold, the Company finally said no. It was not interested in changing the façades or Fortuna's image.

Alexandre Ribeiro joked about it, feigned indifference, but when he got back to the Village he let the firm's directors have it. His public threats against them were incredibly aggressive, and he insinuated that naturally they were going to use his idea without paying him a cent. Greta attributed the project to an attempt to raise rent money to pay his sister, who was no longer willing to let him stay for free. Ângela had mentioned in a telephone conversation that she had given her brother a deadline to make a decision. Either he paid half the amount assessed, or he left the premises. Even if it meant going to court to obtain an eviction notice.

There was no doubt: the Village representative was backed into a corner. A stable, responsible person would have resolved the matter with his sister much earlier, thus averting a crisis. Instead, he preferred to tighten his own noose.

The amazing thing was his obsequiousness with Fortuna and his arrogance and domineering manner in the Village. As if he were two people. The worms will devour his soul.

◊ The water was turned off in the Village of the Bells: the community's bills hadn't been paid.

The stench was unbearable.

◊ An invitation to the opening of Doris's show: *Life and Death of a Woman.*

Greta didn't go. When it was time to dress she was certain that she stank. The stench in the Village permeated her body.

The Department of Hygiene and Public Health tried fruitlessly to locate the source of the fetid odor. Nothing was found. The empty houses continued to await new tenants. The evil smell turned away those who visited the Village. It was even worse in the cemetery.

♤   A visit with Camilo. Greta has never seen him so chipper. He takes Ivo out for walks along Ingleses Street, wearing his old silk ascot. He's going to marry the nurse, a fifty-five-year-old widow. A charming, dedicated, and affectionate person. Now it is she who pushes Ivo's wheelchair. Camilo walks beside her, his bearing dignified as it had been long ago. He doesn't talk about death anymore.

"Who says I'm still alive?" He winks.

♤   June. A cold night. The windows of the house have been caulked. Anybody walking along Palm Street holds a handkerchief to his nose. Only ten residents are still holding out—the others have gone away— maybe because they have nowhere else to go. The church bells have fallen silent.

Greta lights the fireplace for the last time. She pops the cork on a bottle of champagne—a homage to what the Village might have been? She will take little from the house: books, paintings, china, a few pieces of furniture, the rugs. Could that be? The rest belongs to the family.

Tina is looking at the mess left by the movers—sawdust all over the parquet floor, crates near the door, boxes piled up—so many!

"What will become of me?"

"Starting tomorrow you can stay around here keeping an eye on the property and dreaming about lost loves and thinking about yourself and your misfortunes, alienated as you are. You'll be the ghost of the Village of the Bells."

"Come off it. You perceived of me or made me this way on purpose. I could have been useful to the community. The hope for love isn't incompatible with life. On the contrary."

"There are more important themes . . ."

"Give me some examples."

"Find out for yourself."

"Do you still believe in the possibility of the individual gesture in the midst of the chaos we inhabit? There's clearly no such possibility. The return to a healthy and ecologically harmonious lifestyle has been negated, destroyed by the originator itself, Fortuna. Why?"

"I repeat, you can't escape reality and hope to avoid implausibility. Imagine if the Village had really developed and become a model. In Brazil? Hahahaha. They won't allow it. Or how about this to feed your romanticism: Leonardo walks into the living room and asks me to marry him. When have the great passions ever led to anything? Never. Let me think of another possibility . . . No. You have to follow the rules. I'm going to drink a toast to those with the talent to change the course of history. If they still exist."

Greta stared into the flames crackling in the fireplace. A spark fell on the sawdust next to the books scattered about the floor. She knew what was going to happen, but she didn't get up to extinguish the flames.